Galactic

Threat of In

by

JC McMillan

Copyright © 2016 JC McMillan

All rights reserved, including the right to reproduce this book, or portions thereof in any form. No part of this text may be reproduced, transmitted, downloaded, decompiled, reverse engineered, or stored, in any form or introduced into any information storage and retrieval system, in any form or by any means, whether electronic or mechanical without the express written permission of the author.

This is a work of fiction. Names and characters are the product of the author's imagination and any resemblance to actual persons, living or dead, is entirely coincidental.

ISBN: 978-1-326-50970-5

PublishNation
www.publishnation.co.uk

Chapter 1

A DIFFERENT EASTER HOLIDAY

"Calm down. We will not get anywhere if we are talking all at once," exclaimed Mary.

"Yes, even more considering that we are in this room. It´s too small and all the noises are heard so loudly," added Maggie.

"I agree. We'd better let Billy go on with his story," said Bruce, lying on his side in the highest triple bunk bed.

"As I was trying to tell you, when we were almost arriving here I saw something very brilliant coming down from the sky."

Tying up her long ginger hair, Maggie said, "It could have been a comet."

"I don´t think so. It wasn't falling in a straight line. It was more as if it was trying to land or something. It seemed to be a small plane or something like that."

"Couldn't you see approximately where it fell?" asked Maggie.

"No. I guess it could have fallen over the lake. I mean, if it was a plane and the pilot was in trouble he would try to land there, wouldn't he?"

"Billy's right, if that´s what you saw, it rules out the comet or meteorite theory," commented Mary standing next to the bunk bed.

"Maybe it was a plane that had to make an emergency landing, or maybe it just crashed."

"Yes, Bruce, maybe it was. Nailbytes is checking the Internet news on his laptop to see if there's anything about a plane accident," replied Mary.

"Talking about Nailbytes, here he comes."

"Why are you talking about me, Maggie? What's going on?"

"Nothing at all," cried Mary. "Did you see something on the Internet? Is there any mention of a plane crash around this zone?"

"First of all, get out of my bed." Bruce came down at once making a face. In reply to Mary's question, Nailbytes continued, "Not really, I looked thoroughly but there isn't anything about plane crashes."

"Guys, it could be a spaceship," cried Denise leaning on the wardrobe. "How exciting."

"Wait. If it was a spaceship we should call the police."

"We have to be sure before we do that, Billy," replied Mary.

"What are we waiting for, let's go to the lake and take a look right now," cried Denise with a broad smile which displayed her brackets.

"No, sis, it's too dark now. We will go early tomorrow morning," said Mary.

"I just hope those aliens will be friendly." Her friends couldn't help smiling at Denise's words.

"Yes, sis, we sure hope so."

"Don't forget we must do our schoolwork. After all, that's the main reason why we are here, isn't it?" exclaimed Nailbytes.

"You had to mention it," replied Bruce with reluctance.

"Don't worry, we'll do it, too," said Mary.

"Let's get out of this room," cried Maggie. "I'm asphyxiated."

Denise seemed ready to make a comment when they heard a voice calling at them. "Guys, could one of you please take the rubbish to the bin?" asked Billy's father, showing his head at the main door of the caravan, looking into the room in which they were talking.

Mr Nearne is a kind and loving man, unlike his wife who is a little rough on the deal. His appearance, short stature, grey hair, a small mustache and glasses, seemed to confirm, somehow, his gentle personality. "I'll go, Dad," replied Billy, stepping out of the room.

Henry Nearne went out to his wife and his son followed him to take the bag.

Billy's thin frame made Mary go after him. "Do you need help?"

Billy was picking up the bag with both hands. As he departed to look for a bin he smiled to his friend. "Thanks, Mary. It isn't so heavy."

Billy's parents and Mary watched him until he was out of sight, occluded by the trees and some other caravans parked nearby. Mrs Nearne turned to Mary and, before taking a sip from her tea mug, she asked, "Please, dear, could you tell Trevor that tomorrow we will have pasta with pesto sauce but that he may have either bolognese or carbonara sauce instead?"

"Okay, Jaime, I will ask him and tell you what he wants."

"Thanks, dear, the truth is that I worry about his allergy to nuts, and I'm not sure if the pesto sauce has any in it, so I'd rather give him another one," said Jaime.

"By the way, Mary, do you know if Trevor was able to fix my laptop?" asked Henry.

"I think he did. He also said it wasn't so complicated."

"Well, maybe for him it wasn't, but for anyone else I bet it would be very difficult."

"Yes, that's why we call him Nailbytes," replied Mary with a broad smile.

Jaime asked, "Whose idea was it?"

"It was Bruce's. He mixed his surname 'Nail' with the word 'bytes' and there it was."

"Always with his jokes," laughed Henry.

"Please ask him about the sauces, Mary," insisted Jaime.

Henry added, "Since you're going in, please leave this box in the kitchen."

"Okay," said Mary and took the biscuits box. She went into the caravan. The small kitchen was just in front of the entrance. She stood on her tiptoes, pushed aside the small refrigerator and put the box on the shelves that were full of food.

She then went to the boys' room. The sliding door was opened. "Hey, Nailbytes, did you manage to fix your electronic chess?"

Nailbytes, concentrating on his chess game on the upper bed, answered ironically, "No, Mary, I didn't."

"I was just asking, you fool. You don't have to answer me that way."

"Okay, but please do not disturb an inspired genius at work," exclaimed Nailbytes lying on the upper bed without taking his eyes from his game.

"I'm sorry, genius. It's just that you told us that your game was broken."

"Yes, it was, but what do you think? Of course I fixed it."

"Jaime wants to know which sauce you want for your pasta tomorrow, bolognese or carbonara."

"Carbonara will be fine."

Meanwhile, Billy was on his way to the trash bins. He observed all the caravans and tents spread over the peaceful field. "Wow! What a delicious smell. Grilled hamburgers," he exclaimed to himself as he saw a family gathered around a barbecue. He went on walking, surrounded by noisy groups of campers celebrating the long weekend. That's a huge caravan over there. A whole neighborhood must have come on that one, he thought, smiling at a much bigger caravan than his own. He continued his search for a rubbish bin until, at last, he found one. "Well, there it is." He walked towards it but, when he lifted the lid, something caught his attention. "Where does that shine come from?"

He leaned over the edge taking care that his eyeglasses wouldn't fall into the bin. It was almost full but, in spite of his short stature, he reached to get hold of a bag which had something very brilliant inside it. "I've got it." He put it on the ground and took out something that was just on the top. "What is this? It looks like a small box with a very strange shape." Suddenly the shine was gone. He wasn't able to decipher the nature of his discovery so he just put it carefully in his pocket.

He then introduced the rubbish bag back into the bin and hurried back to the caravan. When he finally arrived, he saw his parents chatting at the door over a cup of tea.

"Did you find a bin?" asked Henry, serving himself from a teapot.

"Yes, Dad, I did."

"Oh. I forgot to ask Mary whether she called her grandmother," exclaimed Jaime. "If she didn't please tell her to do it at once so that she won't be worried about her and Denise."

"I'm sure she did, Mom. It was the first thing she did when we got here. You know how close they are. Their grandma is the only family Mary and Denise have since their parents died. The only one who hasn't call his parents yet is Nailbytes."

"Of course, dear," cried Henry. "No wonder he didn't. They are in India."

"Anyway, he should send them an email," suggested Jaime.

Billy left his parents and entered the caravan. He looked to the left where Bruce was watching TV in a tiny living room and made a gesture summoning his friend to follow him, and both went into the boys' room. Bruce turned off the TV and followed his friend.

"Guys, look what I just found out there." In spite of his excitement, Billy kept his voice low as he put his hand in his pocket and took out the box.

"What is it?" asked Bruce, standing behind him.

"Now, what do we have here?" asked Nailbytes, still sitting on his bed and setting aside the chess game.

Mary heard their voices and came in a hurry. "What do you have there?"

Billy gave her the box.

"It has some buttons on it," commented Bruce.

Suddenly a light went on and Mary shouted, "Oh, there's an orange light on now."

"Is there any problem, guys?" asked Henry when he heard Mary's voice.

After a short silence, Bruce answered, "No, Henry, everything is all right."

Then turning to Mary he continued, "Mary Ann Wright, you almost got us into trouble."

"Sorry."

Mary's shout had also brought in the other girls. "What happened?" asked Denise coming into the room, followed by Maggie.

Still sitting on the upper bed Nailbytes answered, "We are now intrigued with a little box."

Billy lifted his eyebrows in surprise. "Mary is right; there is an orange light on. I hadn't notice all these buttons."

Maggie commented, "Look, Billy, it is very small, it looks like the earphone my grandma uses."

Suddenly, something drew their attention. "Silence! Listen," cried Mary.

They all came very close to the strange device.

Bruce asked, "Did any of you hear something?"

"Silence," insisted Nailbytes.

"Yes, something like... Marwel, Marwel."

"I agree with Billy. It sounded something like Marwel," commented Denise.

Bruce said, "That is not much, what does it mean?"

"Please let me handle it for a moment," said Mary taking it in her hands.

"What happened now? I can't hear anything."

"Neither can I, Mary, it seems that the battery, or whatever makes it work, is downloaded. It's totally dead," commented Nailbytes doubtfully, already standing on the floor.

Billy said, "At least we can say that it looks like a communications device, because, apparently, someone was trying to talk through it."

"But we can't hear any more sounds now," commented Maggie.

"No problem," cried Bruce. "Nailbytes, do you know how to load it?"

"I would have to examine it thoroughly, but I can't distinguish whether it's a battery or something completely different that makes it work."

Mary was repeating to herself, "Marwel, Marwel... What does it mean? Could it be a code or a name?"

Bruce said, "Tomorrow we will try to find out where this device comes from and look for that object Billy saw today."

"No doubt something very odd is going on in this place," mumbled Mary, nodding her head.

"But how did it end in a trash bin?" asked Denise.

"Maybe someone found it, couldn´t figure out what it was and just threw it away," replied Billy, shrugging his shoulders.

They all had tired faces and some of them started to yawn. Billy saw that and said, "We had better go to sleep now. We will have a big day tomorrow so let's save our energies."

"Yes, we have a lot ahead of us," insisted Denise as she, Mary and Maggie returned to their room.

"Yes, let's go to sleep, but you can't expect me to sleep well on those sheets. Who knows how they were washed. I prefer my own. I use a very special soap," replied Maggie entering the girls' room.

"The only special thing here is you, Maggie," mumbled Bruce from his room.

"I'm not special, mastodon, it's just that..."

Denise interrupted, "The sheets are quite clean. Let's go to sleep."

"You and your silly comments, Maggie," continued Bruce in a harsh tone of voice. Finally they were all in their beds ready to get a good night sleep, and a short time later they were all sleeping soundly. Well not all. One of them was turning around in her bed unable to fall asleep. After some time Mary pulled out of her sheets and, seeing that everyone around her was sleeping peacefully, decided to take a walk outside. She put on her raincoat and went out of the room. She tiptoed very silently passing near her friends' parents, opened the door and was, at last, outside the caravan.

She spent some minutes walking without a definite direction. It was quite dark so she took out a torch from her pocket as she mumbled to herself, "What if I go to the lake and look around for more tips about this mystery? It shouldn't be too far from here." A light rain started to fall. Mary pulled the cap over her head so that her long, thick, curly brown hair wouldn't get soaked and resumed her walk. She used her torch to see her way towards the lake, following the posters which guided her along a thin path.

She was aware that she was a little far from the caravan now but, at the same time, confident that she would have no problem in finding her way back.

A little later she was aware of the fact that she was also far from all the other caravans and tents, but according to the posters she was now quite near the lake.

For a moment she had to go through a path with dense vegetation which made it difficult to walk, forcing her to avoid some plants with pointed leaves and many flying night insects.

At the end of the path a small trail went straight to the lake. Her thoughts kept her company as she walked. It's quite lonely down here. There aren't any caravans or tents around. Mary had to duck in order to avoid the branches that impeded her passage. After a while, as she stepped on an old, wooden bridge over a little stream, she heard a crackle and smiled to herself. This bridge seems a little feeble. I'd better advise Nailbytes not to step on it. It will fall with him on top. She finally arrived. This is a big lake. It won't be easy to find that flying object or whatever it was. Maybe it sank in the water.

Mary started to walk along the shore. All of a sudden she stopped abruptly.

What is that? Something is floating on the water. The tall trees and the thick vegetation around her made it difficult to see what it was. She couldn't help feeling a cold chill as she went near and had a better view of the object. Could it be the spaceship I'm supposed to be looking for? Her curiosity was bigger than her fear and she went a little closer to the edge. "It seems like a small airplane," she said to herself as she approached the shore. "The wings are too short and it looks more like a war plane." She went a little closer, trying to have a better look at the strange object in the lake. "I can't believe it. It really looks like a spaceship," she mumbled.

Mary felt the sweat on her hands moistening her torch and she shuddered.

Something strange was happening, but what was it?

Chapter 2

A CHILLING DISCOVERY

Still frightened, Mary ran to the caravan. She didn't look back, she just ran.

When she got to the caravan door she stopped for a minute to take her breath.

Then, carefully, she went inside. She looked at Billy's parents' room which was close to the kitchen. It was already dawn and a few seconds later some low sounds could be heard in the boys' room. "Billy, wake up," whispered Mary. Bruce, who was sleeping on the second bed, was the first to hear Mary's voice. "Let's go to see the spaceship."

Billy, still a little sleepy, didn't quite understand Mary's words and answered wearily, "Whatever you want to see we can see it tomorrow. I'm so tired."

"We have to do it now before the people from the other caravans and tents are awake. Can you imagine all the fuss it would cause if they saw it?" Denise was standing on the door. Mary turned around and saw her sister standing behind her. "Why are you awake at this hour?"

"I woke up a few minutes ago and you weren't there. I was so scared," replied Denise showing her brackets. "What happened, sis?"

"I saw a spaceship."

Denise said, "What!"

With a sleepy face, Billy started to dress up and said, "Lower your voices. You will wake up Billy's parents."

Almost all the others were now awake and excited with Mary's story. They spoke almost all at once, trying to keep their voices low.

"If it looks so strange on the outside, imagine how it must be on the inside," commented Mary.

"I have never seen a spaceship," exclaimed Denise, shaking her arms and almost all her body in complete excitement.

"What are you whispering about?" asked Maggie with a yawn, coming into the boys' room.

Denise put her hand on Maggie's mouth. "Keep your voice down."

"Okay, where are you going, guys?" whispered Maggie obediently.

"We are going to take a good look at the spaceship that Mary found at the lake," answered Bruce.

Billy said with a smile, "Nailbytes is still sound asleep and snoring with enthusiasm. Look at him."

"I'm sure he wouldn't want to come with us considering the early hour," continued Bruce.

"Everything is okay but we can't go out through the door. We would wake up Billy's parents," advised Maggie.

Bruce opened the window in the boys' room and spoke firmly, "We can go out through this window. Who is going out first?"

"I will," answered Billy.

"I'm second," said Maggie.

"I'll go after you," replied Denise.

Mary approached them. "Bruce will go after you and I will be the last one."

"How are we going to reach the floor out there? The window is a little high, don't you think so?" Maggie sounded doubtful as she looked at the window.

"That's not a problem," replied Billy. "Remember that all the boxes with my father's fishing gear are right below it."

In view of that fact they started to go out, one by one, keeping very silent in order not to wake Billy's parents. Bruce had just gone out and it was Mary's turn when Nailbytes came near the window and mumbled, still yawning, "What on earth are you doing? Where are you going without me?"

Almost out of the window, Mary answered, "We didn't want to wake you up, you seemed to be so profoundly asleep and snoring quite loudly too. Do you want to come with us? We are going to take a look at a spaceship I saw at the lake."

Nailbytes raised his eyebrows. "Why would I want to do that? I'd rather stay here and get a little more sleep."

"Well, you could really be of great help to us. You know a lot about computers and electronic machines and I think you will keep us from getting into trouble by touching anything we shouldn't."

Nailbytes seemed to be thinking about what his friend was saying and, after a little pause, he agreed. "You are so optimistic to think we will be able to go inside that ship or whatever it is. Well, never mind, I'll go with you." He jumped back, put on his clothes and in a few minutes he was ready beneath the window.

Due to Nailbytes' slight overweight Mary was waiting for him in order to help him go through it. When the others saw Nailbytes' head showing on the threshold they smiled mockingly. "Do you think he'll be able to come through the window?" asked Bruce.

"Never mind. If he breaks it we will fix it. That's what friends are for, isn't it so?" said Maggie with a broad smile.

Nailbytes replied with annoyance, "Instead of making silly comments why don't you help me down?"

Bruce and Billy looked at each other with a little repentance and helped their friend. Once they were all on the outside they started their way to the lake.

"Be very careful, guys. We'd better use just one of our torches. Someone might see us and will want to know what we are doing out at this hour," advised Mary.

"Did someone bring a torch?" asked Maggie. They all looked at each other.

"So nobody did. Well then, we must keep together and walk very silently."

"Are we getting near the spaceship? I can't see anything so I gather that no one can see us either," spoke Denise, her teeth brackets shining a little in the dark.

They went on walking until they arrived at the lake. Mary looked around for the so-called spaceship. "There it is," she said as soon as the dark shape of the transporter appeared in front of her. It was almost covered by some big branches, well secured from curious stares. The ship was next to the shore and they approached it slowly.

Denise exclaimed with a frightened voice, "I sure hope there's nobody inside it."

"We must be careful," advised Billy.

"That looks like a door," said Bruce, approaching the spaceship.

Nailbytes cried, "Wow! It seems to be open."

"That isn't so good. It means that the occupants are not far," replied Mary.

"Well, it may also mean that they are not inside," said Billy.

"Okay, who dares to open it?" asked Maggie.

Bruce cried, "I will." He started to manipulate what seemed like a knob. "It's opening," he exclaimed suddenly. The door opened upwards with a slight noise and a little white smoke.

"Wow! It's impressive," cried Billy.

Mary asked in a loud voice, "Is there someone in here? We are friends."

Denise added with a shy voice, "We come in peace."

Bruce doubted for a minute and then said, "Let's go in." Maggie remained on the outside while all the others entered the ship, one by one.

"We don't have much light in here. We can barely see anything," said Denise.

"There must be some kind of switch somewhere," replied Bruce as he looked around him.

"Wait. I did have my torch with me after all," shouted Mary as she turned it on. "Now we will be able to take a good look at all this."

"Look at all those instruments. I wonder what all those buttons are for."

"I certainly don't know, Nailbytes," smiled Mary.

"Damn," cried Billy.

Bruce asked, "What happened?"

"I hurt myself with these things. I can't see what they are."

Mary turned her torch towards him. "These are seats. There are four of them. This might mean that there are four aliens somewhere around here," replied Mary with a worried voice.

Bruce went towards one of the wings. "Mary, please come over here. I need you to light this place."

Mary went along with Billy and Nailbytes. Denise followed them at once. She directed her torch to where Bruce had told her to. "Well, it's one of the ship wings."

"But look again. There's a seat there with some equipment just in front of it," added Bruce.

"Wait, Mary, don't take your torch away, I can't see anything without it," commented Bruce. "Wait a second, I'm going to see what's at the back of the ship."

Maggie, who was listening to her friends' conversation from the outside, advised, "Hurry up, guys. The owners of this thing might be back soon."

Billy agreed. "She's right, this thing didn't get here on its own."

"Maybe it did. Maybe it got here on remote control," replied Nailbytes.

"What's over there, Mary?" asked Billy.

"I'm not sure but for what I can see this looks like the ship's cargo compartment or something like that."

Although they couldn't see much yet, Nailbytes, Billy and Denise's eyes had adapted a little to the darkness and they could, at least, go around without difficulty. They looked around full of curiosity, staring at the ship's sophisticated instruments. Bruce went to where Mary was. "What do you think is inside those boxes?" asked Mary.

Bruce replied, "Which boxes?"

"Those over there. They have a hexagon shape."

"No idea, Mary," replied Bruce.

From the outside Maggie shouted again, "Get out of there."

Mary jumped at Maggie's shout and exclaimed, "I think I just stepped on something."

"What is it? Did it make any noise?"

"What are you looking at?" asked Billy coming towards them.

Mary picked up a bag. "This bag is made of a completely unknown material. I've never seen anything like this before," she exclaimed, feeling it with her fingers.

"Let's open it to see what's inside," suggested Bruce.

They did so, half scared and half curious.

"Hey, these are like those things you found earlier, Billy."

"That's true," said Billy, taking one of them in his hands.

"This mystery is starting to clear up a little. The device you found seems to belong to whoever traveled on this ship," commented Mary. "Now we have to find out whom, or what, is Marwel."

Billy commented, "It could be the pilot's name."

"That's a possibility," agreed Mary. "Do you think there could be more clues in the cargo compartment?"

"Yes, but we have to be very careful, we don't know what we could come across in there," replied Billy.

They started to search for anything that could help them solve the mystery.

Mary stood with her torch while Billy and Bruce looked into the bags and boxes.

Denise came near to where her friends seemed to be very busy. "What are you doing here?"

"Well, it looks like we were finding out something about the strange device that Billy found inside the trash bin and the ones we just found here," explained Mary.

"It's incredible to think that we actually are inside a real spaceship," cried Billy as he went on with his search.

"What are you two doing on your knees?" asked Denise.

"We are looking for anything that might help us know more about all this," answered Billy with enthusiasm.

"Do you need some help, guys?"

"Okay, Denise, if you want to join us, come on." Denise kneeled down and started to look around.

"However, guys, Maggie is right. Whoever came on this ship could be back at any time," advised Billy with a worried voice.

Suddenly, a sharp cry cut through the silence.

"What is it?" cried Mary.

"I think I touched some hair," exclaimed Denise. Mary and Billy ran towards her and Mary directed her torch to the box near her sister.

"Here it is," shouted Billy as he put his hand into the box. "This is certainly some kind of hair."

Mary touched it and said, "And the worst part is that it doesn't feel like animal fur."

"What do you mean?" said Denise stuttering in fear.

Bruce approached them. "It means that this thing came here to kidnap people and take them to another planet."

Mary replied, also stuttering a little, "It's a possibility. We can't be sure about anything here."

"So there might be human remains in those boxes?" asked Denise.

"Unfortunately, yes," answered Bruce with a solemn tone of voice.

"This is creepy. We might be facing an intergalactic serial killer," replied Billy.

Mary said, "Let's hope it isn't so."

At that moment, as Mary held her torch towards the floor, Billy saw something. "Put your light just right there."

Mary did so at once.

"Oh, what are those stains?" asked a terrified Denise.

Mary replied stuttering, "I think it's blood."

"If what we are thinking is true, we must call the police at once," exclaimed Billy.

At that moment a strong rain started to fall. "This is terrible. I'll get wet in a second," exclaimed Maggie, who was still standing outside the ship.

"You'd better come in so that we can close the door. We don't want anything getting wet in here," suggested Nailbytes.

Maggie obeyed and entered the transporter. Shaking her clothes she asked, "Did you find anything?"

"Yes, but nothing good."

"This is getting really dangerous," added Mary with a frown.

Maggie approached her friends and saw Denise grabbing Mary's arms.

"What happened here? Why do you have those terrified faces on?"

Billy was about to answer when Nailbytes came into the compartment shouting, "Someone is coming. We have to hide." They all ran and tried to hide themselves as fast as they could.

Chapter 3

A TRIP TO THE UNKNOWN

"What is that?" whispered Maggie. A strange creature entered the spaceship, sat down on the main seat and seemed to concentrate all his attention in the panel in front of him.

"I don´t know. But it isn't human, that I know. Lower your voice or it will find us," whispered Billy.

It looked like a strange kind of reptile although it had human traits. However, his clothes reminded those of the explorers they had seen in their history books, ancient explorers like Marco Polo or Christopher Columbus. Though they were made with what seemed to be a silver cloth, the garments didn't fit well in a spaceship. Suddenly the ship lurched. The creature had initiated the take-off cycle.

"We must stop him," Maggie said nervously.

"Do you think so? And how will we do that?" asked Billy trying to sound ironic in spite of his fear.

The creature started to talk to what seemed to be a microphone. "What is it saying?" asked Denise.

Bruce replied, "I can´t understand anything."

"Neither can I. It must be talking in its language," replied Billy.

Mary cried, "Shut up or they´ll find us."

"Well, we already have a big problem here," said Maggie. "We´re on a spaceship on our way to nobody knows where."

"Calm down, Maggie. Despair won´t help us now."

"Calm down you say? What on earth are we going to do, Billy?"

Some of them grabbed their heads in despair. Bruce looked around him with fear and some tears came down from Denise´s and Maggie´s eyes. However, Nailbytes' curiosity about computers and electronics was stronger than his fear. He began to watch how the creature manipulated the sophisticated controls on the spaceship. He was aware of something. The device the creature had on its ears was very alike the one Billy had found near the lake, and the ones on that strange bag they had just found on the ship. He turned to the bag and motioned for Mary to grab it. Mary took one from the bag and put it to her ear. The device looked very much like headphones with a very small microphone, but they had a really strange shape. An incredible thing happened.

"Hey. I can understand everything he says."

"So, what is he talking about?" asked Billy with his eyes wide open.

"Wait a second, I'll fix it in my ear," replied Mary.

"Yes, I hear you... I'm RJ Marwel and I'm on my way to Esmadis. Just let me leave the Earth orbit and I'll be in touch again," spoke the creature as he shook the raindrops from his clothes.

Nailbytes spoke in low voice, "I think these devices will be very useful to us in this unfortunate situation. I suggest we all take one and keep it safe." They obeyed at once, and each of them took one from the bag.

Maggie said, "I insist we have to do something else about this."

"Okay, what do you suggest? We don't even know if that creature is armed," whispered Billy.

"What kind of creature is it?" wondered Nailbytes.

Bruce commented, "Well, at least now we know that those science fiction films didn't lie much."

Maggie replied, "Very funny. I appreciate the fact that you and the others seem to be enjoying all this. However, what are we going to do?"

"Lower your voice," said Mary. "Look, he is manipulating his device again."

The creature spoke, still shaking the raindrops from his clothes. "I'm leaving the Ace planet orbit now. I'll be on Xfay speed." Looking at the raindrops on its clothes the creature continued, "There is something else. I'm not sure what it can be but I have a queer substance on my clothes. It seemed to fall from above. Yes, I'll analyze it at once."

They saw him pushing a button on the panel and a small tray came out. He took what seemed to be a piece of glass, put some drops of rain on it and introduced it into a slot in the panel. After a few seconds, the tray came out again and the creature looked at it for a minute and shouted at the microphone, "You won't believe this, I have Ace all over me. Now I am absolutely sure the Triple Alliance will be rich when Lonar Mayer's army invades this planet. They have so much of it there that it even pours down from the sky.

"Yes, don't worry. I already have the samples you asked for and I'm on my way home." The engine began to make a different noise. "Wait, I have to change to the Xfay speed."

The ship seemed to be traveling in a steady speed now, silently and smoothly. The only thing they could see through the few side windows as well as the bigger pilot window was a yellowish light outside. Inside the ship there was not much visibility either, but they could make out some kind of sophisticated looking equipment. The driving wheel, for instance. It didn't look like the regular ones, it was a half wheel, more like an airplane's.

Mary moved a little forward and looked at the floor. The others looked at each other without saying a word, but they all had the same terrible thoughts in their minds: What was going to happen to them now? The fear of being found kept them silent while the creature rubbed its face with a hand, trying to dry the remaining raindrops on it.

After some time, they saw that it was putting on the device again. "Hello, do you copy me?" Someone was calling the creature.

"No, I didn't copy you. It's because I had taken away my Isikul. Wait, the automatic control is telling me that the Xfay is over and that I must start to work with the manual controls in order to continue my trip.

"Are you asking me where I am? Let me see for a moment... The panel says... Wait a second... Tiron Zone."

"The pirates you say?"

After a few seconds the ship had a sudden shudder. "I'm being attacked," cried the creature. "Due to its camouflage, those stupid pirates must think this is a cargo ship."

Another strong shudder made them jump on their feet. Fortunately for them, RJ Marwel was concentrating in manipulating the screen in front of him. They felt another jolt. The creature seemed to be a good pilot. It managed the computer as if it were looking for something. Once again, a strong jolt made them jump. Their fear was bigger now. The attack could destroy the ship and kill them. Pushing a button, RJ Marwel unloaded an appliance with three screens, something like a triple submarine periscope. Each screen showed one side of the spaceship and had individual shooting command. A strong jolt made them stumble once more.

RJ Marwel went on operating the ship's controls on the panel, shooting in different directions, as he looked at his targets on the three screens he had in front of him. "From what I can see it looks very much like a video game." They all looked at Nailbytes with an angry face.

Bruce replied, "Yes, but the difference here is that you don't gain points or achieve levels, you just get killed."

"Okay, calm down," said Mary.

Another shudder moved the ship. They could see that the ship of one of the attackers had exploded. They heard one more explosion. The spaceship had destroyed another pirate ship. Luckily for them the remaining enemy ships ran away.

RJ Marwel spoke on the microphone. "I left the Tiron Zone but... Wait. Damn. It says here that the attack has damaged some systems.

"Yes, I know. I put on the camouflage system a little late."

"No, I don't know, let me see..."

He tipped something on the ship's computer and spoke again. "Apparently I am not at Sise stage but I will be scarcely able to land in Imhamway, and from there... Oh. To think how I hate to go to the Multipower Center."

"Yes, okay. I'll ask the computer for the list of the things I'll need." RJ Marwel went on, "I have to stop talking now. I have almost arrived to Esmadis. At least that's what the computer is telling me now. Someone might intercept this communication and it would be fatal for me."

After a few seconds handling the ship's controls the creature continued, "I have an order to deliver, I request permission to land in

Imhamway Space Station. I am bringing some equipment for the Esmeraland Fair."

"What is he waiting for?" asked Denise.

"Be careful. Don't speak so loud, please."

"Sorry, sis."

A voice which seemed to be a controller's answered at once. "Since your spaceship is a cargo ship, you have to land on platform ES-036. That one is free."

"Okay, I will do so," answered the creature. "Control center, I copy you. My screen shows I will be the second ship coming in. Another ship will land before me."

After a few minutes the voice spoke again. "Cargo ship starting landing operations." The spaceship disguised as a cargo vehicle began its landing maneuver over Esmadis. All they could see from where they were was complete darkness, a fact that did nothing but increase the uncertainty of what was to come.

In a few moments the ship slowed down its speed which could be the normal procedure before landing.

Suddenly Nailbytes directed his eyes ahead and touched Mary who was at his side. She also directed her eyes forward. Within seconds everyone could see through the pilot window some lights in the distance. The ship was slowly approaching the lights. The creature spoke loudly, "I'm almost in position.

"Yes, I'm already in front of the Imhamway mountain.

"I need permission for landing.

"Okay, confirm if ES-036 is my landing platform."

Now it was clear that the lights they had seen in the distance illuminated the four levels to and from which spaceships arrived and departed. It certainly demanded expert pilots because the space station was on top of a huge mountain, very close to the cliff. Even the building had its six floors or levels almost on the air. "Okay, here we go."

The ship entered the first level very slowly. From the pilot's window they could see the first station level. It was big. It reminded them of those huge hangars where aircrafts are repaired, but this seemed much bigger. Although with difficulty, they could see that there were many different intergalactic ships parked around. The ship was moving very slowly as if it was just floating in the air. It was flying at a certain height and, due to the ship's material, they could hear the noise made by some smaller load vehicles and creatures moving from side to side underneath it. "Okay, the computer says that we've already landed on platform ES-036.

"I'll be ready for inspection so please send an inspector at once because I have to go to the Multipower Center to get some repairs."

The answer was, "Okay, copied. An inspector is on his way right now."

A few minutes later the ship stopped. The creature began to arrange some papers it had near him. When the ship stopped completely, even with so little visibility inside the ship, the Earthlings tried to see through the pilot window; from that height they could only see some spaceships parked around them.

It was incredible, they were on another planet but the noise that came from the outside was very much the same as the ones that could be heard in any airport or bus terminal on Earth. But at this point what really mattered to them were two things: first, how would they avoid being captured, and second, if they achieved that, would they be able to return to the Earth? Could they do it on this ship? It needed repair, and it was obvious that the pirate attack at the so-called Tiron Zone had been quite hard and had caused damages.

Another thing to have in mind was that the creature could need something from where they were hiding and then... The creature was getting ready to go out. It stood up from his seat and started to go back. The Earthlings looked at each other in terror. And now what are we going to do? they all thought. But something happened. The ship's door opened as RJ Marwel waited with what seemed a file under his arm. Once it was wide open another creature followed by two armed guards went in.

"That is good, I get greeted by the Thiller guards and one of my partners." RJ Marwel cried nervously. "It is an honor."

"Leave us alone, Thiller guards," cried his partner addressing the guards who had come in with him.

"Okay, Diemor," replied one of the guards. He made a sign to the other one and both left the ship.

"What is happening? What are you doing with that disintegrator?"

"Nothing my, dear RJ, the fact is that it is not profitable for me to share all that wealth at the Ace planet with you."

He walked slowly to the other side of the ship while RJ looked at him and pleaded. "But what are you saying? We will be more than rich. You can´t imagine all the wealth there is in that planet. Enough for the three of us: you, me and **Herni Delucano**."

Diemor smirked and pulled out a strange weapon as he replied harshly, "I do not share your optimism, my dear RJ."

"But what are you doing? We are the Triple Alliance. Are you crazy?"

"Yes, I am crazy, but I am crazy for power, ha ha ha." Diemor shot him with his disintegrator and RJ Marwel turned into dust in seconds.

"Thiller guards, you can enter now. The guards came back to the ship. "Get that dust out of here," demanded Diemor Diamadar. "Send a mechanic and check all over the ship."

"Yes, sir," cried the guards.

"And you don't know anything about this." The guards walked towards the dust and picked it up. Then the three of them left the ship.

"This was terrible," said Denise in a frail voice.

"It´s incredible, he was turn to dust in a second," added Nailbytes.

"And now what are we going to do? We don´t have the least idea of how we can go back home."

"Maggie is right, guys. We are in real trouble. I'd like to think this is just a nightmare," commented Nailbytes.

"Thank you for your good wishes."

"This is serious, guys. Unlike of what we watch in the movies or read in books we don't have any special powers, no magician that will help us with his wise counsel or anything like that. I don't have the palest idea of what we are going to do about this situation." Nobody spoke, they just looked at each other in dismay.

Chapter 4

STRANGE CREATURES

"What's that noise?" asked Mary.

"It seems to be coming from the outside." In spite of the situation, Denise spoke with a broad smile displaying her brackets as she always did. Through the opened door they could hear a voice coming from the outside. It spoke with a strange accent but completely understandable due to the devices they had on their ears.

"Hey, Tantoon, do you have this ship's documents? I can't find them."

"Everybody down on the floor," advised Mary in a low voice.

"Now what?" replied Maggie. All of them sat on the floor trying to go unnoticed.

Bruce said, "Well, if you are in such a hurry, you could go outside and take a look."

Maggie replied, "I wasn't speaking of going outside. I meant that one of us could try to peek out from one of the windows and see what it is like out there."

"Well, you try it then."

"Maggie is not tall enough, Bruce. It has to be someone a little taller so that he can look through a window and tell us what he can see," advised Mary.

Bruce cried, "Okay, I'll do it."

"Fine. Please tell us what's going on out there," said Nailbytes.

Bruce began to climb up on some boxes to reach a small window above him but he slipped and made a noise. Maggie said, "Careful with what you're doing, mastodon. You can break something and it will be even harder for us to go back home."

"Calm down," said Billy sitting on the floor.

"Why don't you come over and climb it yourself?"

"Forget it, Bruce, keep going," said Mary soothingly.

Bruce finally managed to reach the window and took a long look at the outside. "What the hell are those creatures?"

Maggie exclaimed, "Just tell us what you see, you fool."

"Calm down. Give him a little time," said Billy.

"Well, I can see a ship floating slowly towards the exit, but I can't see very well because some spaceships are blocking my sight."

Nailbytes commented, "That is not too bad because they can't see us either."

Mary said, "Go on."

"Well, there sure is a lot of movement out there. All sorts of strange creatures walking around. Some of them are carrying lumps and using weird kinds of trolleys. And those other things look like robots."

"Describe them you…. Tell us what they look like so that we may have an idea," exclaimed Maggie.

Bruce was about to answer when Mary interrupted, "Try to describe them using images we are familiar with."

"That's a good idea. I'll try to do that. There are a lot of different creatures but from what I'm able to see from here, most of them look like a rhinoceros, huge and fat, with something like a horn coming out from their noses."

"What are you saying?" asked Denise, sounding terrified.

"It's just as you heard. I can only see their heads and arms from here."

"What about their bodies? Can't you see more?" asked Nailbytes.

"They are wearing a sort of greenish gown."

"What horrible creatures," cried Maggie.

"They look like you when you get up in the morning," joked Bruce, but suddenly he bent down.

"What happened?" asked Mary.

"Some of them were passing near, and I think they were looking at this window."

"Did they look like rhinoceroses too?" asked Nailbytes.

"Yes, they walked close together and wore strange uniforms."

"We'd better look out through another window, now. Maybe those creatures are still looking at us," advised Mary.

Billy stayed quiet for a while.

Denise replied fearfully, "So we are on a rhinoceros planet."

"Okay, sis. First of all we must keep calm. We have to think of something to do."

"We have to be very careful then. They might be looking for this ship," said Mary.

Bruce was already looking out from another window. "That one looks completely different from the others," said Bruce.

"Does it look like you?" asked Maggie ironically. Bruce didn't bother to answer.

"This is serious, guys," demanded Billy.

"What can you see now?" asked Mary.

"There are some creatures quite near our ship, I can listen to them."

"What do they look like?" asked Billy.

"That thing is not at all like the others. It is black. With his long nose and big ears."

"What?" asked Maggie.

"What you heard. The others are grey. This one is black."

"Is it wearing the same kind of gown?" asked Mary.

"No, it looks more as if it were going to play cricket. It is wearing a cap, shorts and a T-shirt."

"Keep quiet, all of you. Listen."

They all went down on the floor. Only Bruce stayed in his place in order to listen to the creatures who were talking right beneath the ship's window.

"Okay, check out everything and hurry up. I have to go to the city in order to have everything ready for the fair," said a cheerful voice.

"You are not the only one, Edison," replied one who sounded more like an inspector. "We have too much work with the fair."

"That's true. I'm in a hurry too. Please let me check out my ship first so that I can leave right now," replied a third voice.

"It seems that there are three people talking now," whispered Bruce.

Maggie exclaimed, "People? You mean monsters."

"Well, three talking things," answered Mary lifting her eyebrows.

"Keep quiet, let me hear," asked Bruce.

The creatures went on talking. "You always make me wait too much. We have too many ships and boxes to look in to, I can't look to your stuff first. As I already told you, you are not the only merchant on this platform."

"But I'm the one that brings more merchandise than anybody else. That's true, isn't it? Look at the Stingray on Platform, E-037, it came in full but I have already unloaded all the boxes. They are on the right, by the ship, do you see them?"

"Yes, I know that, Edison, but you are just arriving and I want to leave before it gets too late. I risk meeting those crooks by the Tiron Zone," answered the other merchant.

"Do you see? Ugarra is right. The Stingray has just arrived and the Fortune Voyager has to go before it's too late, Edison. If not he will certainly meet those thieves on the way."

"Give me your papers."

Ugarra replied, "Here they are. Go through them quickly, please."

"See what I mean? You'll take a long time looking into his papers and I'll be waiting here until late, I know," exclaimed Edison.

He turned to the E-036 Platform and cried, "That's the ship where that Enphaler was?"

"Yes, I think so, but he is dead," said the inspector. "But we'd better change the subject. Talking about it can bring us big trouble. Even a trip to Atilkawa Fortress."

Ugarra commented, "Yes, the inspector is right. Why don't you tell me where I can get that tile to protect my energy box instead?"

"In the Multipower Center," answered Edison.

"Are you going there? I can give you the rutters so you can buy it and give it to me when you're back."

"No. I have to go to Esmeraland to see some things about the fair."

"You can never do a favor, can you?"

"Leave him alone, Ugarra. That's his way with everything. Anyway, let's change the subject once more. Did you watch the Nweph-Shake game last darkness?" said the inspector. "The Tigers team was losing and the poor Green Vest team. Despite of having Ilse Banser in their team, the best Bular-Ufu of the season."

Edison added, "They are…"

Inside the ship, Bruce spoke. "I think I've heard enough. Some weird creatures we have here, we could even begin a collection."

"Have you seen more of them?" asked Denise.

"Besides the rhinoceros and the black thing there is a third one named Ugarra."

Mary asked, "Okay, tell us everything you could hear. We didn't hear much, at least I couldn't."

"It seems quite simple. There are two ships, spaceships of course, one is coming in and the other is going out, and both want to be inspected first."

Billy said, "I heard something about a center or something like that too."

"You're right. I forgot about it and it's very important. If we want to get whatever this ship needs, we have to go to that Multipower Center and get the spare parts they were talking about."

Still on his knees, Billy commented, "First we have to know which parts we'll need to repair this ship."

In the same position Mary added, "And then we must go to the city. Maybe someone over there will tell us where the center is."

"RJ Marwel mentioned the name Esmeraland," commented Bruce.

"And how do we get there?" asked Nailbytes. "We have to think fast, it won't take long until they come to take out all the boxes and then they will find us."

"I have it. One of those talking creatures, I think it was Edison, said something about having unloaded some boxes with merchandise from his ship, the Stingray. Isn't it so?"

"What kind of merchandise, Bruce?" asked Billy.

"I didn't get it all, but we could take a look and see what's in those boxes. Maybe we are able to get into them."

"Which of the creatures is Edison?" asked Denise displaying her brackets.

"We still have a problem though. If we go out through the ship doors they will see us, we have to find another way out," said Nailbytes.

Billy commented, "I think I have it. Look over there, it looks like an emergency exit. Maybe there's another one near the window from which Bruce was looking out."

"Yes, good idea. Let's check it out," cried Mary.

Followed by all the others, Billy went to the right wing. "Yes, there it is. We just have to open it and one of us can go down and crawl to those boxes. As a matter of fact, they should be right underneath this wing."

"Okay, but who will do that? And how?" asked Maggie.

They looked at each other and around the spaceship.

"What's that thing on the floor next to that central barrel?" asked Nailbytes pointing to what seemed to be a piece of cloth.

Mary approached it and took it in her hands. "It's an old tunic, it probably belonged to one of Marwel's companions."

Billy stared at the piece of cloth and, after a few seconds, he exclaimed,

"We could use it to make a rope so that we can go down to that black thing's boxes."

"Wonderful idea," replied Mary.

They hurried to tear up the tunic and used the pieces to make the rope.

Mary looked at it attentively and commented, "I don't think it is long enough to reach the floor."

"Well, then the tallest one of us must go first," replied Nailbytes. All eyes turned to Bruce.

He answered with a grin, "Being the tallest and the strongest sure brings disadvantages."

"Easy, mastodon. It's not so complicated, you just have to go first and we will follow you," replied Maggie.

"Why don't you go first if you think it's so easy?" demanded Bruce.

"Because she'll have to jump and could get hurt and we have enough problems already," answered Mary.

Bruce made a face again but agreed.

"And how do we open this door?" asked Billy.

"There must be some sort of sign somewhere," replied Bruce

"I think I can see the sign." said Mary, standing right behind them.

"You're right, let me turn around this handle. Presto!"

"Well done, Billy," cried Nailbytes.

"Wait," cried Bruce.

"Don't shout! What's the matter?" asked Denise.

"I didn't shout. It's just that someone could see us if we open that small door too much. It would be better if we open it just enough to pass the rope little by little."

Nailbytes said, "But you told us some spaceships blocked your sight on the outside and that means they can't see us either."

"Yes I did, but we have to be careful anyway."

Billy agreed with Bruce and, very carefully, he started to open the emergency door on the ship wing.

"Okay. Can you see anything?"

"Not much, just some ugly creatures walking around everywhere."

"Mary means if you can see anyone near Edison's boxes."

"Don't be pissed, Bruce, it was a joke. But no, there's no one near."

"Okay then, here I go, wish me luck, guys."

"Good luck. But remember, if you get caught you came alone."

Bruce didn't bother to answer to Maggie's words, he just turned his face to her and gave her a harsh look. "That's enough," said Billy. Bruce prepared to go out of the ship. "Where can we tie this rope?" asked Billy, looking around him.

"Over here, this handle looks quite strong, I think it will resist our weight," advised Bruce, ready to leave the ship. He opened the door a bit more and began to go down the wing, trying not to be seen.

"Be careful, Bruce," whispered Mary.

"It's not so high really. The problem is not to be seen by those creatures," replied Billy, standing by the door with Mary.

"Okay, who's next?" whispered Mary.

"I am," answered Billy.

"Wait a minute, guys," cried Nailbytes. "Have you realized that we can breathe perfectly here?"

"That's true. We were so worried about everything else that we didn't notice something so important!" exclaimed Mary. "We should have known that from the moment the door was opened and we didn't feel any problem with the air coming from the outside."

"The atmosphere on this planet must have the same components as the one on Earth. Remember that the creature wasn't wearing any breathing device when he was out in our beautiful planet."

"Enough, Nailbytes, we have to hurry," interrupted Billy.

"Let me step away a little so that you can go down," said Mary, moving away from her place at the door. "You should better take a look and see if Bruce has been able to open some of the boxes."

"Yes, he has opened one already and he is hiding behind another," commented Billy as he put his head out through the door.

Bruce could smell the smell of new clothes like when you are in a store.

From where he was standing the boxes seemed to be full of clothes, some kind of tunics and coats. They could push them down a bit and fit into these boxes without any problem.

Billy started to go down the rope.

"Have any of you thought about how are we going to breathe inside the boxes until we get to Esmeraland?" asked Nailbytes.

"Once more luck is on our side. Look, the boxes have some holes in them which will allow us to get some air," exclaimed Mary, cheerfully.

"Okay, it's my turn, now," said Maggie.

"Come here and hold the rope. Start to go down carefully. Wait, someone is coming."

Mary closed the door silently before Maggie could start her way out. One of the creatures walked by the boxes but, fortunately, completely unaware of what was going on. "He's gone. Okay, you can go now."

Maggie stepped on the wing holding the rope. "This warm sensation is just like the one I felt like when I went very close to a bonfire," she said as she went down.

"I agree. It feels as if the heating was too high," agreed Nailbytes.

"The most important fact is that we can breathe normally," added Mary.

Maggie got to the floor and Bruce helped her into a box.

"Hurry up, Denise, let's go before they come back."

"Take it easy, sis. Don't get upset, we're doing fine so far."

"Shut it!" cried Mary, as she saw something coming towards them.

"What's the matter, sis?"

"I saw a robot walking by with two armed rhinoceroses." The three of them waited for a few seconds until the creatures had gone away.

Mary opened the emergency exit again and took a look outside. "Let's go now." Denise went down and got into a box.

"It's just you and me now. Go!" ordered Mary.

Nailbytes walked carefully towards the wing and started to go down the improvised rope. Just at the moment she saw her friend already on the floor, she heard a voice calling at the spaceship door. "Is there anyone in here? I need your documentation now. Hurry up."

Rapidly, Mary made a sign asking Nailbytes to throw her a sort of tunic that Bruce had previously taken from one of the boxes trying to make place for all of them.

Nailbytes threw her the tunic and she put it on as quickly as she could. Fortunately, it had a big hood. Withdrawing the rope, Mary crossed her fingers to her friend. After a few seconds, once she saw that they were all out of sight, she closed the exit door.

Chapter 5

SLINKING TO ESMERALAND

The voice insisted harshly, "Okay, if you don't open this door at once I'll be forced to break in."

Mary took a deep breath and, well covered by the tunic, opened the door.

In spite of her fear, she tried to speak in a harsh tone herself. "That won't be necessary, but it's a pity that one can't have a little privacy for one's calls," she cried, opening the door holding the Transler in her ear. She tried hard to talk naturally. "First of all, my clerk has the travel documents. He's the one who brought me to this fair" The inspector, accompanied by three guards, stood looking at her.

"Well, don't just stand there. What explanation can you give me after all this fuss?"

"I don't know what you are talking about. I'm just asking you for your travel documents. If you have any troubles with your agent that's your problem."

"Is that so? I'll never come to another fair in Esmeraland again." Mary made her best to sound furious.

"You better go down so we can discuss this quietly." The inspector sounded a little friendlier now. They all left the spaceship, Mary covered with her tunic, the inspector and the guards behind her.

Once on the floor Mary tried to keep her face covered and, in order to avoid more questions, she began to complain. "Of course, my transportation has not arrived yet. I insist this is the last time in my life that I will come to this city. No one has bothered to pick me up." The guards just stood still listening to her complaints.

Mary continued, "It's incredible. All of this is taking too long now. I hope I won't be late for the fair's first day."

"The fair doesn't start until after tomorrow."

"I have to prepare my stand, inspector."

Mary saw the creature called Edison coming out of one of the offices nearby. He walked towards them and, taking a look at the complaining figure, he asked, "What's the problem here, Inspector Dalmin?"

"I really don't know. Maybe you can explain it to me. This creature says that she is a merchant but she has no papers. She claims that she gave them to her agent. At least that's what I have understood until now.

Edison looked at Mary head to toe and as he had suddenly remembered something, he cried, "Of course. You must be from Caution Rai colony. The Supreme invited them to this fair."

"I... Yes, of course, I come from there."

"Dalmin, if she's been invited by The Supreme you'd better let her go, don't you think so?"

The inspector looked doubtful for some seconds but then he spoke. "Okay, she can go, but I'll ask the Trading Secretary to give me a list of all the guests of The Supreme. Otherwise, it will be a complete madness."

Mary couldn't believe her luck. "That would be a very good idea. It will certainly avoid having to go through so many problems the next time I come to this city. That is if I ever decide to come back here!"

The inspector seemed relieved, but looking around him he asked, "Where is your merchandise? I have to look into it."

Mary doubted for a second before answering in a highly arrogant tone of voice, "My agent brought it a few days ago. I'm too important to travel with a lot of trash, don't you think? And I must see that this ship is repaired if I pretend to go back home, can you imagine? I had my share of trouble, don't you think so?"

The inspector just nodded his head and made a sign to the guards who followed him as he started to walk towards the offices. As he walked away from them the inspector shouted to a guard nearby. "Hey, you, send a mechanic to this ship. I think Benji is available."

Mary and Edison stood silent for a moment. "Who is Benji? Is he good mechanic?" asked Mary.

"He's one of the best around here," answered Edison. "There he is. Benji, it's this ship!" shouted Edison, pointing his finger to the E-036 platform.

The so-called Benji approached them rolling on his four wheels. "Benji at your service."

"You're a robot. But you speak like a human!" cried Mary

"He speaks like what?"

"No, I mean that in spite of being a robot he speaks like us."

"And what else could a mechanic be?" asked Edison, sounding puzzled by Mary's words.

"I mean… Well, okay. You have arms so I suppose you will be able to repair my ship," she exclaimed as the robot went up the ramp to the spaceship. While Benji looked into the machine, Mary was aware that, no matter what, she had to go on with her drama. With a sigh, she exclaimed sadly, "Unfortunately, my problem subsists. I have no way to get to the city and I must go there to prepare my stand."

Edison looked at her for a few seconds and answered, "Don't worry, I'll give you a lift."

"Thanks. Where is your transportation?"

"It's quite near, but first I have to find a slovo to help me with those boxes. I don't have an agent to do that for me." Mary kept quiet, smiling at his words. Edison looked around him until he could see an inspector. "Hey, please, get me a slovo at once." The inspector took a whistle from his pocket and put it in his mouth. A high-pitched noise forced Mary to put her hands on her ears with a gesture of pain. She didn't know what the slovos were like until she saw five small creatures running towards them. They were small sized creatures, mustard colored and with big ears.

"Let's see… You, in the red vest, come here and start carrying these boxes," said Edison.

"What's inside them? Something fragile, perhaps?"

"That's none of your business. Just carry them carefully. If you do it well you will be rewarded, but remember that if you drop or damage anything you'll pay with your life. Did you hear me?"

Mary was frightened at the thought of the weight of those boxes with her friends inside but, luckily, the so-called slovo seemed to have huge strength in spite of his small size.

The chosen slovo didn't take long to put the boxes on a pallet pulled by a pump truck he had brought with him. "Where the hell am I supposed to take this?"

"Beware of your manners if you wish to be rewarded."

Mary couldn't help replying, "You should be nicer to him."

The slovo looked at her with surprise. "Okay, I will," answered Edison, a little surprised himself. Mary followed Edison and behind them came the slovo, carrying the boxes. The noise made it difficult for them to keep a conversation.

"That's better. I'm sure that he will do his work quite well. Where exactly is your transportation?"

"Wait a second. I will bring it to the land vehicles entrance," answered Edison as he walked, manipulating a strange bracelet on his right hand. Mary jumped backwards in surprise at what she saw. From his bracelet came a hologram that showed the inside of his vehicle. Edison began to manipulate it as he drove the vehicle through his device to put it where he wanted. "Just follow me," he cried.

While she walked along with Edison, Mary watched all the intergalactic ships which were parked on the other platforms. She looked up and saw some spaceships floating over their heads, either coming in or going out.

A strange and strong smell of burnt cables caught her attention. She could also feel some other odors which she quickly associated with the ones found in a garage. Mechanic robots worked on some of the spaceships, letting tools fall on the floor around them making a peculiar noise.

"I hope you'll pay me well, these boxes are too heavy."

"You're exaggerating in order to get more, aren't you? I don't remember putting so much weight in them."

Mary hurried to reply soothingly, "That often happens to me. Every time I go to a fair I intend to pack a certain quantity, but I always end up taking too much merchandise and I'm not able to sell it all."

"I don't care what's in here. I just want to be paid fairly," cried the slovo

"You will be, my friend," risked Mary. Once again, the slovo looked at her in complete bewilderment.

Mary kept trying hard not to show her face. She couldn't help being surprised at so many intergalactic creatures, as well as sophisticated robots walking around her and all those strange devices which carried the merchandise from one place to another. However, she didn't see any creatures that looked, even by far, like her and her friends. There were also armed rhinos guards everywhere watching over everything that went in and out. "Watch out!" cried Edison pushing Mary slightly to one side. A slovo carrying other customers' merchandise almost hit Mary with a pallet truck. "These slovos are not careful at all," commented Edison in a high voice.

Everybody seemed to be in a hurry and Mary had to be careful, trying not to bump into anything or anyone. She was concerned about being able to get the list of the parts needed for the ship in order to return home, so she occasionally looked back to see if Benji was coming after them. However, she thought, even if we get the parts will we be able to go back home by ourselves?

At the end of the platforms, she saw a lot of intergalactic creatures as well as their burdens going up and down along two wide ramps in spiral on both sides. These ramps were made of smooth stone and led to the different levels. Next to each of them there was a door of what appeared to be a big lift for cargo and passengers. They were also quite crowded. It was very noisy and Mary tried to talk to Edison keeping her face well covered. "There is a lot of movement here, isn't there?"

"This fair is very attractive and many visitors from the whole galaxy come to Esmeraland," explained Edison. "It is one of the most famous fairs around here."

Mary felt a little relieved because she no longer felt that burnt cable smell or any of those other odors which had given her a headache. She felt quite cold now, like if she were inside a cave.

After passing some ramps there was an exit that led to a very huge parking lot where the creatures left their land vehicles. Next to it was a main hall. Once at the hall Mary could see a lot of creatures of all types and sizes waiting and talking to each other. She saw what seemed to be the front door of the station and a lot of creatures like rhinos going in and out. They didn't look like guards, they were dressed with knee pants, a vest and a cap on their heads, all in an ocean green color. Mary thought they looked like taxi drivers waiting for clients.

"Turn right there and you will see my transporter. I set it up very close to the entrance. There you have it, the *Loader Vargas*. Isn't it a beauty!" exclaimed Edison.

"It looks like a minivan to me but with a much more aerodynamic design of course," said Mary.

"What do you mean?" asked Edison, a little disappointed at Mary's lack of enthusiasm.

Mary was far from wishing to upset her host and tried to correct her mistake. "I think it seems to have a very practical design, not to mention the color. I find that navy blue astonishing."

"I don't know about the color but it's certainly an extremely special transport." Edison was pleased now with Mary's last words.

The slovo interrupted, "Okay, enough conversation. Where do I put these boxes? Hurry up with my payment and make it worth, please."

"Wait a moment, slovo. I'll open the back door so you can put in the merchandise," said Edison, manipulating his bracelet once more. "Okay, put here this terribly heavy merchandise as you want me to believe..." The slovo hurried to obey. Once all the boxes were in place, he extended his hand expectantly to Edison. "Here is your payment and I hope you are satisfied because I'm not giving you anything more than this."

"It won't make me rich but I guess it's alright. Good fair for both of you," answered the slovo, counting the objects in his hand as he started to walk away in the search of more work.

"How much did you give him?"

"Five rutters, that's the usual payment for their job." Edison looked a little surprised at his companion's ignorance about what should be everyday knowledge for a merchant.

"Well, I'm not the one that takes care of these matters as you can imagine," answered Mary, feeling the astonishment in Edison's voice.

"Wait!" shouted Benji, the mechanic robot, as he hurried to where they were. "I made a quick diagnosis and here I have a list of the spare parts you'll need for your ship."

Mary took the paper trying not to show her face. "Thank you." Benji just rolled away towards the take-off platforms. Mary and Edison entered the *Loader Vargas* and Edison started the engine. The vehicle rose a little as if it were floating in the air. They left the station quickly, almost running over a clueless creature that was in the outdoor. At the entrances and all around the Imhamway Space Station there were many military vehicles, big and small, with armed guards watching around.

Mary saw something else that caught her attention. "What are those green vehicles parked in a line at the main door?" Some slovos put load on the towbars

"They are Wonners. They take visitors and traders coming to the fair to their accommodations."

"That is as a taxi?" What Mary was referring to were small vehicles that looked like small automobiles with a back cargo trailer.

"I don't know what that means. But they are smaller vehicles that transport creatures and their dependents."

At last, they were on their way to Esmeraland. As they left the space station behind a huge desert appeared in front of them. Mary looked around hoping that Edison would not see her expression. She couldn't believe that she was on a strange, far away planet, although up to that moment she had seen enough to be convinced of the reality of her awkward, to say the least, present situation.

Some creatures as well as some vehicles passed them on the road. "If you are planning to go to the Multipower Center it would be better if you know what you need so that you won't lose time over there."

Mary withdrew the list from her pocket and tried to read it. "I don't know, I really don't understand what's written here. This looks like a lot of scribbles to me."

"That's because it's in Esmadian. You'll be able to understand them if you use the Transler you have in your ear. Take it off and use it, slowly, as a scanner over the paper. First you have to pass it horizontally and then vertically from top to bottom," explained Edison with a surprised expression on his face. Mary obeyed and withdrew the device from her ear taking great care so that Edison wouldn't see her face. "Do it quickly as long as that violet light is on." Mary could hear Edison's voice but, without it in her ears, she didn't understand a thing he said to her. However, she realized that she could hear his words translated to her language coming out faintly from the small earphones of the Transler.

When she did what Edison had told her, some words began to appear on top of the strange signs she had seen on the paper. She could now read the list perfectly. "It says that I need the energy cartridge, a power regulator, one wall of the esbastic box and some other things I don't know what they are for."

"If you go to the Multipower Center they'll tell you what they are for and where to find them."

"Thank you."

"You are welcome. To get back to the Imhamway Space Station, you'll have to ask someone who is going there," advised Edison. "But you have to be very careful, this is a very dangerous planet, you could get killed just to steal some rutters from you."

"How terrible. What do you mean by…?"

Suddenly an explosion shook the *Loader Vargas*.

"What was that?" asked a terrified Mary.

"I'm sure they are those misfits from the Liberator's Army."

"Why do you call them misfits? If they are fighting it must be for a reason."

"It's a useless fight," answered Edison. "However, I must admit that things are very hard around here. Eliom and Lonar Mayer are taking Esmadis to its total disaster." Mary listened keeping her face covered by the tunic cap. She tried to wipe off the sweat from her face. "I know it's quite hot in here but the Esmadisans don't have anything, not even the Ace Basic," said Edison when he saw Mary's gesture.

"What's the Ace Basic?"

"Wow! Where are you really from? It's what you drink when you're thirsty."

"You mean water?"

"If you call it that way back home, so be it. Your galaxy must be really very far from here. Everybody around here knows it's called Ace."

"Yes, you're right. I just forgot it for a moment. But tell me, why don't you have water, excuse me, Ace?"

"Well, because there are no rutters."

"Do you mean money?"

Edison stared at her speechless.

"Don't look at me like that. It's really my first time in Esmadis and I hope to make some good business here," said Mary with a firm voice. "It's a terrible thing that people here don't have Ace. They can die of thirst."

"What does mean people? You meant creatures?"

"Yes, I do."

"Anyway, you can get some Ace pills, but it's not easy I can assure you. Now, Elion and his lieutenant, Lonar Mayer, are not really worried about the lack of Ace anymore. It seems they have had very good news."

"What news?"

"There is some hearsay about a big discovery," answered Edison with a calm voice. "A group of Enphalers went to investigate some far away galaxies and found a planet with plenty of Ace. It's incredible."

"And what are they planning to do now? Are they going over there to get more information about it?"

"I don't know what the next step will be, but I can assure you that the advisors of The Supreme Elion, a big bunch of crooks all of them, are looking forward to the profits they could get, not only from the Ace but also from the slaves they will be able to bring here."

"But do you know how are Eliom and his army planning to conquer that planet?"

"I don't know much about it, it's all pure gossip. Anyway, I only care about the rutters that will come of all that mess. I may be able to make very good business myself."

"You mean selling Ace and slaves?"

"That also, but I'm sure there will be other business related to whatever they bring from that planet. As I always say, 'Where there are rutters, there is Edison'."

"But how are they planning to invade my... the Ace planet?"

"I heard they were thinking about making a kind of bacteria to kill the inhabitants of that poor planet."

"When?"

"I don't know, but that knowledge can cost you your life or a trip to Atilkawa Fortress, and I really don't know which would be worse."

"I've heard something about that fortress. Where is it?"

"It's a little far from here. I have to go there sometimes. I supply some..."

"It's all business for you, isn't it?"

"Well, I told you that where there are rutters, there is Edison..."

"Yes, but sometimes you should try not to..."

"Wait a moment. Look up, that's an Ulphavisor coming towards us. They are trying to find out about the attack we just heard. They are afraid of the Liberator's Army."

Once the military ship was still Edison began to slow down his own vehicle and stopped. "What are those Liberator forces?"

"Please, keep a low tone, you can get me in trouble." Then he added, "Where do you come from?"

Mary doubted for a minute and answered, "I told you, I came to do business." Edison looked at her but kept quiet. He opened the door and, just before he could get out of the van, Mary grabbed his arm and begged, "Please, tell them I am your companion. I'll explain everything to you after."

"Okay, I will tell them that."

He went out to meet the guards. Mary followed him with her eyes without removing her cap. When he was out of her sight she took it off and took a deep breath. The only thing she could do at the moment was to wait for Edison's return hoping that everything would be okay. "Don't get nervous now." Mary jumped on her seat. "You scared me."

"If you keep doubtful before you answer his questions he will begin to suspect that you are lying," said Bruce.

"Did you hear what he told me?"

"Yes, we all did. When we get to the city we'll have to make a plan."

"Yes. First we have to get the spare parts and then see how we can go back home. I'm afraid that will be the difficult part," exclaimed Mary. "There he comes. Go back to the box." She hurried to put on her hood.

Edison came near the *Loader Vargas* and spoke to Mary before coming into the van. "It's alright, we can go now."

Mary was truly thankful to whom she had started to consider as a new friend. "That's wonderful, thank you so much for that. Let's go."

Edison came up and began to drive. "Are you going to tell me where do you really come from and what are you doing in Esmadis?"

"I already told you, I came to do some business here."

"That's not true. You don't come from this galaxy or from any other nearby."

"Yes, I do. As you yourself told the inspector, I come from the Cocktion Rai colony."

"You don't even know how to pronounce the name. It's Caution Rai. And that colony wasn't invited to the fair, the creatures there are not merchants, they are all miners. I said that to save you from the inspector. I knew he wouldn't know about anything at all as he's quite ignorant"

Mary didn't say anything.

"If you don't tell me who you really are we will go back at once and I will give you away, not only you by the way, but also all your friends that are inside my boxes. I just hope they haven't damaged my merchandise."

"How did you know that I wasn't alone?"

"It was that smell. I've never felt something like that before," answered Edison, sniffing the air with his long nose.

Mary kept still for a moment then, slowly, began to take off the cap over her head.

"Wow! You are certainly not from this galaxy. Where are you from?"

"I come from the planet that Lonar Mayer is planning to submit."

"So they have sent a mission to try to do something about it. I'm surprised though, that they've sent their younger inhabitants."

"I can assure you that nobody sent us. We can say that we are here due to a mistake. As a matter of fact a huge mistake. But as long as we are here, we have to do something to avoid the invasion of our planet and the annihilation of the human race."

"Well, I sure hope that you and your friends have a really good plan to defeat, according to the Dragadan Prophecies, one of the Seven Devils of Shigahell."

"What is that?"

"Forget about it."

"Tell me, why didn't you give us away if you knew I had been lying all the way?"

"I didn't do that because I don't like Lonar Mayer at all. This planet is getting worse every day. Furthermore, I was curious about you all. By the smell I could say you didn't come from Esmadis or from any nearby galaxy, and that you were not part of the Liberator's Army either. I was curious to know exactly where you came from."

"We're looking for some spare parts for our ship so that we can go back to our planet," said Mary. "Do you know Marwel?"

"Do you mean RJ Marwel? That Enphaler is well known. I'm sorry but I have to get rid of you at once."

Chapter 6

ANOTHER UNEXPECTED ENCOUNTER

"I don´t really know him. I know he belongs to the Triple Alliance which is the name of the group of Enphalers. From what I´ve heard, they have an agreement with Supreme Eliom to explore and invade the Ace planet."

"What does Enphaler mean?"

"They are Intergalactic Explorers but I don't have time to tell you more about that."

"So you were on the ship that landed at the E-036 platform and you and your friends were waiting to crawl into my boxes."

"Exactly," said somebody from the back

Edison turned back to the boxes for a second and asked, "And who are you?"

"My name is Bruce."

"Glad to meet you. What's the name of your companions?" The rest of them pulled out half their bodies from the boxes

"I'll tell you their names. This is Denise my little sister, and these are my friends, Nailbytes, Maggie and Billy. By the way, my name is Mary Ann."

"Thank you, Mary Ann. I really hope you will take care here, it's a very dangerous place if you don't know your way around."

"Now that you know who we are can you tell us where the Multipower Center is?"

"It is not too far away from here, Mary."

"But you can take us there to buy the spare parts we need for our ship can't you? You were talking about it," insisted Bruce.

"I'm afraid that's impossible."

Bruce said, "Just tell us where we should get off your transport and we'll go on by ourselves. You have helped us a lot already."

Edison took a detour on the road as he spoke. "I can't leave you in the city. As I just told you this is a very dangerous planet. If any of the supreme guardians or even any of those ambitious competitors of mine sees me with a creature not known to them I'll be in great trouble, you can be sure of that. I'll leave you at some place in which I can park without being seen. You're right, I've already done too much by bringing you here." Edison stopped the *Loader Vargas* behind some kind of dunes. "I'll leave you here, guys, it's quite safe and there's nothing around. Let me open the back door for you."

Mary got off followed by Edison. When he opened the door the boxes opened as the Earthlings stepped out, one by one. "Please excuse us for taking advantage of your kindness, but can we take one of these garments for each of us? That way we won't arouse any suspicions because of our looks," asked Billy.

"Yes. Please, Edison," added Denise showing her brackets.

Edison couldn't help smiling at her. "These garments are called tongs. Okay, my little friend, but don't get used to receive anything from me just for free. I can't live on gifts you know."

"Thank you," said Billy.

Maggie spoke in a low voice. "I really don't know what you are thanking him for. These garments are not a bit fashionable."

Billy whispered, "You'd better keep quiet. We have enough problems already."

"And I really don't know what you're talking about. Look at all these colors and sizes. This brown and red one looks very nice," replied Denise.

"I'll have that one," exclaimed Nailbytes.

Denise continued, "And what about the yellow and cream? And this…"

Edison spoke a little harshly. "I am in a hurry. I don't have the whole brightness to stay here with you. You better take the tongs quickly and get going."

Mary and Bruce looked at the road ahead of them with a worried frown. "Where is the Multipower Center?" asked Mary.

"It's towards your right. It's a little far if you have to walk, I'm afraid, but that's what you'll have to do."

They started to get off the *Loader Vargas*. Maggie shook her hands trying to refresh her face. "We will fry in this heat."

"I can't understand you but I think you are talking about the Iriage?"

Accidentally, at the moment he was getting off, Billy caused a small bottle to fall on the floor. Fortunately, it didn't break. "I'm sorry," he cried.

"What is it? It looks like some kind of golden grease."

"Yes, Mary, as a matter of fact, it is grease. They use it on the energy ducts at the Atilkawa Fortress. They have problems with the lijas and this grease keeps them away."

"lijas? What are those?"

"I'd have to spend a lot of brightness explaining all this to you. Anyway, they are animals I hope you'll never get to know face to face."

Billy asked in a soothing voice, "Just tell us enough to keep us alive in this place."

"It's not like if I was your father. Okay, sorry, guys, but I guess you're smart enough to go on by yourselves so I can go on myself too."

They were all as ready as they were able to be covered up with the tongs Edison had given to them all but one. Billy exclaimed, "What are you waiting for, Maggie? Take a tong now."

"I'm still looking for the right one for me. I don't know which to use."

Bruce shouted at her, "Just take one! Hurry up!"

"Don't shout. You found a grey and blue tong and, I must say, it becomes you. You don't look so bad, but me..." Bruce just looked up to the sky with a deep sigh. "Take the same color as that of Denise, ocean green and white," asked Mary.

"Oh, there are too many of those. I bet they are very common around here."

"I insist. I don't have all brightness, Maggie. Hurry up!" cried Edison

"Then take one like mine," suggested Mary

"Well, this design looks nice on you, the light brown shades matches your hair and the green goes well with it, but it´s not my style."

Edison spoke in a low, angry voice. "Is she always like this?"

Her friends looked at each other and answered all at once, "Yes."

"This could be the one," said Maggie looking at the tong in her hands. "I like these shades of pink and lilac."

"Hey, that´s one of the most expensive ones," cried Edison.

"Please, let her take it so that we can go now," begged Billy.

Edison didn´t say anything, he just lifted his arms in a gesture of defeat, walked towards the front and started to climb up to the driver's seat.

"Hope to see you soon, my friend," said Billy.

Edison answered without turning his head to them. "I think it will be better for all of us if we don't."

After a minute he stopped and returned to where they were standing. "I think you will need these."

"What's inside this bag?"

"Take them, they are Ace capsules. You'll find them useful when you get to the city, the Iriage is quite strong. One capsule will help you for quite a long period of time." After that, Edison just turned around, got on the *Loader Vargas* and drove away.

"Well, now we are in Esmeraland, but how do we get to the Multipower Center?"

"Just walk, Maggie," answered Bruce. She didn't answer and started to walk with a bad face.

The heat got worse as they started to walk. "It's terribly hot," said Billy, rubbing his forehead with his hand.

Mary replied, "You have to hold on. There's nothing we can do about it."

"He is right. This heat is going to kill me," exclaimed Maggie. Heat or Iriaje, it was unbearable. They could not even see the road with ease because the sun went straight to their face. They didn't have any choice but to dry the sweat on their faces and keep on walking. There was nothing at the horizon, only some sand dunes around and a few spots of vegetation, one of which, luckily, was very close to them.

Suddenly they heard something. Billy shouted, "Cover your faces and run to those bushes. There's a patrol coming towards us." They managed to hide behind the bushes and remained unseen as the patrol car went by.

"That patrol looks like a London taxi," commented Mary.

"How I wish I were in London right now. I don't like this place at all."

"Okay, Maggie. Complaining won´t help now. We´ve been lucky not to be seen by them. Edison said we would be dead if they find us," commented Denise.

Maggie replied with a tired voice, "Yes, that's the truth. And to think all this is happening because of that awful caravan trip."

"Okay, guys, whether we like it or not we are all together in this and we must work as a team to get out of it. We have to concentrate on getting the spare parts for the spaceship so that we can go back home," said Mary.

"I wish it will be as easy as it sounds," replied Nailbytes.

"I know, but that's exactly what we have to do."

Billy added sounding exhausted because of the heat, "We also have to try to frustrate the plans of that Lonar Mayer."

"Look, the only thing I am interested in is to find those parts and go home."

"I know you think only of yourself, Maggie, but there's a small detail you should have in mind. If we don't do something to avoid the invasion of our planet, we might not have a home to go back to."

Mary added, "And even if we can go back, we might not be there for too long. Since we are trapped in this planet we should at least try to do something about it."

For a while they kept walking towards the city under the burning heat, or Iriaje as it was called in this planet, until they saw they were very near it. "There's Esmeraland," said Bruce with an exhausted voice.

"At least we're alive. Until now, of course," added Billy.

"Yes, there's a lot ahead yet. To begin with we have to found out how to get to the center," said Nailbytes, walking with difficulty.

"I know, but let's rest a little, please. Ouch, my poor feet are hurting," cried Maggie, "and I feel sticky with this terrible heat."

"We can't stop now, we have to get there as soon as possible," replied Billy.

"But look at this place. It seems that we have arrived to some ruins not to a city."

"I agree with you. Look at all these destroyed or half-made constructions. Nobody can be living here."

"You are wrong. Look at that thing standing over there. It seems to be looking for something," said Denise.

"Where?" asked Bruce.

"Over there, that creature with a rhinoceros face. It looks like the ones you saw at the station where we landed."

"It will be better if he doesn't see us. Let's go and hide in those barrels by the big stones."

They ran towards the barrels and hid behind them just in time before the creature came nearer. Billy commented, "He is holding something like a machine gun. He seems to be looking for someone who's not really very popular around here."

"I think so too," said Mary.

"But have you seen those garments? He is a…"

"Shut up, Maggie!" replied Bruce. "We must think of something."

Nailbytes suggested, "Why doesn't one of us go and ask him about the Multipower Center?"

"It might be a good idea. That way he'll think we're just merchants looking for the center. Who's going? You are?"

"I don't think so, Bruce. It's my idea, let someone else carry it out."

"I'll go."

"Are you sure, sis?" asked Denise.

"Yes. I'll ask him. I think my voice will not frighten him."

"Please be careful. We don't know how he will react. Keep your distance."

"I will, Billy."

Mary walked to the creature who seemed to be a guard. When she got near him she kept her head low, covered with the tong's hood, and asked with a soft voice, "I'm sorry, I've got lost. Could you please tell me how to get to the Multipower Center?"

The guard turned to her and spoke in a harsh way. "Don't waste my time, I'm busy. Go and find it yourself, I'm looking for a young spy, I don't have time for lost idiots." Mary stood there and the guard spoke again fiercely, "What are you waiting for? Get going, you idiot, or I'll capture you for obstructing the work of the Supreme's guards." Mary didn't answer but hurried away to where her friends were, unaware that the guard's eyes were following her.

"I don't know if you could hear how nice that rhino was," she mocked.

"We heard something, definitely that thing needs to have better manners. I would have broken his ugly nose," commented Bruce.

"I don't doubt it. What do we do now?" asked Billy.

Nailbytes asked, "He said something about looking for a spy, didn't he?"

"A spy? Who can it be?"

"That would be me," said a voice coming from one of the barrels.

"Who said that?" asked Billy. They were all surprised.

Before they could find out who had spoken the guard appeared in front of Mary. He was already aware that she wasn't alone. He shouted at her, "Who else is here? You are not alone, are you? If that's the spy I'm looking for, you will certainly regret it." Denise thought fast and jumped into a barrel, the rest of them kept well covered and quiet. "Okay, who are you?"

Mary tried to keep her voice calm, "We are merchants. We're here to make some business at the fair, but our ship is damaged and we must get some spare parts."

"So you are merchants are you? And what's in those barrels?"

"Just some terrible smelling garbage," answered Denise, from inside of one of them.

"What are you doing in there?" replied the guard.

"We are very hungry. By the way, do you happen to have something to eat?" answered Billy.

"Do I look like your mother? Get your own food, you idiot."

"We'll do that," said Mary.

The guard insisted, "Whoever is inside there, come out immediately."

They all looked to each other and Mary spoke, "Okay, Denise, come out, but be careful with your face."

The guard sounded bewildered. "Denise? What a strange name. You must be from a very, very far galaxy, aren't you?" Denise came out with her face completely covered by her cap and her tong covered by garbage. "You're too short so you're not the spy I'm looking for, but I have to see your face right now."

"Okay, you can see it, but I must warn you that we have a terrible disease. If you look at our faces you will get it too and will be dead in no time. Back home we can live with it for a long time but foreigners are not strong enough and they die soon."

The guard put his sleeve to his big mouth. "On second thought I don't have time for all this. I'd better go look for the spy before he gets too far."

"Oh, but stay a while and tell me about the Nwephe-Shake game. It was quiet hectic don't you think? The Tigers were…"

"Are you crazy? I can't stay to chat with you. However, it was kind of hectic, you know. After the first set when the Green Vest expelled three of their players I thought things would get terrible, but… Wait! Wait! Wait! Shut up and don't make me lose my time." The guard walked away and disappeared from their view.

Mary cried, "Well, that was brilliant, Bruce."

"Yes, it occurred to me on time."

"But we still don't know where the Multipower Center is," said Nailbytes.

"I do," the voice in the barrel spoke again.

"If you do, why don't you come out and tell us?" said Mary.

A small creature started to come out of the barrel removing the dirt off his body. He looked like a grey reptile with small ears, very slim and quite short. He wore military green bermuda shorts as well as a shirt of the same color. His hat was similar to those worn by fishermen and it was the same color as his whole outfit. "What's your name?" asked Billy.

"My name is Centromaltidanuy," answered the creature looking calmly at the guys gathered around him.

"What?" asked Nailbytes.

"You can call me Centi if you wish."

"That's better," commented Mary with a smile.

"And who are you if I may ask?"

"Well, I'm Bruce, she's Mary and that one's her small sister, Denise. He's Billy, this one is Nailbytes and the one with the annoyed frown is Maggie. Now, tell us, are you the spy that thing was looking for?"

"Not really. That guard thought that I had a message from the Liberator's Army, but what I really had was one of the Dragadan Prophecies."

Billy asked, "What is that?"

"Have you never heard about the Dragadan Prophecies?" replied Centi. "The mystery of the Shigahell Temple? Where are you from?" The confusion among them was total. Centi took something from the side of his hat and read it to them. "It's convenient to avoid the alignment of the Seven Devils of Shigahell, our end will come if this happens, there will be eternal darkness for every living creature in the galaxy."

"What does that mean?" asked Billy.

Centi answered, "It is one of the prophecies of…"

"How interesting," cried Maggie. "But enough of horror and witches tales. It would be much more interesting if this reptile could lead us to the Multipower Center so that we can buy what we need and get out of this hell."

"Yes, Maggie, I'll do that, I know where it is," answered Centi with a gentle voice, despite Maggie's harsh words.

"Okay, let's go," cried Bruce.

After walking for a while they were sweating all over. The heat was terrible and they could hardly keep on walking anymore. They had to wipe up their forehead to avoid getting sweat drops into their eyes because they walked with their heads down which was quite tiring. "Centi was right in advising us to walk this way so that the sun won't blind us," commented Billy with a deep sigh.

"Keep walking and think about something else," advised Mary. "If we try to think about something different, maybe we won't feel so hot. What were you doing here, Centi? Nobody can live in this heat."

"That's exactly why I thought that no guard would be able to find me there, but I was wrong."

"He mistook you for a spy," replied Billy. "Do you like topics about prophecies and that sort of things?"

"Yes I do."

"Please keep walking," cried Maggie.

"At some point I will go to Kuntur-Maphre and then I'll go to the Shigahell Temple," commented Centi. "My mom doesn't want me to go there though."

"Where is Kuntur-Maphre?"

"It is a city not too far from here, Billy." Centi continued. "The last thing I read on the Dragadan Prophecies tells something about an invasion to a planet of a very far away galaxy it seems."

"What are you talking about?" asked Bruce.

"According to the prophecies, Lonar Mayer is one of the seven devils. They need new souls for Egold Amanda and that far away planet creatures might supply them. She knows that, and for that reason she is making new weapons. Creatures in the mines are working tirelessly through darkness and brightness in order to make them."

"If she is a devil how can anyone defeat her?"

"Well, it seems that it is not absolutely impossible, Mary. One of the prophecies tells that very deep in The Lost Temple of Shigabell there are Golden Pentagons which are the…"

Maggie interrupted, "If we keep talking we will never get to the center. Let's walk fast before this heat burns me up."

"What's that noise?" asked Bruce looking back.

Centi shouted, "A contingent is coming."

Chapter 7

GETTING TO THE MULTIPOWER CENTER

Billy shouted, "Quickly, let's go behind those dunes!" They all obeyed at once.

Mary and Centi popped out their head a bit to see what was going on. Several army vehicles carrying contingents of guards passed near them.

Standing behind Mary, Centi explained, "They are part of the Amarphy Army. I wonder where they are going."

"Can we go out now?" shouted Maggie.

"Yes, we must go on."

Coming out of his hiding, Bruce said, "I couldn't see much but I'm sure there were well-armed soldiers on those vehicles."

"As I just said, they are going somewhere to put down a revolt or something of the sort. That happens every day around here."

The group continued their walk towards the Multipower Center. "How far are we now, Centi?" asked Bruce, taking off his tong hood.

"Not much. As a matter of fact we are almost there."

A little time later Bruce exclaimed, "I think I can see a town. At least it looks like one."

"All the constructions are made in stone."

Denise added, "Yes, sis. And, in spite of the fact that we're supposed to be in a city, these roads are not paved as we could expect, they are just like the ones at the desert."

Maggie commented, "What? There aren't any paved streets here? This isn't a bit fashionable, you know."

"Tell me why would they need paved streets if all the vehicles here float over the roads? You and your silly comments," replied Bruce.

"But she is right about one thing though. Most of the creatures wear the same color of Denise's tong, ocean green with white."

"How interesting," Nailbytes replied. "That's my most important worry about this adventure."

"Be careful not to show your faces, guys," advised Centi as they walked by a group of creatures gathered in front of a stone house. All of a sudden a creature came running out from a building stumbling over Bruce.

"Hey, you, be careful," cried Bruce lifting his arms.

"Take it easy. He didn't mean to push you, he almost fell too. Don't be mad at him," replied Centi.

The creature spoke to him in a harsh voice. "We will fix this later, you and me." He then turned to the creature he had been talking to before and continued, "And you, asshole, you don't have any reason to complain. It's a fair deal. I'm first in the row, you arrived after me."

The other creature replied angrily, "It's been a long time since I could get any Balotelas."

"If you don't get out of my place I'll..." He withdrew a small knife from his pocket. The other one did exactly the same.

Some creatures that were passing by stopped to see what was going on.

Billy whispered. "This is getting dangerous, let's go."

Bruce replied, "Wait, this is getting interesting. I thought those rhinoceroses would fight with their horns not with knives."

Maggie said in a low voice, "I don't think all this is funny."

Mary asked in the same voice, "What is this fight for?"

"It's obvious. One of them was standing in line and the other, for some reason, tried to sneak in."

"And this is the way they settle their problems, with knives?" asked Denise.

"Yes, that's the way things are here. You don't like something you attack."

"Be careful," cried Nailbytes to one of the fighting creatures. Turning to his friends he exclaimed, "Did you see that? He almost stabbed him but the other was lucky enough to avoid it on time."

Billy said, "We'd better go on, we won't get anything positive staying here, guys."

"And this multitude might bring an Amarphy patrol to take them all away, at least the ones that are still alive by then."

"Okay, let's go," said Maggie, trying to go through the creatures gathered around the fighters.

"Don't push, just try to walk away quietly so that they won't notice us," advised Centi. Once they were far from the fight Centi asked, "Nobody is missing, is it?"

"No, we're all here," replied Mary.

A contingent of armed guards on their vehicles parked just in front of them near a stone construction. "Quickly, let's go!" shouted Maggie.

"Don't shout. We'll just go on slowly as if this isn't about us at all," said Centi. The guards pushed their way through the creatures. "We'll follow down this street and turn left at the next corner." They walked obeying Centi's instructions.

"It seems that fights are very common on this planet," commented Mary.

"Yes, they are, especially over food coupons and Ace pills. Here prevails the law of the strongest."

Denise commented, "Life isn't too happy here, is it?"

"I'm burning," commented Nailbytes. "With these temperatures those Ace pills must be well appreciated."

"They certainly are. The merchants who manage them make many rutters.

"What's that?" asked Bruce.

"It's their money. They call it rutters," explained Mary.

Maggie said, "This chat is very nice, but this heat is at boiling point."

"Okay, we'll ..."

Suddenly they heard screams. "Stop or I'll..."

"Sithel Isban."

A creature, pursued by three guards who were shooting at it, was headed to where they were. They dropped to the floor but one of them remained standing, apparently unable to react. "Nailbytes, be careful!"

There was another shot and a beam came out from one of the guards' weapon. Mary stood up, pushed her friend down and both fell on the floor.

The persecuted creature was also lying on the floor but she stood up quickly and went on running, but a guard pointed his weapon to her. "No, please, wait. Oh no!" shouted Denise.

The guard shot and the poor creature turned into dust. "But what did that creature do to deserve such a death?" asked Denise.

"I don't know. I think I saw a bag in her hand. She must have stolen some food from a delivery store." Nobody spoke. They just looked at each other.

"Where's my sister?" asked Denise after a minute.

"She's there, under Nailbytes," said Maggie with a smile. "Hurry to help her. With that weight on her she'll soon be disintegrated too."

Billy went to help lifting Nailbytes from the floor.

"Well, if this planet doesn't kill me, something like this again will certainly do it," exclaimed Mary lying on the floor.

Nailbytes replied, cleaning the dust from his tong, "Don't complain so much. Let's go."

The group continued on its way. Maggie commented, "From what I could see the supreme guards have a curious costume."

"Yes, they look like Roman guards with helmets and armors and they seem to be using sandals," added Nailbytes.

"Yes, I can remember something like that on our history books, but they are a little chubby. I would put them on a diet, and that terracotta color doesn't go at all with their terrible rhinoceros complexion."

Bruce interrupted, "That's enough, Maggie. I insist, you and your silly comments."

"Leave her alone, it's no use. I hope we are near that famous Multipower Center."

"Yes, Mary, so do I. Where is it?" asked Maggie.

"We are getting close."

"I hope so, but I don't believe you anymore."

"This time it's true, I promise."

After a few minutes Centi pointed at a big stone construction. "The Multipower Center. There it is." They kept walking until they arrived to what seemed to be a parking lot. There were all kind of transportations parked.

"It's a huge building but it seems to be made of stone," commented Bruce.

"Yes, as a matter of fact it looks more like a big cave," said Billy.

"I don't know what you mean. But there you have the Multipower Center you were looking for. By the way, what exactly are you looking for?"

"We need some spare parts for the ship we flew in, Centi."

"You'll sure find them in there. They have all kind of pieces for any ships, whether they come from this planet or from any other galaxy."

"Thanks. We have to go in at once," exclaimed Mary with enthusiasm.

"Wait a moment. I can't go in. There are guards there who know me and they will capture me. I'm sorry, but I must stay here."

"But we don't have an idea of what to do. I mean, do we go in there and just ask for spare parts?" Looking at the list in her hand, she continued, "We give them the code or what?"

"I see what you mean. If the guards see you so lost they will get suspicious…"

"You see? You have to go with us," exclaimed Billy.

"But I told you, if I go in there I will go straight to the Atilkawa Fortress, and it will be the end for me."

"If you can't help us maybe some of us have to go and try to get the spare parts so that we can get out of this hell," said Maggie.

"It's not that I don't want to help you, but I have to take care of myself. However…" Centi walked a few steps away but, suddenly, he turned around and came back to them.

"I have an idea. As she just said, you should go in but not all of you. Large groups bring too much attention. I'll stay here with some of you and we will communicate through the Transler RX7 which works as a radio as well. Just put it in low sound and nobody will know that you are talking to me. That way I will be able to tell you where to go and what to say. I know the Multipower Center very well."

Mary cried, "That's a very good idea!"

"I think so too. Now we must decide who goes in and who stays here,"

Billy commented, "This won't be easy. If you get caught they will take you to the fortress and I can assure you that it will not be at all like a nice vacation."

"I'll go. If you're so afraid that they will get you, you can stay here with the girls."

"I didn't say that I wouldn't go, Bruce, I just said that the ones who are going in there have to be very careful."

"Let's not lose time in discussions. We'd better decide now who is going in."

"Nailbytes is right. Well, there is Bruce and... I will go too."

"Okay, so it will be Mary, Bruce and me."

"Good luck to all of you. You know that I get claustrophobic when I am in caves."

"We know, Nailbytes. And anyway, one of us had to stay here and take care of the girls," said Bruce.

"I'll do that."

"Now that it's all set please go and find those parts so that we can go back home."

"We are going in right now, Maggie," answered Billy.

"First allow me to adjust one of your Translers to a very low sound." Mary gave hers to Centi. He manipulated it until he left it in the right level of the communication they would need inside. "Okay, take it and go."

Mary, Billy and Bruce walked towards the big entrance of the Multipower Center surrounded by all kind of creatures and taking good care not to show their faces. Centi started to use his Transler. "Testing, testing, can you hear me, Mary?"

"Yes, I can hear you clearly."

"Tell the guards at the door that you are in a trade mission and that you were hit on your way here by the bandits of the Tiron Zone.

That's very common around here, but don't let them see your face. Keep it covered."

"Okay, thanks."

The three Earthlings went up the stone steps leading to the front entrance.

Two guards stopped them at the door. "What do you want here?"

"We are part of a trade mission. We came to the Esmeraland Fair," answered Mary, keeping her head low and well covered.

The guards looked at each other and one of them asked. "What products do you sell?"

"We sell clothes, garments for everybody," answered Billy. They had to move aside in order to let some creatures go out the door. One of them was manipulating a bracelet on his right wrist.

"They probably came to buy some parts too," commented Bruce in a low voice as they walked by him.

"So, you are merchants, aren't you?" insisted the guards.

"We can show you all our merchandise. We have the latest outfits. I'm sure you and your family will like them. I can go to my transporter and bring some brochures," said Mary, pretending to go back to the parking lot. As she walked a few steps she turned to Billy. "You can show them our jewelry too. I'm sure they'll love it."

Suddenly, a vehicle parked right in front of the door and the creatures that had just passed by them got on it and went away in a hurry. "It's okay, that's enough. I can't buy anything now. Just go in," ordered one of the guards.

They entered the center with mixed sensations of fear and curiosity. "Did you see that? As far as I could see that vehicle came here all by itself. There was no pilot," commented Billy.

"That's the same thing Edison did back at the station. It seems that the vehicles here have some sort of remote control which brings them to their owners."

"Okay, guys, we'd better move quickly so that we won't raise any suspicions," said Bruce. They walked away from the main door.

"Wow! More strange creatures," commented Billy, looking around him.

"Some of them are just like the ones I saw at the station," replied Mary. "Watch out, there are armed guards everywhere." Mary then put her hand on her ear and spoke quietly. "And now, Centi, where do we go?"

"If I'm not mistaken you are in the entrance hall. Is that so?"

"Yes."

"Right in front of you there are many passages with a lot of stores, aren't there?"

"That's right."

"Well, you have to take the first one on the right."

"Copied," answered Mary.

The three Earthlings walked in the direction Centi had indicated. The big noise made difficult any conversation and, as they walked along the small stores, they kept close to each other. "Well, well, well, this looks like one of those galleries back in London, don't you think? All those small stands, one besides the other," commented Billy

"The stands look like small stone caves with counters."

"Everything here is made of stone," added Bruce.

The three Earthlings had to break through the crowd of intergalactic creatures going from one side to the other, trying not to push anyone or be pushed by them.

Mary spoke to Centi. "We can only see a lot of stores, or caves."

"Keep walking. Go to Platform Two, Wing Five. I think you will find the spare parts there."

"And where are the stairs?" said Mary. "We only see a lot of stone stands on both sides."

"You'll see them soon. Just keep walking."

The three friends kept on talking among themselves about the things they saw. "Look at that reptile, he's showing a Transler to the other one."

"Look over there, Bruce. Those things look like tablets."

"Mary and Bruce, take a look at your left, those seem to be gas masks. I guess they use them for protection against a chemical attack or something, don't you think so?"

"I have no idea, but here you can find anything you may need for a spaceship, just as Centi told us," replied Bruce.

"Yes, they have everything in there. But tell me now, where are you?" said Centi.

"We are still on the ground floor and now we can see some stairs right in front of us to the right."

"Okay, Mary, go up to the first floor." They obeyed Centi's instructions and went up.

A strange creature rushed to the stairs almost pushing them to a side. "Let her pass," said Mary. Bruce stepped aside.

"That thing was in a real hurry," said Billy.

"Yes, she sure was," smiled Mary. They could luckily dodge two rhinoceros armed guards who were going down in a hurry. The guards just passed by their side and walked away.

As soon as they arrived at the second floor Mary spoke. "Here we are in Platform Two, Centi, where's the Interior Five?"

"There it is," Billy hurried to answer pointing to a sign but unaware that his sleeve was showing his arm under his tong.

"Be careful, Billy. Cover your arm at once."

"I am sorry."

"This floor looks just like the one below. Small stands like caves everywhere around."

"All the floors are the same, Bruce. Just go to number five," said Centi.

Billy commented, "There are too many corridors. Anybody could get lost." They walked to the Interior Five but two guards who were passing by turned around and came towards them.

Mary turned slowly and told her friends, "They are coming after us."

"And now, what?" muttered Billy.

"Just keep walking. Let's go to the Interior Five," replied Mary.

"But they are following us."

"Do as Mary's telling us, Billy."

"Don't shout, Bruce. And you, Billy, don't worry, we just have to walk a little faster but trying to keep them for noticing us."

"I think they've already noticed us."

"Well, we'll just stop and find out what they want."

"I sure hope you know what you're doing, Mary," replied Billy.

"I think I do."

The guards reached them. Both had strange black modern rifles and wore terracotta color uniforms. One of the guards asked, "Where are you from? Why are you here?"

"We are members of a trade mission," answered Mary.

The other one spoke harshly. "Quickly, give me your trading documents."

"We don't have them here, we left them at our ship. They told us we wouldn't need them here."

"What are you saying? If you don't have them you must come with us," said the first guard.

"We are in a hurry. We have to find some spare parts for our ship so that we can bring more merchandise," explained Mary in a soothing tone.

"I sure hope it's not too late already," added Billy.

"Hurry, Mary, tell them that you are Eliom's guests," said Centi through the Transler.

"Please, we are special guests of the Supreme Eliom. He invited us to the fair and he's certainly waiting for us right now." Mary tried to speak firmly.

"And where is your invitation? Show it to me," asked one of the guards.

"Wait a second, I have it somewhere..." said Billy as he pretended to look into his pockets.

One of the guards showed a gun to them. "Take off your caps. Let's see where you are from."

"Don't do that! Run!" cried Centi through the Transler.

"We can do that another day. Let's go!" cried Mary as the three of them started to run.

"Stop or I'll shoot you."

They ignored their pursuers and kept running as fast as they could. One of them shouted, "Isis Isban."

Suddenly, they heard a sound and Billy, who ran a little behind his friends, fell down with a gesture of pain on his face "What's the matter?" asked an anguished Mary.

"I felt like a strong current on my leg."

"Your Isban is regulated to disperse mobs, you idiot. Put it on direct attack level," cried one of the guards to his companion. The other one did so as he kept running towards the fugitives. Mary ran towards Billy when a kind of trolley passed by them. She pushed it towards the guards trying to hold them back for a moment. It helped but not for long.

"Run! It'll be better if we split up!" said Bruce in a high voice. They started to run in different directions and the guards went after two of them. The creatures around looked curiously to what was happening.

"Wait there or it will be worse for you," cried one of the guards who ran after Billy. Billy ignored him and kept running. The guard went after him trying to shoot him but, fortunately, there were more creatures now walking around the center, although most of them kept aside to avoid getting into trouble because of some strange foreigners.

The guard lost view of Billy for a few moments when he turned over a corner. Billy saw that a trash chute was quite near him and that it seemed big enough for him to go through. A little far from him yet, the guard realized what Billy was thinking about and smiled to himself. "Poor idiot," he mumbled as he approached the trash chute. Billy wasn't around anymore and the guard pushed the crashing button. "That's the end of that poor creature."

He went to join his partner with a smile on his face.

Chapter 8

A RISKY SWOOP

Mary kept running, looking back from time to time. As soon as she saw that nobody was coming after her, she stopped and started to walk so that she wouldn't catch the attention of the other guards. Bruce wasn't that lucky and was still being pursued by the guard. He went towards the stairs which had led them to the first floor. He had started to go up to the next level when, on the landing, he saw a small opening on one of the walls. He looked through it. There was a grill running over the whole external wall from the ground floor up to the top of the building. Making a quick decision he went out through the hole. A few seconds later his persecutor was on the landing but, unaware of the grill, continued his way upstairs.

In the meantime, Mary had realized that she was completely lost within the galleries around her. Unable to find her way out she kept walking, trying to keep calm and go unnoticed, when something caught her attention. "Where are those creatures going?" She went a little nearer to take a better look at a group that had been walking a little ahead of her and, to her surprise, had disappeared when they went near a wall. She was sure that they had gone inside some entrance on the wall. She couldn't see any door but then, she thought, there must be a secret entrance. She began to touch the wall with her hands taking care at the same time that nobody was looking at her. Finally, she smiled. "This is it."

A small opening had appeared in front of her. She saw an empty room and a small corridor at her left. The ceiling was a little low but she would be able to walk along it if she bent a little. "Let's see where it goes."

She went down the corridor, more like a tunnel, trying not to make any noise. It was really a series of ramps, one after the other, in an "S" kind of shape.

She hoped she wouldn´t meet any undesirable creatures. She finally arrived to what seemed to be a warehouse with loaded shelves and boxes on the floor all over the place. A little light entered by the only window and also from what looked like another entrance. She suddenly heard a voice coming towards her. She ran to hide behind a shelf.

Mary saw a creature very alike the ones at the Imhamway Station, a kind of rhinoceros, although this wore a different outfit. "Okay, I have just a few more to go and I will finish up with this order." Talking to someone on his Isikul, the creature went on, "Where do I have to leave this order? What? Can you repeat that please, I didn't get you. At the reactor BB Down, okay, it is right outside of the Atilkawa Fortress, isn't it? Okay. What? What do you want sell to me?"

"A bracelet you say? And how is it like?"

"Okay, at what price?"

"That is too expensive."

"It's expensive even if it´s pure gold."

"Okay then but it must be in good condition."

"I knew it, what is written on it?"

"Just Toby? I think that can be easily removed."

"Okay, I´ll take a look at it when I get there."

"Okay, bye now." The strange creature took two boxes and walked towards the entrance.

As soon as she saw him leaving the room Mary went near the window, climbed on a shelf in order to reach it and went out. She had to jump to the floor beneath but, luckily for her, it wasn´t too high. She looked out to see where she should go from there. Once more she was lucky. Not far from her Bruce was already waiting outside with his friends.

Denise's brackets shone all over when she smiled broadly not fully believing what she saw. She cried out Mary's name. "Make a sign to her so that she can see us," advised Centi. Nailbytes raised his hand calling her name. Mary hurried to meet her friends. "What happened? Bruce just told us that the guards almost caught you," exclaimed Centi.

"Those Roman guards are really dangerous," commented Mary. "Their helmets are very alike the ones used by the Roman soldiers we've seen in history books."

"Yes, she is right. Thinking about it even their vests are alike, at least those of the guards at the door," added Nailbytes.

"How did you manage to escape?" asked Centi.

"We split and then I found a secret passage."

"How's that?" asked Maggie.

Mary replied, "I'll tell you all about it later. But where is Billy?"

"Here I am," answered her friend appearing behind them with a broad smile on his face.

"How did you and Bruce escape?"

"I don't know about Billy, but I came down a grill on the outside wall."

"And what did you do, Billy?" asked Mary.

"I ran as fast as I could and hid behind the counter in an empty stand."

Centi asked, "Didn't the guard see you there?"

"No. He thought that I had gone into the rubbish chute. I think it was because a creature had thrown something into it and it made quite a noise. He thought it was me who was inside so he pushed the crashing button and went away."

"You were lucky," cried Denise.

"He certainly was." Centi seemed quite impressed.

"We'd better get moving, guys. Those guards might still be looking for us," said Billy.

"Yes, we should go elsewhere before Lonar Mayer comes to check over. Just follow me, guys."

"Follow you where to, Centi?" asked Mary.

"We're going to the city. You'll see."

They began to walk towards the city and Mary told them about her experience at the secret tunnel and the creature she had seen there. After a while, they saw a big vehicle flying above them, more like a spaceship. It was not too big but looked quite impressive. "What's that strange transportation?"

"It's the *Landthunder*. It's the most powerful vehicle on this galaxy. It could invade any planet all by itself."

"Who's the owner?" asked Billy.

"It belongs to Lonar Mayer, she´s Eliom's general, and it seems to be going to the Multipower Center."

"It looks like the Batimovil, though it's dark green."

"It looks like what?"

Bruce said, "Don't pay any attention to Denise. Who is that Lonar Mayer? How bad is she?"

"Okay, I'll tell you, but where can I begin? Extortion, smuggling, torture, murders, abductions, you pick one. They say she will be Eliom's successor."

"Wait a moment, where's Bruce?" asked Mary.

"He's standing on that dune," answered Maggie.

Centi asked, "What are you doing there, Bruce, are you out of your mind? Someone can see you. Let's go."

"I'm going. I just wanted to take a look to that Lonar Mayer you talk so much about. It was the opportunity to do so since the spaceship was flying so low."

"You'd better listen to Centi. Let's go before they find us."

"Okay, Mary," replied Bruce, coming down the dune. "I couldn't see her well but she looks like something in between a human being and a condor."

"What´s a condor?"

"Forget it, Centi, it´s a huge bird we have in some countries back home. I saw someone moving inside the *Landthunder* with her. I couldn´t see it well but it was small and walked with a limp," said Bruce.

"Definitely, that was her lieutenant, Ultro the Yagoon."

"And who is him, or what is it?" asked Maggie.

"We´d better stop this chat, I´m burning out here."

"Okay. Let´s go."

They went on walking through the desert towards the city of Esmeraland.

On their way some creatures, as well as many strange vehicles passed near them.

"We have to be careful with those vehicles, we might get hit by them," advised Centi.

"It's so hot," complained Maggie.

"Yes, it feels as if we were walking by a bonfire," commented Nailbytes.

"It's more like we were walking through a bonfire," added Denise.

Nailbytes said, "I suppose that's why everybody around here wears those greenish tunics."

"They are aqua green," corrected Denise.

"You should be grateful that we are not in Benza. We can get up to 120 irios there."

"How much would that be in Celsius?"

"I've no idea."

Bruce said, "Really, Nailbytes, that was a foolish question. How could Centi know anything about Celsius?"

"Okay. Let's make the conversion then."

"There you go again with your calculations and mathematical nonsense."

"Leave him alone, Bruce. It might be useful for us to know that," replied Mary.

"Can you see now, Centi? That's why we call him Nailbytes."

They went on walking under the scorching heat towards Esmeraland. Centi shrugged his shoulders. He really couldn't get what his new friend meant.

"We'll get a beautiful tan with this heat," commented Billy.

"Leave those foolish comments to Maggie," exclaimed Bruce. Maggie didn't say anything, she just made a face.

"Someone is coming," cried Centi. "Let's go to that ravine." They all went down the small ravine. A huge vehicle passed by.

"What was that?"

"It's a prisoners transport. I don't remember it's name."

"So there are prisoners inside it?"

"Yes, I suppose so, but it has no escort. That's strange."

They resumed their walk. After a while Billy exclaimed, "Hey, guys, look at that. I think there are a lot of houses over there." There were a series of flat constructions surrounding what seemed like a square. He sounded surprised as he came closer to what he had just discovered. "I can only see the roofs. And they are a kind of gable roofs."

"You're right, Billy, they are queer. They have a small window on one side and something that looks like a door on the other," commented Bruce. "They look as if they were made of concrete."

Suddenly, Bruce said, "Be careful. What noise is that?"

"What's the matter?" asked Centi as they walked through the square which was full of creatures. At that moment they all saw a big vehicle stopping nearby. In a few minutes other smaller ones arrived and a bunch of "Roman guards" as the guys had named them came out of them and approached the houses.

"What's going on?"

"Don't say anything, Mary, just keep calm," advised Billy.

They heard the shouts, "Guards, Isis Isban."

Mary asked in low voice, "What are they shouting?"

Centi made a gesture to make her keep quiet. In a few seconds the whole square was full of Amarphy vehicles and supreme guards. The guards pushed the creatures towards the center of the square. One of the creatures, who looked quite old, almost stumbled and begged, "Please, I can't walk so fast." They were gathered in groups around the vehicles.

"What are they doing?" asked Bruce in a very low voice.

"They are looking for members of the Liberator's Army or for any opponent of the government."

"Or they might be looking for us," said Billy.

"Don't say that. Let's hope that's not happening," said Nailbytes, speaking low but in an angry tone.

"What did the one with the bracelet on his arm say?"

"It was an order, Mary. Isis Isban means, 'have your Isbans ready for punishment'."

"Yes, I remember now, those were the same words the guards shouted at Billy before they shot him," replied Mary.

There were many small vehicles which looked like a mix of scooter and water motorcycles, Alphavisors as they call them in this planet.

At that moment all the inhabitants from the houses were outside being registered and questioned by the guards. "They are coming towards us. What are they going to do?" shouted Maggie.

"I don't know," said Mary.

"Hey, don't point that thing to me," demanded Bruce.

"Don't provoke them. Supreme guards are brutal, they will shoot you for no reason," advised Centi in a very low voice.

They heard one of the inhabitants begging, "I don't have any more papers, these are all."

"Well, if you don't have all the papers you need you'll have to come with us to the Provisional Precinct."

A female voice cried, "No, please, my partner is ill, leave him here."

"And what is he doing here if he's sick? He should be dead."

"No, no, he's not so sick. What I meant is that we have three small children..."

"Shut up! Come on, take him."

"No, please, I beg you..."

The guards beat the couple until they were on the floor. "Stand up, now!" shouted one of the guards.

"Just shoot them and let's finish up with these idiots at once."

"Hey, wait a minute. That's enough!"

"And who are you, you idiot?"

"I'm Mary, but that's none of your business."

"Well, look at this one. We have a brave stupid who wants to be disintegrated in a minute."

Laughing mockingly the guards took out their strange rifles, the Isbans. One of them shouted to Mary, "Where are you from? Take off your cap immediately." Mary obeyed. The guards stared at her in surprise.

"What planet are you from?" shouted one of them and his voice brought over other guards who were dealing with the creatures.

"Look, it seems that we have visitors from far away galaxies."

Centi hurried to where they were and spoke firmly. "Sorry, guys, I don't know where she's from but she is here to work in the laboratories."

One of the guards said, "I know she is not from anywhere close to this galaxy. Why does she have such a pale complexion?"

"Well, I didn't want to talk about it but this poor creature has a disease. Of course it's not supposed to be too contagious, but you never know…"

"If she's ill she must be disintegrated. Rules are rules," replied one the guards.

"That's right, she must die. And who are you? You look familiar," added another guard.

Centi replied cautiously, "I'm from Esmadis. I live in Esmeraland, Glover Zone."

One of the guardians insisted, "Let me see your papers again." The others stood nearby paying attention to the discussion.

"It's useless," spoke Bruce in a low voice as he started to walk away.

"Where are you going?" asked Billy.

"Just watch me," he answered, running towards one of the vehicles which looked like an aquatic motorcycle. He took it and rode away.

When they heard the sound of the vehicle, the guards, pushing their way through the creatures around them, ran to their own cars crying, "Hey, you, leave that Alphavisor at once, it's not yours. Come back here immediately!"

Bruce's action caused a great confusion among the guards and the creatures around them. It was a complete chaos. "Let's take advantage of the situation to run away from here."

"You're right, Mary. We have to get away from here as fast as we can," added Nailbytes. The creatures who had been detained started to go away and so did our friends.

"We have to go that way," advised Centi.

"Are we going to your house?" asked Maggie.

"Yes, we are."

"And where is Bruce? How will he know where to look for us?" asked Mary with a frown.

"I don't know," answered Billy.

"No problem. Bruce knows well how to look after himself," cried Nailbytes." Once we get home we'll see who will come back to wait for him."

"We must go now. I sure hope Bruce will be okay."

"We all do, sis," added Mary.

Somewhere not far from where his friends were, Bruce went on driving the Alphavisor followed by some of the guards. He realized he wasn't running too fast. He wondered what he should push or pull to make it go faster. Bruce kept his eyes both on the road and over the panel, trying to find the way to increase his speed. He was running over a road surrounded by deserts. "Oh, damn, it's going even slower. What's the matter with this thing? And those guards are getting closer."

He looked at one side and saw there was a sand bank. "It's now or never!"

He thought in a minute and jumped out of the vehicle. The small Alphavisor went on by itself for a moment until it crashed against a big bank and exploded.

Bruce had the exact time to cover himself behind a sand bank just before the explosion. The guards arrived at that moment. "Where did that creature go?" asked one of the them still sitting on his Alphavisor.

"I don't know but let's just leave him alone. If, by any chance, he was lucky enough to survive the crash he will be a delicious lunch for the scoorts."

"Yes, we'd better go before one of them smells us." Both guards turned around and went away.

Bruce came out of his hiding place and walked to the path, shaking out the sand from his clothes and the tong he was wearing on top of them. "What were they talking about? What are those scoorts supposed to be?" he asked himself with fear. Suddenly, he heard a growl. He turned around, trying to find out where it was coming from, when he saw the sandy soil moving near him. As he started to run Bruce said to himself, "I'm afraid I will be meeting one of those scoorts very soon if I don't get away from here at once."

When he thought he was already far enough from that sound, Bruce took a deep breath and started to walk. "I'll have to walk to the city under this heat, or this Iriaje, as they call it here." It went unnoticed to Bruce that his tong's cap had slipped leaving his face uncovered. The few strange creatures that passed by looked at him just the same way he looked at them. Sometime later he had to get off the road because an Amarphy convoy was coming.

Meanwhile, the others were still walking towards Centi's home. "We are almost there. Hold on, guys."

"I hope so. My feet are hurting so much after walking around this horribly hot planet of yours."

"You are not the only one, Maggie," replied Nailbytes with a plaintive voice.

Strange creatures went from one side to the other, some of them waving their hands to give themselves some air.

"We can see many creatures walking around but not so many vehicles," said Billy.

"The ones you see on the road belong to the government or to the Amarphy. Also to the merchant's who come to the fair. The inhabitants don't have any vehicles. They have to walk…"

Maggie interrupted ironicall,: "How interesting. When are we going to arrive at your house?"

"There it is," cried Centi, pointing out to a house with a finger as he walked towards it.

"It looks like all the others," cried Maggie.

"You can't help yourself from criticizing everything you see, can you?" commented Billy.

"Well, I'm sorry if you don't like them but all our houses look the same."

"Don't pay any attention to her. Thank you so much for allowing us to come with you," said Mary.

"You're welcome. But to tell you the truth I'm not so sure that my mom will let you stay until the shadows go away. She is very distrustful."

"Well, we're lucky," murmured Nailbytes.

"Easy. You will see that Centi's mother will be as nice as he is."

"I sure hope so, Denise," said Centi.

They came to the door and waited for Centi to be the first one in front of it.

"Please open it at once so that we can get out of this heat," asked Maggie.

"I will do that."

They went through the door but all they could see was a spiral stone staircase surrounded by walls. "Is this staircase your whole house?"

"Of course it isn't, Maggie. All houses here are like this. We have to go down the stairs."

"Well, everything is so queer in this planet that I wouldn´t be surprised if it was," insisted Maggie.

"Well, let's go, then," said Nailbytes.

"Be careful. Come down slowly," advised Centi. They took off the caps from their heads as they went down the stairs. "Well, this is my home."

Nailbytes said, "We sure came down very quickly, didn't we?"

"It's a short staircase."

"Your house is very fresh and nice," cried Denise.

"Thank you."

Maggie replied at once, "Really? I wouldn't say that. What's that other staircase over there on the other room?"

"It leads downstairs to the bedrooms."

"And that curtain just in front of us? What does it hide?"

"It doesn't hide anything, Maggie, that's the place where we make our meals."

"I would certainly paint this living room in a brighter color and change that curtain. It would look much better. That grey doesn't become this place at all."

"Anything else, Maggie?" asked Mary with a frown.

"Well, if you ask me, this stone decoration is not so bad but it's a little too much here. Everything is made of stone." Maggie didn´t pay any attention to Mary´s previous complaint and continued. "There is not much light here, you can barely see anything."

Being built underground the house was quite cool but, on the other hand, the rooms were small and lighting was very weak. Some tubes, which ran along the upper corners of every room, provided a soft, white light. Billy was frowning when he addressed Maggie. "You can save your decoration tips for another time, Maggie."

They heard a voice coming from behind the curtain. "Is that you, Centi?"

"Who's she?"

"That's my mamay´s voice, Mary."

"Who is she?"

Two creatures came out the kitchen. They seemed to be female and one looked much older than the other. Both were just like Centi, some kind of small grey reptiles. "Wow! It was about time this specimen decided to show up and in a strange company too," spoke the younger one.

"Stop, Mom, I was looking for another prophecy," explained Centi. "But a guard took me for a spy and they saved me."

"Wait, Esther," intervened the eldest. "We were worried about you, dear."

Esther said, "I do not think that matters much to this specimen, mother."

"At last you're here. I was starting to get worried about you, son," continued the one Centi had called 'Mamay'.

Denise approached politely. "Good afternoon, ladies, I'm very pleased to meet you both."

Mamay answered, "Thank you dear, who are you?"

"They are some friends I met when one of the supreme guardians was after me and they really saved my life."

"What kind of trouble did you get in this time, Centi?"

"It wasn´t a big deal, Mom, but they helped me to escape and now they are the ones who need help so that they can go back home."

"And where are you from, guys?" asked Centi´s mother.

"We come from a very far away planet, madam. My name is Mary, she is my sister Denise, she is Maggie and those are Nailbytes and Billy."

"I'm pleased to meet you. By your appearance I guess you come from the Hantyl Protectorate, don't you?"

"I thought so too when I met them, Mom, but no, they don't."

"We come from the planet that Lonar Mayer and his accomplices are planning to invade. That's why we're here."

"Wait a moment. You come from the Ace planet?"

"What's Ace?"

"It's the resource used to give our bodies the liquid it needs, Maggie. In this galaxy Ace is very scarce, almost inexistent." Maggie's expression showed she didn't understand what Centi's mother was talking about.

Nailbytes said, "We certainly have plenty of Ace in our planet. Three quarters of it are water, I mean Ace, as you call it."

"That's exactly why Lonar Mayer wants to invade it."

"What's your name, madam?"

"Oh, I'm sorry. My name is Esther."

"She's one of the leaders of the Liberator's Army, aren't you Mom?" Centi sounded very proud of his mother.

Mamay commented, "Please, Centi, don't say that, it might get all of us in serious trouble."

"And are they willing to help us?" asked Esther.

"I'm afraid we should begin by helping ourselves."

"What do you mean, Nailbytes?"

Mary explained, "What Nailbytes is trying to say, Esther, is that we must get some spare parts for our ship, the *Iron Warrior*, so that we can fly back home."

"I understand that you will find those parts at the Multipower Center."

"We went there, Mom, but we couldn't get anything," answered Centi, but his mother was now speaking to someone at the door.

"What's the matter, Mom, who is here?"

Esther was already inviting the visitor in. "Hello, Yami. Come in and let me introduce my friends to you."

"Hi, Centi. Who are your friends?"

"Hi, sis."

Centi introduced his sister to his new friends.

Denise hurried to answer. "Hi, we come from the Ace planet."

"She doesn't know much about it, Denise."

"Sorry, Centi."

"Here I go. Excuse me if I hit someone with my cane," exclaimed the new arrival with a smile on her face and a cane in her hand.

Chapter 9

STRAIGHT INTO A TRAP

"Let me help you."
"Thank you, dear. You are Denise, right?"
"No, I'm Mary."
"Your voices are much alike."
"Yes, that's because we are sisters."
Maggie spoke to Centi, keeping her voice very low. "Your sister can't see, can she?"
"No. She has been blind for quite a long time now."
Yami withdrew something from her pocket. "Look, Mamay, I just made this. What do you think about it?"
"It's beautiful. You're getting better every day in making these Berma figures. You're quite an expert now."
"Yes, it's very nice. Could you make one for me to take back home please?" exclaimed Mary.
"Of course I will."
"You can make one of me with my Gafunder uniform," exclaimed Centi.
Esther made a grin and he realized that his comment had not been well received.
Then Esther said, "Instead of wasting time in searching for prophecies and all that nonsense, you should be…"
"Those are not nonsense, Mom," cried Centi. "There are things even you cannot explain."
Esther looked at her son with annoyed and piercing eyes. Mamay said, "Oh no, you will begin to argue again."
"In the depths of Kuntur-Maphre many mysteries need to be solved…"

"Enough, Centi."

Mamay didn't say anything, she just watched them with a gesture of fear. The Earthlings looked at each other. "But Mom, it's just that…"

"Shut up!" said Esther putting her hands on her face.

"One of those mysteries is that the body of Lautana Martin was never found," insisted Centi.

"It must be buried there," continued Mamay. Esther dropped her hands with a deep sigh.

Centi continued, "It is believed that her body was taken away by…" Suddenly a big shout shook them all.

"Stop it, please!"

It was Yami with tears in her eyes. "I told you so. Shut up!" said Esther. Mamay approached her daughter and hugged her. Esther rejected the hug and went into the kitchen. There were a few seconds of silence which increased the tension.

Mary said in a low voice, "We should go and look for Bruce."

"Great idea," said Centi. "I'll go with you. Hearing the same thing over and over again bores me."

Billy said, "I will go with you as well."

"Thanks."

Mary, Billy and Centi went up the stairs. Down at the living room Denise spoke with a frown, "I hope Bruce is safe. I'm so afraid he might get lost."

"I don't think he will. If he is as smart I think he is I bet he has gone back to the place where the guards made that rally," commented Nailbytes.

"What is your name? Mamay?"

"No, Maggie, I am Elgateralynaina. My grandchildren call me Mamay."

"What was your name again please?" asked Denise with a smile.

"Okay, you can call me Elga."

"It's very nice to meet new friends, but I'm really very hungry," commented Maggie.

"You are not the only one," replied Denise.

They had kept their voices low but Elga had heard them and said kindly, "I think I have something from our underground orchard for you to eat."

Nailbytes asked, "Do you have an underground garden? How's that possible? Can you grow anything down here?"

Esther had joined them again and explained patiently, "Yes we do. Zanas, potoes and other things."

"And how is that possible without any daylight?" said Maggie.

"It's probably because these things don't need light to grow," explained Nailbytes.

Elga offered, "And would you like some dessert also?"

"And what's that supposed to be?" asked Maggie.

"It sure sounds nice," commented Nailbytes trying to be polite.

"It's the only dessert we have for our little ones here."

"You mean that it's like a treat for us?"

"What does it taste like?"

"Well, I put some chockey to melt on a pan, mix it with some products I grow down here and then pour it into small containers. We call them Liberator's ammunitions and, of course, the people at the Supreme Council say that they are subversive products. Can you imagine?" Denise, Maggie and Nailbytes just watched and smiled. Elga added, "They say the same about the Escapers but we don't make those here, they are made elsewhere."

"Could you please show us the Escapers?" asked Nailbytes.

"Of course, come with me to the food preparation room."

"You mean the kitchen?"

"Yes, Maggie, they call it different here," explained Nailbytes.

"Let's go to the kitchen," replied Elga cheerfully.

They pulled the curtain aside and, once in there, she showed them the Escapers. Nailbytes cried, "It looks like the chocolate bars we have at our planet."

"These so-called ammunitions seem to be very tasty too, Elga. What flavor is the red one?" asked Denise.

"That's rojano flavor."

"And the yellow one?"

"Let me see. I'd better tell you what the four flavors are. They are all natural from our orchard. The red one is rojano, the yellow one is planton, the green one is martan and the orange, ornela. As you can see they come in small bags. Take as much as you wish. I have more for your friends so they can taste them as soon as they are back."

"And the Escaper, how does it taste?"

Turning to Nailbytes Elga replied with a smile, "Have a piece, dear, you'll like it."

"I better don't. It seems to have nuts and I'm allergic to them."

"I'm sorry, Nailbytes, I'd forgotten about your allergy," exclaimed Denise.

Maggie doubted at first but once she saw that everybody tasted the candy she took one. "It's just like a chocolate bar with nuts and peanuts. It even has some sort of a caster. It's delicious!"

"Well, that's the Escaper. All creatures here eat a lot of it. It sure helps when food becomes scarce. It is more than just candy, it's nutritious too."

Meanwhile, not far from Centi's home, another conversation was going on. "Why are we going this way?" asked Billy.

"We must be cautious. It's safer to take different roads in case they are making another rally."

"This looks like a deep cliff towards a huge desert."

"That's how the landscape looks around here, Mary."

"A slip and we are dead," exclaimed Billy.

"Just walk carefully over the edge," advised Centi. "Now, we turn here."

Billy cried, "Wait a minute. Can you hear those screams? Can it be a rally?"

"I can hear them but don't worry. That's not a rally, they are playing Nwephe-Shake."

"Where did I hear that name before?"

"I'm sure you have heard it before. It's the most popular game in the whole galaxy."

"And how do you play it?"

"Just wait a moment, Mary. We will go near the field where they are playing it right now and you'll see by yourself."

A few minutes later they left the cliff and walked to a field. "There you have it."

"So that's the famous Nwephe-Shake," cried Billy. "Hey, can you see that? Isn't that Bruce?"

"Where?"

"Over there, right across the field."

They approached the place where they believed their friend was. "Bruce!" cried Billy

"Hi, Billy. Hi, Mary. Hi, Centi."

"How did it go? You did get rid of the guards?"

"It wasn't easy, Mary. I almost became the supper of the scoorts."

"Wow! Those creatures are terrible. They eat anything that comes their way."

"Yes, I heard them when I was hiding in the sand banks."

"They also hide there and very often they fall asleep making their digestion but if one of them gets you, you're lost."

"How did you get to this field?" asked Billy.

"I walked to where that rally took place planning to wait for you there. Then I heard some creatures shouting but, fortunately, in a cheerful sort of way. I thought it would be better to be in a place surrounded by other creatures instead of being alone, so I followed the noise and came here. We're just at the back of the place of the rally."

"That was a good idea. You certainly were a lot safer here," cried Centi. "Let's go home now."

They resumed their way home, still looking at the game as they walked by the field. "I have been watching this Nwephe-Shake game and it is very much alike the cricket we play at home."

"Mary is right," said Billy. "Look at that. She hit the ball with her hand instead of a bat."

Mary commented, "And what a coup that she gave it. Look up where she sent it, far away."

"The one who hits the ball is called Pharir, and the further away you can send it the better."

"And they don't use any protection. If the ball hits your face you're done."

"If you want to take someone from the other team out of the game, Bruce, you have to hit him hard," explained Centi.

Mary kept looking at the game. "Did you see? The one that threw the ball ran all around the field while all the players shouted Subatha – Taya."

"That is when someone runs all around the square without stopping at any base."

"Well, like a home run. It sounds like baseball," commented Bruce. "Those who are in other bases come to the main base as well. From here I see four bases I think."

"There are four bases," explained Centi. "The Nwephe-Shake is the main entertainment around these galaxies. They all play in the…"

"Watch out!" shouted Billy.

"That ball almost hit you on the head, Mary!" cried Centi. "Give it back, Bruce."

Bruce threw it heavily towards the big square. "The ball is half green, half purple," commented Billy.

Bruce added, "It looks like a tennis ball but quite bigger."

"Okay, guys, let's go home."

Mary and Centi talked cheerfully as they all walked to Centi's home, but suddenly…

Centi exclaimed, "Wait!" Billy and Bruce, who came just after them, stopped at once.

"Oh, oh, something is happening over there," commented Mary.

"Those are armed guards. What are they looking for?" said Centi. They were stopping almost all the creatures, apparently to question them. "Okay, we must split so that we won't arouse any suspicions." They did so. Mary and Billy took one way, Bruce and Centi another.

The way Bruce and Centi took was calm but Mary and Billy were not so lucky. The guards stopped some creatures which walked just ahead of them. They could only wait to see what was going to happen next. "Let's see. Where are your papers? Where do you come from?"

One of the creatures said, "We are from this place." One of the guards looked at the papers as the other one pointed his strange weapon at them.

The one reading the documents asked, "Do you know anything about the murder of a member of the Royal Minta?"

"I don't. But come on, guard," cried one of the creatures, "you know what has happened. Surely he was killed due to rivalries between them." The guards didn't answer. They just went on registering them.

Another detained creature added, "These sects are always in trouble with each other."

"I am sure he was part of one of their famous sacrifices," added one of the creatures behind them.

The guards let them resume their walk. Trying to distract the guards, Mary exclaimed as she walked by them, "You can't walk around here anymore." The guards just made a face to her.

The four friends gathered a little further. "Hey!" shouted Billy.

"What is it?" asked Mary.

"That guy pushed me."

Bruce said, "He is going towards the tumult over there."

"It looks as if someone is giving a speech," commented Mary.

"Then it must be one of the Mayellis," explained Centi.

"Let's go and hear what he's saying."

"Wait, Mary, it can be dangerous," advised Centi running behind her. They followed Mary to where the crowd was listening to a preacher.

The Mayelli was a creature with human features, mustache and white hair, some wrinkles on the face and pointed ears. With his husky voice he shouted, "They are already here." He continued, "I am sure. We should never lose hope. We must go on fighting from our trenches." His medium height made it difficult for them to take a good look at him among his audience. The Mayelli took out what seemed like a papyrus from his sky blue and white tong and began to read. "From far away galaxies the saviours have come. They escaped from their own destruction and, by accident, will save the Esmadis galaxy from the Seven Demons of Shigahell. Suffering will stop temporarily."

A voice came from the crowd. "But when will those Stelars arrive?"

The Mayelli shouted, "I don't know, but I do know it will be soon."

"I hadn't heard that prophecy before," said Centi in a low voice. He then whispered to Mary, "Let's go now, the guards will be here soon."

When they were on the road, far from the crowd, Centi suddenly shouted,

"Be careful!" and pushed Mary aside. A group of guards passed them on several vehicles.

"I'm afraid that poor Mayelli is lost," commented Mary.

"What are they going to do to him?" asked Billy, looking backwards.

"They'll sure take him to the Atilkawa Fortress and disintegrate him for inciting to violence," explained Centi. "We'd better go home."

They went on chatting until, finally, they arrived at Centi's home. "Hi, guys, I see you found Bruce," said Denise with her mouth full.

"What are you eating?"

"It's called Liberator's ammunitions. They are like lentils with different savors stuffed with something they call chockay which is almost a chocolate. If you want some Elga told Nailbytes to take a few for you. I don't know why she didn't ask me to do that. I guess she thought I'd eat them all."

"And she was so wrong, wasn't she, sis?" laughed Mary.

"Hi, Bruce, you got away," said Maggie coming out from the curtain.

"Yes, fortunately I was able to get away in one piece."

Nailbytes said, "Okay, now, if we want to go back home we have to get those spare parts. It's all very nice here but we must not lose sight of our main target."

"At this moment, my dear Aceiters, I think your main target should be to find a way to prevent the invasion to your planet. Then you can plan how to go back to it," replied Esther.

They looked at each other in silence, surprised by the word Esther had just used to call them, until Mary spoke. "We can try to do it simultaneously. But, anyway, I think it would be advisable to have those parts as soon as possible. By the way, that's a funny name you gave us, Esther. I think that's a good name for us. Of course our enemies should never hear it."

"You're right, Mary. Well, now about the spare parts, I propose that we go to the center when it's dark and try to get in without anyone noticing us," suggested Centi.

"We might be able to do that through the tunnel I found when they were after us."

"I don't think so, dear. If that's the tunnel I'm thinking about it will be too dangerous. I'm sure they use it to get a lot of merchandise out illegally with the complicity of some of the guards. If they see any strangers they will shoot them immediately."

"I agree with Esther. We'd better try to get in climbing up the rail I used to get away."

Centi commented, "We'll have to wait until it gets really dark so that they won't see us."

Billy replied, "But it wouldn't be advisable that all of us go together. A big group would be easier to be seen and would certainly arouse suspicion."

"Who will go?" asked Esther.

They looked at each other again but no one spoke until Mary took the initiative. "You should go, Bruce. You know where that rail is and how to climb it."

"Okay, I will go."

"Well, now it's the turn of the ones who didn't go the first time," said Billy.

Maggie asked, "What's the matter? Are you afraid to go there again?"

"That's not the reason. It's just that I think it's the turn of those who didn't go before."

Bruce said, "Then it's Maggie's, Nailbytes' and Denise's turns."

"Hold down. I will go in my sister's place."

"But I'm a big girl now. I can take care of myself," insisted her sister.

"Yes, you are a big girl, but I will go instead anyway. That's a very dangerous place."

"Okay, then it will be Mary, Nailbytes, Maggie and me."

"Well, as a matter of fact, I'm not feeling well. I think I'm coming down with a flu," replied Maggie, acting as she was having chills.

"Of course, I believe you… First you accuse me of being a coward and now it's you who is making up excuses so that you don't have to go."

"Let her. Maybe it will be better if she doesn't go after all. We'll go, Nailbytes, Bruce and me," decided Mary.

"But I think I have a fever too," said Nailbytes putting his hand on his forehead with a theatrical gesture. "Oh, I think I have the flu."

"You don't have anything. Start walking," replied Bruce taking his friend by the arm.

"I will go with you," said Esther.

"I will too," added Centi.

Esther put a bad face. Elga addressed her daughter. "Be careful, Centi and Esther. And, just in case, don't forget to take your bag, dear. You might be able to get some Berma on the way."

"Yes, mother, you're right. I might find a queue for Berma."

Darkness came over them and the chosen group went out heading to the Multipower Center. They walked hurriedly. What they saw outside wasn't very different from what they had seen during brightness. The only big difference was that it was terribly cold. There were very few creatures walking around and no vehicles at all on the roads. After walking for a few minutes they saw some creatures sleeping in a row next to a stone building. Centi advised, "Be careful, everyone. Keep close to the row."

Some vehicles passed flying low over their heads. "Those are supreme guards, they watch the city at darkness on their Alphavisors. We were lucky to be near that row so we could pass as pacific citizens waiting for Berma. If not they would have taken us for interrogation."

"Hey, go back and take your place in the row!" shouted a strange creature.

"Do you think you are a Supreme so that you don't have to be on the row?"

Bruce made an angry gesture but Centi summoned him to keep quiet.

A little further back Nailbytes walked unaware that there was a creature lying down on his way. "Ouch! Look where you go," shouted the creature, rubbing his hand.

"I didn´t mean to hurt you."

Standing up the creature replied angrily, "Who are you yelling to?" It was a big and strong creature. "I´m going to deflate you, fatty."

Nailbytes turned pale and answered with a shrill voice, "But... but... I really didn´t mean to..."

"Well, I will give you a good spank, and I do mean it!"

"I... I... Bru... Bru... ce... Bruuuuuce, come please."

Esther approached them. "It´s okay, he won´t do it again I promise. We will just go our way." Nailbytes tried his best smile. The creature sat on the floor as Esther and her friends resumed their walk.

"You are so pale," commented Mary walking at his side. "I thought he would put your face just like your tong, all brown and red."

The group resumed their walk. When they turned to the right they saw another long row. There were all kind of creatures, some of them sat down on the floor and others were standing up, all of them very close to the stone buildings.

Mary asked, "Do these stores open all night long?"

"No. The stores open early in the brightness but food is really very scarce around here so they have to wait through the whole darkness so they will be able to get anything at all..."

Nailbytes commented, "It must be very hard to stay here the whole darkness with this cold."

Centi added, "Not so much. Do you remember the game we saw during the last brightness? Most of the teams are made by creatures which are in the different food rows in all the darknesses. They spend the darkness chatting about the last game and planning the next one."

The Aceiters couldn´t help smiling at Centi´s remark. "There are the Bermas, the ones that get Berma, the Sautins, the ones that get Sautin and so on," continued Centi

"Hey, guys, we'd better hurry," cried Nailbytes.

"We're almost running now," replied Esther. They heard a loud noise. Something was approaching. "Be careful," cried Esther, pushing all of them to a side. They could barely see two flying motorcycles passing by in a high speed.

"That was near. How irresponsible. They drive too fast," exclaimed Mary.

"I think those flying things were carrying one more creature each," said Billy. "I thought they were individual."

"The Alphavisors are individual but those were irresponsible young Esmadians which love to…" Esther turned to look at Centi and asked him, "How do you call that thing they are doing?"

"It's called pique. They do that during darkness. It's quite intense."

"I'm sure it is. Many could have died, and I'm sure many did, because of those piques as you call them."

"Okay, Mum, we'd better forget about that. Let's go on."

Mary and Bruce walked a little ahead. "Where do we go from here?" asked Mary in a loud voice.

Esther answered making a gesture for her to low her voice at once. "Turn over there."

They turned and went out of sight for a moment but someone spoke. "Well, well. What do we have here? Two creatures that will make me the Solten…"

"We'll not make you anything at all, you stupid."

"Oh yes?" said the unfriendly creature taking out a small knife. "What do you say now? Will you make me the Solten?" At that moment the others had come near.

When Esther saw what was going on she came forward and said, "Don't lose your time, we don't have any rutters."

"You'd better have some if you want to stay alive."

Bruce insisted, "You talk too much."

"And you won't have a mouth after this darkness."

"I don't think so. Just try."

"Calm down," begged Mary.

"This assures me that I'll get what I want," said the creature lifting his knife.

"Take this!" shouted Bruce as he raised his foot and kicked his hand forcing
the assailant to drop the knife.

"I don't need it to kill you, you horrible creature."

"If you want to see something really horrible look at yourself on a mirror," exclaimed Mary.

They started to fight. After a while, Bruce, who had always been a good fighter, succeeded to control his attacker. "This won't end this way," said the creature with a bloody big nose and full of bruises.

"I'll be waiting for you, Jackass," replied Bruce, quite bruised himself. The crook walked away with difficulty.

"Wow! You are a very good fighter," commented Centi.

"Your skill will be very useful. There are a lot of crooks around here," added Esther with a smile.

"Let's go on now. What way should we go?" said Nailbytes, standing behind them.

They all turned around and Mary asked, "Where were you? I didn't see you around."

Nailbytes said, "I... I was... I was taking care that nobody would come near us."

They walked until they arrived to an open field. "Look at those youngsters gathered over there," said Centi. "That's the finishing line for the Alphavisors."

"So, you are telling us that the Alphavisors races are illegal?" asked Bruce.

"So it seems," added Mary.

Billy asked, "And how do they get them?"

"Some of the participators and also some creatures from the public have relatives at the Supreme Party," explained Esther, "or they just steal them. Of course, if they catch you, you'll be in serious problems." Looking at Centi she added, "Isn't it so?"

Centi replied, "Are you going to start that again?"

"You have to be more responsible. What if they..."

"I told you to forget about it. It won't happen again so please don't go on."

"Okay," cried Billy, trying to change the subject, "are we still too far, Centi?"

"No, just a little more and we will be there."

After a short while they arrived to the center. "Where's that rail?" asked Nailbytes.

Bruce replied, "Just follow me."

"There you have it."

"You go first, you know how to do it."

"Okay, here I go."

"Who is looking out in case someone comes near?" asked Nailbytes in a worried tone.

Esther said, "I am, but it's very strange. I don't see any guards around.

"Maybe they are quite foolish," said Billy.

"I still think it's very unusual," replied Esther with a frown.

Bruce went to the rail and started to climb. "Well, he sure climbs fast."

"We will talk about it later, Centi. Who's next?" asked Billy.

"I'll go," cried Nailbytes.

"I will go after you."

"Centi will go third, Billy goes fourth, then goes Esther and I'll go last."

"Are you sure, Mary? I can go last," said Esther.

Almost everybody had gone up. Only Mary and Esther were still waiting their turn to climb up the rail. "Yes, you go now, it's your turn."

"Wow! They have gone up really fast!" Esther and Mary went up the rail and arrived at the second floor.

Once they were all together Nailbytes spoke in a low voice. "Okay, let's go to the second level. It's this way but be careful, I can't see anything, it's too dark."

"No one thought about bringing a torch."

"You're right, Nailbytes. I admit I forgot," answered Mary.

"Are we there?" asked Esther.

Mary replied, "Don't worry, we are on our way, but this darkness makes it more difficult for us to find level five and the stands where we saw the spare parts."

"We will be right behind you," said Nailbytes.

"Yes, it's quite dark in here but I insist. It's very strange that there are no guards around." Esther seemed worried.

Mary said, "It's opened. I thought there was a protective rail in level five."

"Forget it. Let's go in."

"Let me see… The stand I saw is over here."

"Hurry up!" cried Nailbytes.

"Don't shout, just take it easy," replied Centi. "Yes, let me look. Here it is."

"Pay attention to the parts' codes, Mary."

"That won't be easy, Bruce. I can hardly see anything."

"The letters on the cartridge are quite huge. You'll see them even if there is a little light," commented Centi.

"You're right, here they are. I will take two."

"I told you it would be very easy to catch them. They fell in our trap."

"Who said that?" muttered Nailbytes.

Suddenly, all the lights went on.

Chapter 10

THE ATILKAWA FORTRESS

"It was quite easy. Lonar was right, we just had to leave a crack opened and wait for them to jump in," said Ultro the Yagoon as he walked limping around them with his dirty tong.

"What do we do now?"

"Take them to the Atilkawa Fortress."

"But there was no trial!" shouted Bruce.

The guards grabbed him tightly. Ultro smiled mockingly. "This was a quick trial and this is your sentence."

Esther made her best to go unnoticed among the group of prisoners. "Start walking," commanded one of the guards.

Accompanied by a strong contingent of armed guards, the prisoners walked down the stairs leading to the ground floor. Ultro followed with difficulty due to his limp. The prisoners were practically shoved down the stone stairs, separated from one another by the guards, and taken to the exit. When they got to the front door Bruce said in a low voice, "Wow! There´s an entire Roman army out there." On the street, right in front of the main entrance, they saw a lot of well-armed supreme guards, all of them holding Isbans which looked like submachine guns with a queer design.

Esther added, "It's a whole contingent. Definitely, they were waiting for us."

"Shut up and walk!" shouted one of the guards.

They walked down the stone steps of the Multipower Center entrance. The guards pushed their way among their armed companions to take the prisoners to one of the huge vehicles parked outside. On the back of the vehicle a guard shouted to another one, "You! Put them on the magnetic rings at once!"

The guard approached them yelling, "Put your hands in your back now!"

He then took what seemed a TV remote control which made a low noise when it was aimed to their wrists.

"I can't separate my hands, it's like if they were tied up," muttered Bruce.

"Except for that one you are not from this galaxy, are you?" said Esmiro, one of the guards pointing to Esther.

Other of the guards spoke timidly, "It's strange, but I counted five of them in there, but I see that one is missing now."

"You were wrong. We're only four," said Mary.

"Shut up, you idiot," answered angrily one of the other guards. The prisoners looked at each other in silence, realizing the fact that Centi had been able to escape.

They were forced to board a big, dark green vehicle. One guard, climbing to the roof by a lateral staircase, yelled, "Let's go, Boshwaqo One!" The vehicle started to move fast.

In the back part of the huge vehicle, "What are we going to do now?"

"Low your voice, Nailbytes. I don't know, but I'm sure I will find the way to escape from this vehicle. If any of the guards recognizes me I'm dead."

"It won't be easy, Esther, it is fully armored. It really looks like an armadillo," remarked Mary

"I don't know what that is but this is a Boshwaqo, a very powerful vehicle," replied Esther.

"What will happen to us, now?" asked Nailbytes.

"You heard Ultro, they are taking us to the Atilkawa Fortress."

"So that was Ultro the Yagoon. What a nasty creature."

"Nailbytes is right. It looks like a frog wearing a white wig," said Bruce.

"Yes he does. But right now we're in a huge problem and we have to find a way out of it," replied Nailbytes, and added, "Being in this position is killing me."

Bruce said, "Don't complain. You sound like Maggie."

"Well, sitting on the floor with your hands tied at your back is terribly uncomfortable," replied Nailbytes.

Mary intervened. "We are all feeling the same."

Esther whispered, "Please speak in a low voice."

"Sorry," replied Mary, "but look. We are not alone."

They had an escort coming behind them, Alphavisors and Ulphavisors with armed guards inside. They were part of the Amarphy, like a police force. "We were lucky that this vehicle is not taking more prisoners."

Nailbytes commented with sarcasm, "Yes, we are so lucky to be the only ones. We are in paradise."

"That's not what I meant, you fool, I was talking about having to share this transport to that horrible place with other creatures. It's quite crowded with us."

After a long journey the four prisoners were about to arrive to the sinister Atilkawa Fortress. "What's going on? I think we have stopped or is it my imagination?" asked Nailbytes.

"We did stop. I think we arrived to the Atilkawa Fortress," replied Esther.

But the vehicle moved again.

"What happened? I thought we had arrived," asked Mary.

"We did. We only stopped to wait until the front door was opened," explained Esther.

"Come down, all of you," commanded one of the guards at the back door of the vehicle when it stopped again.

"Ouch! I couldn't stand being seated anymore," cried Nailbytes, standing up with difficulty. They went down as they coul, with their hands tied up at their back.

Once outside the vehicle the guards shouted at them, "Start walking, I'll show you a beautiful place, your new home. Ha, ha ha!"

They looked at the huge wall around them which was made of big stone blocks, one next to the other, just like those ancient stone buildings they had seen in their history books. There were many strange creatures wandering about. "This is worse than I thought."

"Yes. Look, some of them walk talking to themselves," added Bruce.

The guards shouted at them, "Okay, come this way."

Another guard added, "And be careful with the crazy ones."

Nailbytes asked in low voice, "What does he mean by that?"

"He's talking about the creatures you are looking at. I suppose they have gone crazy after spending too much time in this place. There are more over there, be careful," replied Esther.

They came to a stone door at a different colored building. One guard sent an order through his Isikul. "The door, Vajot." The door opened in four pieces, two to each side. Followed by several guards, they entered an environment where, once more, stone was the predominant element. They saw some sophisticated computer equipment and a few stone doors and small windows around. A cool breeze started to blow and they felt a little better. "Alright, walk."

"Hey, don't push me."

"Just walk."

Mary commented in a low voice, "That must be a prisoner." Two guards with a creature between them went to the door. When it opened they went out, turned right and disappeared.

"And what do we have here? Where are these creatures from?"

"Hi,Tonkol. They are spare parts thieves and…"

Suddenly, one of the guards spoke pointing to Esther. "Hey, Esmiro, she's Esther, an active member of the Liberator's Army."

"Well, well, so we have a member of that terrorist group."

"We are not terrorists. We fight against the abuses of your leader."

"Just shut up! I'm sure that when Lonar Mayer finds out about your presence at the fortress, you and your friends will not have a pleasant experience."

Esmiro said, "So keep her for Lonar Mayer, I'm sure she will want to see her."

"I certainly will. Are the others also members of that terrorist group?"

"I don't think so, they are not from this galaxy, I can tell that. We have to know where they come from, so just put them in the political criminals' pavilion until we find out more about them."

"Well if they are with that idiot they sure belong to that army as well."

"As I just told you, Tonkol, I'm not sure yet, but I understand that Lonar Mayer's orders are that all strangers should be first taken to the laboratory just in case they are enemies wanting to attack us with a hidden bacteria or something like that."

Another guard standing by a stone desk intervened. "But, Esmiro, you know Elhan, she'll sure want me to put them in different pavilions. They shouldn't stay together."

"Romey is right," added Tonkol.

"I know that but what if they are carrying some bacteria? You want us to have a lot of pavilions infected?"

"But, Esmiro, you…"

"It's enough, Tonkol. This isn't your problem at all. Do exactly as I'm telling you. If Elhan says anything about it tell him to talk to Lonar Mayer. You'll see he will shut up then. He's terrified with her."

"Okay, let's go to the political pavilion now. Esmiro, give me the capture report," said Vajot. "After the tests at the laboratory we'll make the individual cards."

"At the moment they are Opasays," said Esmiro.

"I hope they take the exams as soon as possible. This creature looks like he can work very well. He is tall and strong," said Vajot looking at Bruce.

Esmiro added looking at Nailbytes, "And this fat one, after the exams, where are we going to send him? To the kitchen?" Everyone in the office laughed at that comment.

"Just walk over there, all of you," said one of the guards going towards a door.

Esmiro spoke before they left the room. "Communicate with the laboratory so that they will have the identification tests ready. That way we'll know at last where they come from."

"You have a call from Ultro."

"What does he want now?" answered Esmiro, walking towards the communicator. The others just waited.

"Hello, Ultro."

Bruce commented in a low voice, "Something bad is going on." Mary and Nailbytes just looked at each other.

"Silence!" shouted one of the guards trying to listen to the conversation.

"But, Ultro, I've already sent my best guards, I'm getting short of guards and I need them here too."

"They seem to have some problems," whispered Mary.

"I told you to shut up!" cried a guard as he hit one of them on the leg.

"Are you okay, Nailbytes?" asked Mary, bending over her friend.

"Okay, Ultro, I'll see you later." Esmiro hung up and turned to the others.

"What happened there?"

"I'm sorry but some creatures just can't understand that they have to keep quiet." Esmiro didn't bother to answer. "What did they want, Esmiro?"

"They need more guards. The problems with the Caution Rai colony are getting out of control. I told him that we're working in double shifts because we're short of guards around here. Of course, Ultro doesn't care about it. Okay, take them away, they don't need to hear all this."

"Walk, all of you!" shouted the guard as he turned to his Isikul. "Requesting reinforces to take the prisoners." The door opened in four pieces, just like the one before. The prisoners went out with one guard, the others remained at the office.

"Wow! This courtyard is enormous," cried Mary.

"Silence! Turn left and be quiet!"

All of a sudden, there was an intense heat or Iriaje, just like the one they had felt when walking through the desert. Although the Iriaje would not let them raise their heads much, they could see that on a corner at the right there was a corridor which connected this yard with another one surrounded by other buildings.

Outside, a dozen guards were ready to escort them to their cells. In that big courtyard in the distance they could see what seemed to be three dining rooms in different places in which probably the prisoners took their meals. Each had stone tables with large stone benche, covered by small ceilings. The group walked towards the political prisoners´ pavilion. The intense sun had blinded them a bit so it was hard for them to keep their eyes looking forward for long. The guards, however, did not seem at all affected by the bright daylight. After crossing through the huge courtyard from one extreme to the other, they finally reached what seemed to be the political pavilion. "Here we are," exclaimed one of the guards.

At the door the Aceiters saw a terrible scene.

"No, please, I don't know anything about it, I swear. Let me go," screamed a prisoner as the guards dragged him out of his cell.

"The lijas will sure have a banquet with you," answered one of the guards with a derisive laugh.

"What are lijas?" asked Nailbytes.

"You'd better not ask," said Bruce with a shiver.

"They are monsters you'll sure meet later, but I don't think you'll be able to tell anyone about it," answered Vajot.

The guards in charge of the pavilion door stood aside to let the group in.

Some guards from the escort stayed outside. The prisoners went in with Vajot and a few others. There was a wall right in front of the pavilion door which forced them to turn either to the right or to the left. Mary started to go to the left when one guard shouted at her, "No! Don't turn to the left, that's the way to the infirmary. We have to go to the right."

Mary mumbled, "I'm sorry."

They continued walking down a steep ramp and, turning to the right again, they went down a few meters. They saw small cells on both sides with strange creatures inside. These cells were right under the large courtyard they had been on before. "Be careful, Nailbytes," shouted Mary, holding his friend's arm. "You almost fell.

"Thank you. These irregular stone blocks on the floor made me stumble."

"Shut up and walk!" cried Valjot angrily.

They continued their way down the ramp. It was a spiral ramp surrounded by tiny cells. As they descended the cool air which touched their faces grew more intense. A few minutes later one of the guards ordered them to stop at the door of what seemed to be an empty cell. Vajot talked to his Isikul. "Vildan, open cell 312."

He turned to the prisoners. "Go in there and wait."

"Aren't you taking off the magnetic rings?" asked one of the guards as the prisoners entered the cell.

"Well, I don't see why not. Cover me, and in case they do something foolish just Isis Isban," answered the guard in charge looking at his companion who was pointing at the prisoners with his Isban.

"Okay, you will stay here now," cried Vajot. Relieved from the rings, they started to rub their wrists as Vajot talked once more to the Isikul. "Vildan, close cell 312." The guards went away.

"These cells are so small," commented Nailbytes. "We can hardly move in here." He stood in the center and spread his arms. "Look at this, I can almost touch the walls with my spread arms."

"And who cares about that? We are aware that we can hardly move in here."

"Let it go," cried Mary. Wrinkling her nose she exclaimed, "There's also a terrible smell in here."

"It smells like rotten milk," added Bruce with a gesture of disgust.

"I hadn't noticed it until now," commented Nailbytes putting his hand on his mouth. "It's making me nauseous."

"Wait a minute. I think I have something here," said Mary as she looked into her pockets. She smiled and, holding something in her hands, she added, "These are mint drops. They'll help us endure the stench."

Nailbytes added, "But it's not only the stench, the floor is so dirty."

"We don't have a mop with us."

"I was just saying so."

"You will only find desolation here." The voice came from somewhere in the cell. They looked through the darkness around them trying to see who was talking.

"Where does that voice come from? Can someone tell me?" asked Nailbytes.

"I don't know. I can't see much outside. There isn't much light in here."

"Mary is right. The light is very weak," exclaimed Bruce.

A couple of tubes that ran down from each top corner of the spiral ramp to the bottom emanated a faint greenish light. That was the only light they had. "I am not on the outside. I am here, right next to you."

"Who are you? Why are you here?" asked Mary approaching her cell's door, still unable to know exactly where the voice came from.

"I opposed the government back at my village and they thought I belonged to the Liberator's Army."

"And do you belong to it?"

"No, I sympathize with their ideas, but I'm not part of it."

"And that was enough for them to sentence you to disintegration," commented Esther with a sad grin.

"And who are you? Where are you all from? You sure look very strange. I have never seen anyone like you before."

"She's Mary, and these are Bruce and Nailbytes. They came to our planet with a few other friends."

"Anyway, be careful then. In this place if you are a different species they send you to the laboratory to be analyzed, and they make you go through a lot of experiments." They looked at each other terrified at these words.

"Take it easy, you're scaring them to death."

"But it's true. Your friends are in a big danger. Those scientists have no pity." They turned to the other side of the cell looking for the new voice that had just spoken.

"Who said that?" At that moment a small piece of stone fell down from the wall, and through a small hole they could see a creature in the next cell. "What's your name?" asked Mary.

"I am Baldon. I don't belong to the Liberation Army either. I was brought here for stealing in a medicine warehouse. My daughter was ill and I didn't have any choice."

Esther asked, "But if you're a Blissay why are you here?"

"Because I am a political enemy as well. I tried to form a workers trade union when we were doing a building in Ragazza-Bela. They labeled me as an Opasay."

"And how is your daughter now, is she okay?" asked Mary.

"Yes, thank you for asking. She's safe along with her mother and my other son. We pretended a fight with my wife so that the guards would leave them alone. If I could ever run away from here they would retaliate against them. That's why I prefer to stay here. It's sad but at least they will be safe."

"Why do you say that we are in great danger?"

"Because they all can see that you are not from a known galaxy and this will arouse suspicions among the guards. They will sure bring over someone from the laboratory to get you analyzed and you'll be submitted to all kind of tests."

Bruce asked, "And how could we avoid that?"

"I am afraid you can't."

"I didn't see you earlier. Where did they take you? I was afraid they had disintegrated you," exclaimed one of the prisoners.

"I was taken to witness the disintegration of an active member of the Liberator's Army," answered his companion.

Nailbytes asked, "Why did they take you? Do you enjoy seeing that?"

"Of course we don't. Whenever they plan to have disintegrations they take witnesses from all the pavilions so that they can tell their fellow prisoners about it. It's supposed to keep us from wanting to escape."

Another voice spoke. "Okay, that's enough. Now do your magic and take us away from here."

"And what's your name?" with his face close to the bars of his cell Bruce addressed the prisoner at the cell across the corridor.

"I'm Burna. I'm not from the Liberator's Army either, but they caught me just the same and I am sentenced to be disintegrated. What matters now is that you start using your supernatural powers and help us out."

"What do you mean by asking us to use our powers?" asked Mary.

"Don't tell me that you don't have some secret powers. You look so weird. You must have some sort of courage belt, miraculous cape, shields, powerful sword, strength ring or something like that."

Mary replied with a sad voice, "Unfortunately, we are plain and common Earthlings."

"How sincere," cried Nailbytes.

"Then it will be very difficult for us to get away from here if you can't do anything about it. Goodbye," said Burna and moved back in her cell.

"Really, in order to solve a problem like ours, it's not necessary to have all those things you mentioned. What we need are our own abilities. It's no use to depend on supernatural forces or objects," spoke a new voice.

"Master Cantelot, I thought you were asleep," replied Burna, appearing once again at the front of her cell.

"I was but your conversation woke me up."

"Do you teach at a school?" asked Nailbytes looking at the cell next to Burna's.

"Well, I did. They brought me here along with my family," answered the so-called Master Cantelot with a deep sorrow in his voice.

"Where is your family?"

"My daughter Camila and grandson Toby are somewhere in this terrible place, Nailbytes."

"Why did they bring you here, Master?" asked Nailbytes.

"I had the bad idea of saying on one of my classes that the dictatorship of Eliom was not the best thing for our galaxy, and that we should change to the least worse of governments, the one that allows free elections. And my daughter and my grandson stole food from one of the big stores, so they are in the Blissay pavilion."

"And what does Blissay mean?"

"We don't know what Opasay means either, Mary," commented Nailbytes.

"These are the names they give to the pavilions. The common law detainees are called Blissays and political prisoners are Opasays," explained Baldon.

Mary said, "And what will happen to you now, Master?"

"I don't know. The only thing left for me is to wait for their decision."

"Well, I don't want to go on listening to all these pessimistic thoughts. We must devise an escape plan. Is it really so difficult to get away from here?" asked Mary.

"Please, lower your voice. Yes, it's very difficult. All the surroundings are full of sand tramps with voracious animals eager to eat anything that comes around. We could only escape by air."

"The Master is right, guys. There are other problems like the extremely low temperatures at dark and terribly high ones when the light comes. There are also many guards all around the walls with ferocious black panthers," said Baldon.

Nailbytes commented, "It seems that you have studied the subject very well."

"In fact we have. Every day you hear about escape attempts, but most of them, if not all, fail. They end up eaten by the beasts or killed by the guards".

Eshtor added, "The only advantage of being here is that there aren't any surveillance cameras as they have in the other pavilions. It seems that they don't consider political prisoners as highly dangerous creatures."

"That's something positive after all," replied Nailbytes with a faint smile.

"Well, we'll have to wait until someone comes up with something."

"That's very optimistic of you, Mary," replied Esther.

"Not really, we just have to wait until Billy, Denise and Maggie come up with an idea."

"Wait a moment. Let me see if I understood what you just said. Are you implying that Maggie is going to take us away from here?" asked Bruce in an ironic tone of voice.

"Well, not only her, also Billy and my sister, Denise."

"If you are relying on Maggie to save us I have only one more question to make."

"And what's that?" asked Mary.

Bruce turned to Burna. "Does the disintegration hurt much?"

"Please."

"But, trusting our life to Maggie is really too much."

"I have already told you that it's not only Maggie, but anyway people sometimes surprise us."

"That wouldn't be a surprise, it would be a miracle."

"I'm sorry but I agree with Bruce."

"Come on, guys. You both have to be positive. I'm sure our friends will give us a big surprise or even a miracle as Bruce puts it."

Burna commented, "I have lost all hope. It's very difficult to escape from the Atilkawa Fortress. To think it would be possible is just a waste of time."

"Don't discourage our friends. If they think they will be able to do it maybe they will."

"You are very wise, Master Cantelot, we all respect you a lot around here, but believing that anyone can get out of here is very imaginative, and even more for these inferior creatures," talked Burna with a tired tone of voice. Turning to the newcomers she added, "Don't waste your time." She then withdrew to the back of her cell.

"It's nice to have dreams, Burna. No creature can live without something to live for."

"Dreams may be good, Master, but not these unfeasible fantasies. On top of everything you already mentioned, if someone succeeds to escape the guards will go after him at once with the Hangescapes ready to track him."

"Sorry, Master Cantelot, what's that thing you have around your neck like a necklace?"

He looked down and touched the necklace that Nailbytes had mentioned. "It's like a location sensor. Each inmate has one. This way they used to control the prisoners."

"Don't they use it anymore?" asked Mary.

"They had a problem with the central system and they are no longer operative," Master Cantelot explained. "They say that they will be working again soon."

"Ha, if I had an extra ration of food each time I hear that something will be repaired soon around here I would be better fed," commented Burna.

"Hey, all of you, I have been listening to you for quite a while talking about things that could put us in trouble, so shut up before one of those officers hears you." The voice came from the corridor just outside the cells.

Burna replied, "Look, Doldo, we pay you very well to leave us alone, you and your superiors, so don't bother. Remember you can get more treats from us like some Escapers as the one you are eating just now."

"Take it easy, Burna."

"I am sorry, Master Cantelot, it's just more than enough to be in here and on top of that to deal with these guards."

"Do you think we guards have it easy around here? We all have a rough time."

"If you say so."

"Wait! Where are you from?"

"Her name is Mary, but that doesn't matter right now."

"Of course it doesn't. I'd better go hear Nwephe-Shake game, it's terrific," said Doldo. He started to walk away but then he stopped and turned to the prisoners. "I forgot I was bringing you some news. That's what you pay me for, don't you? Elisa and Lonar Mayer will be here any time now and so are some scientists. I am sure they are coming to analyze these specimens." He added with an ironic laugh, "I'm so sorry for you."

"If you are through go and eat elsewhere, fatty," said Bruce.

"I don't know who you are, you idiot, but you'll pay for your bad manners," cried Doldo still laughing as he went away.

"I know that creature is repulsive but try to control yourself. The only thing you'll get by talking to him like that is that he will want to take revenge."

"I'm sorry, Master Cantelot, but it gets me so angry to hear him so delighted with those news."

"I hope that Maggie, Denise and Billy will come up with a good plan, and quickly too," sighed Mary.

Chapter 11

MAKING DEALS WITH A CROOK

"They should be back by now. Something terrible has happened. I'm afraid it's obvious that they have been caught," said Denise.

Billy cried, "Unfortunately, it sure looks like it."

"And we don't have the spare parts," added Maggie.

"That's not the real problem now, is it?" replied Billy.

"You are not sleeping yet?" said Elga, coming out of the kitchen curtains,

"We can't. We are worried," explained Billy. "Our friends have not arrived yet. They have had plenty of time. We're sure the guards caught them."

"If they have them they will take them to the Atilkawa Fortress," said Elga. "That's where the guards take all the prisoners."

"They are in big trouble," cried Maggie.

"If it is so we will not be able to do anything about it. My poor daughter. I told her not to get involved in the Liberation War but she wouldn't listen to me and now look what has happened. I don't know what to do."

"Don't worry."

Denise said, "We must listen to Billy. We just have to know how to get to the fortress and we'll go and rescue our friends."

"You don't understand. Very few people know exactly how to go there, and even if you could it's heavily guarded in brightness and darkness. It's too dangerous, we don't know of anybody who got there and back."

"But I remember that Edison…"

"That's it, Denise! Edison!" shouted Billy. "Remember what Edison told us on our way to Esmeraland? He mentioned that he went there often."

"Even if it's so how do we find Edison?"

"Well, that's simple. Let's look for his mobile number."

"Mobile number? What number is that?" asked Elga.

Billy explained, "I'm sorry. Our friend Maggie thinks she's still back home."

"Sometimes I do forget that we are in this hell," sighed Maggie.

"Where are Mom and Centi? It's late," said Yami coming into the room yawning broadly.

"They will be here in no time, dear."

"Don't lie to me, Mamay, I know something has happened to them. I heard you talking about it."

"Forgive me for lying to you, dear, it's just that I didn't want you to get worried. All this looks like a big nightmare and I wish it could be over soon," cried Elga. "You know at first we thought that all this would end quickly, but it's been too long now. Food is scarce and now my only daughter and my grandson are prisoners. Relatives disappear every day without anyone knowing about them anymore."

Billy said, "I'm sure this will be over, Elga. Now, we need to find Edison."

"Wait a moment, he said he had to go to the Esmeraland Fair, he must be there," commented Denise.

"Yes, I remember that too. Let's go there at once," cried Billy.

"That will be easy. It's very near, you will be there in no time," said Elga wiping her tears away.

"Can you show us the way, please?" asked Denise.

"Of course I can. But we must wait until it opens to the public. That will happen as soon as brightness begins. The buyers start to arrive quite early."

Billy said, "We'll wait. It's the only thing we can do. If Edison helps us we will be able to go to the fortress and rescue our friends."

"Go slowly. The big legend about that place is that no prisoner has ever been able to get out alive," insisted Elga.

"We have to try. We can't just abandon our friends. We'll go there, Edison will know how."

"Please, guys, bring back my mother and my brother."

"We will, Yami, I promise you," replied Billy, "but why don't you make more sculptures?"

"Yes, they are beautiful," added Denise.

"At least you like my sculptures," commented Yami, "my mom never talks to me about them. She doesn't care."

"I have already explained it to you many times, my dear. It's not that she doesn't care, your mom is too busy."

After she heard her grandmother Yami left the room and went to the kitchen.

When Elga saw that Yami was gone she spoke angrily, "That stupid Liberation war!"

"What do you mean?" asked Billy.

"What Jami just said is true. Esther gives too much time to the Liberation War and I do not know how to justify her absences to her children." They all kept silent.

Sometime later, somewhere around the Esmeraland Fair. "There it is, just as Elga told us," cried Billy. "Do you see? It wasn't so far."

Maggie replied, "Yes, but look, there are guards everywhere armed with those strange rifles and big vehicles as well."

"Relax. Just walk naturally towards the door. We have to stick together and, of course, find the clothing area. That's where Edison's stand should be." The three of them walked to the door and went in trying not to raise any suspicions, mingling among all the strange creatures which had come to the fair.

"We are inside. Now what, Billy?" asked Maggie.

"We've to go the clothes area."

"Fine, but in case you haven't noticed there are armed guards everywhere."

"And many flying motorcycles too," added Denise.

"You two please relax. There are also a lot of visitors, so it will be easy to sneak off in the middle of this multitude."

"Oh, how I hate crowed places, you have to walk with everyone pushing you around," commented Maggie. "We're lucky it's held in open air. Imagine how it would be like under a closed place. The smells would be unbearable."

"Spare us your comments. Let's just look for Edison," insisted Billy. "We have to keep our eyes wide open in order to find his stand."

Maggie advised, "Yes, but be careful not to show your face. The guards might see us."

"We know. But we'll have to make our way by pushing people," replied Billy. They went on walking through the multitude of guards and visitors from all galaxies who walked from one place to another looking at the stands around them.

"Hey, Maggie, don't push me," cried Billy.

"I'm sorry but I can't help it. It's too crowded," said Maggie.

"Hey, be careful, man."

"It's not a man," cried Denise.

"Shut up! This is horrible and they all smell so terribly. Don't they take a bath every day as everybody does?"

"Calm down," said Billy. "You'd better let that creature and his merchandise go by."

Maggie moved to one side.

"That must be merchandise for a stand," commented Denise.

Looking around him and trying not to show his face, Billy added, "There are rhinoceroses carrying those pallets trucks everywhere around."

"But be careful. Don't push."

"Calm down, Maggie," asked Billy.

"I'm calmed. There they go again. Hey, stop pushing me."

"I'm sorry, it's just that they sold me this tong and it's a wrong size. I have to go and change it at once," explained a strange creature.

"Who sold it to you?" asked Billy.

"It's that creature from the clothing section."

Denise looked at the garment and cried, "It's just like the ones I saw in Edison boxes."

"You know Edison? Well, he's really famous around here," replied the stranger.

"So you know him too?" asked Denise, taking good care not to show her face.

"That Edison comes to every fair that's held here at Esmeraland. He must have won a lot of rutters already."

"Where is him?" asked Billy.

"He's right over there, but I have to hurry before he tells me that it's too late to change the garment."

"Okay, we'll see you. Good luck," said Billy.

"Thanks. Goodbye," answered the creature as he walked away in a hurry.

"We'll follow him."

"Why couldn't we go with him?"

Billy explained, "It could be dangerous. He could have asked us questions about our relation with Edison and it's better to go unnoticed. Okay, let's hurry or we will lose him."

"I'm walking as fast as I can," said Maggie.

"Just hurry."

"Excuse me please."

"Move over, let me pass."

"Maggie, just apologize like I do," said Billy.

"It makes me mad not being able to walk freely."

At last they arrived at the clothing section but remained at a little distance.

"There's Edison," cried Denise.

"But let's wait a moment."

"Why is that?"

Billy said, "It's very simple. We don't want that creature to know that we've followed him."

Denise said, "We can go closer without it noticing us."

"We'd better wait until he makes his change before we get closer."

"But we have to hurry up to get our friends out of that place."

Billy looked at Denise and at Edison's stand for a second and answered, "You are right. You go and try to talk to Edison, but please be very careful."

"Don't worry, I will."

Denise walked towards the stand looking to the clothes around her until she came close to Edison. The creature was already there with the garment in his hands waiting for Edison to finish attending a client. "Do you want to try this on?" he was asking politely to his customer.

"I don't know. Is it made of a rough material?"

"Of course it is. And it's quite washable too."

"I'm not sure yet."

"What are you exactly looking for?"

"Well, I want something that will last, easy to clean, not too heavy and for daily use."

"Well, this is exactly what you need. Light and very easy to clean. I assume you want it for going to work, don't you?"

"Yes, but what's the price?"

"It's only 260 rutters or eight food coupons."

"That's too high."

"Well, you may be right but you'll be saving a lot when you get to clean it."

"Yes, and you say I can wear it everywhere? But the price is still too high."

"I agree with you about the price being a bit high, but if you compare the pros and cons of price and benefits you'll see that it's a 'win win' purchase."

"You are right. I'll take it," said the customer as she took the money out from a pocket, paid and went away.

Denise began to walk towards him when someone pulled her arm and got there first. "Look, this tong is too small for me. Can you change it please?"

"No problem," answered Edison, taking the garment and searching in some boxes behind him.

"Here, I have that same model but in the right size."

"Thank you so much. Good bye."

"You're welcome."

As soon as the creature went away Denise hurried to go near him before another client would come. "Do you remember me?" she asked in a low voice, carefully showing him her face.

"Of course I do. What's the matter now?"

"I'll be brief. My sister Mary, Bruce and Nailbytes, Centi and his mother, they have all been made prisoners and I'm afraid they have been taken to the Atilkawa Fortress."

"Well, that's not good at all, and I can imagine what you want to ask me for, but I'm sorry. I have no business to attend there at the moment and, furthermore, if I take you there with me I'll sure get into big trouble." Billy approached them along with Maggie. "I'm sorry but I can't help you, guys."

"But you're the only person we know that knows how to get there."

"You're Billy, aren't you? Look, I do know how to get there but I have many things I have to take care of at this moment. I'm sorry."

"What can we do now?" asked Maggie. "It was your idea to look for this guy," she cried, addressing her friends.

Edison replied, "Don't get mad at me. I don't know how you manage yourselves in your galaxy, but here you have to take care of yourself in order to survive. Nobody helps anybody around here, at least not for free, as I think I told you before."

"But please, Edison."

"Sorry, Denise, and now go. One of the best customers I could have is coming. Halondra the Great is one of the richest queens of this and many other galaxies around, but I have never been able to sell her anything. Go away so that I can concentrate and try to sell her something at last." Billy, Denise and Maggie walked away with sad and worried faces.

"I didn't go well at all," cried Denise.

"Well, I hadn't noticed," replied Maggie and added in a harsh tone, "and Billy thought that bug would help us. He's nothing but a selfish, self-centered creature." Billy and Denise just looked at each other with a sad smile at Maggie's remark.

"Well, that creature over there must be Halondra the Great," said Denise

"And she comes along with a huge entourage too. They must be her bodyguards or something like that."

"So it seems. And she certainly knows how to dress. She's wearing very nice jewels as well. I think she could be considered as fashionable."

"If you say so," said Billy.

"She really looks like a Martian cow, but I must admit that she is wearing some nice clothes and accessories. However, I would advise her to wear a tunic or tong in a lighter shade. I'm sure it would become her dark complexion."

Billy said, "That's enough. You can tell us later about your fashion tips. Now we have to think about the way to get to the fortress before it's too late for our friends."

"I'm sorry. The fact is that we don't know how to get to that terrible place and, even if we knew, we don't have a plan to rescue them."

"Maggie is right, we have to think about a plan." Billy just nodded in agreement.

Halondra's bodyguards turned to them when they heard them speaking.

"We'd better keep quiet now," said Denise.

"Yes, let's pretend that we're looking for something to buy until they go away," added Billy in a low voice.

"Let's take a look at this stand. Maybe you'll be lucky today and I will buy something from you at last."

"It would be an honor for me, your Supreme Majesty," answered Edison with a reverence.

Halondra began to look at the tunics one by one. "The truth is I can't find anything interesting here, as always."

"My Supreme, maybe you haven't looked well," insisted Edison in a shy voice.

"Don't tell me what to do, servant."

"I'm very sorry, Your Majesty."

"Let me see this one," she said, putting a tunic close to her huge body.

"That's very nice and it can be washed very easily."

"Look, you foolish worm, I don't have to wash anything at all. I use my clothes only once and give them away to some unfortunate creatures."

"Once again, I'm sorry. I'd better keep quiet."

Hearing the conversation at distance Billy commented, "Edison is a good salesman but that lady makes him very nervous."

"That lady is not looking for easy to wash clothes. She wants something that will become her and Edison is unable to see that. He has to make a completely different approach. It's so exasperating," exclaimed Maggie.

"You are a fashion expert. You go and try to sell something to that cow as you just called her," replied Denise with a harsh tone.

"Are you crazy? Don't pay attention to her," advised Billy.

Edison was still trying to convince his possible customer. "That brown tunic will look very well on you, Your Majesty."

"Do you think so? I think this color doesn't show all my beauty."

"That lady sounds so vain and disgusting."

"I don't think so. She only wants something that will become her, that's all."

Billy replied with an ironic smile. "As always, Maggie, speaking for people who think exactly like her."

"It's not that I defend her, it's that because of his nerves Edison doesn't understand her."

Halondra turned to where the voices were coming from and saw them standing a little far from her. The guys kept quiet. Edison insisted, "What do you think about this other tong? And I can offer you a hat that will go with it. You can use them for any official events."

Halondra took the tunic and put it on her body. "I don't like it. This dark blue doesn't suit me at all." At that moment, she turned to the guys and saw Maggie, whose face was a little at sight. "Hey, you, come here," she said, pulling Maggie's arm and bringing her close to her. She put the tunic on Maggie's chest. "Look, what do you think? But take your cap off, my friend." Billy and Denise were terrified about what would come next. "Where are you from?" The bodyguards looked at each other.

Edison hurried to answer. "She comes from a far away galaxy. She came to work with me in this fair. Okay, you, go and put some order in those boxes over there and hurry up."

"Wait. She has a lighter complexion, that's why it suits her but not me. I'm really losing my time here, I'd better go look somewhere else."

"Just a moment, Halondra. I think you'll find what you need here. You need a color that will emphasize your beauty." Maggie spoke in a soft voice.

"Well, show it to me."

Edison smiled broadly at Maggie's comment and at the queen's answer. He stepped aside while Maggie looked into the boxes and Halondra waited. Billy held Edison's arm and took him aside. "Let's make a deal right now. If Maggie sells something to the queen you take us to the fortress."

"But couldn't she make that just as a favor to a good friend?"

Billy sounded a bit angry. "Now who is talking about friendship? Didn't you say that nobody does anything for nothing? It's a deal or not?"

Edison smiled and asked, "Do you really think she will able to do that?"

Denise said in a low voice, "Just look at her. Halondra's gestures show that she's convinced of what Maggie is telling her. She'll do it."

Billy agreed. "If there's something she does very well it is to talk about fashion. I'm sure she'll sell her those tongs."

Edison looked at Maggie and saw that she was showing the whole box of tunics to the queen. "Okay, Billy, it's a deal."

"Done!" cried Denise.

"I'll take all these tongs. You're right, I must wear light colors, they are the ones that fit me. Do you think this cap will highlight my make-up?"

"Of course it will, Halondra. You're so lucky. When you have that beautiful dark complexion of yours it's better to wear lighter shades of make-up. I have to put on pounds of protection against this Iriaje and wash my hair every day."

"But your red hair is lovely and it goes so well with your blue eyes. You'll look fabulous in that pink tong."

"Thanks."

"You're welcome. I have to go now. Take care and I wish you the best in this fair."

"I hope to see you soon and exchange tips so that we both can look fabulous," replied Maggie.

"Why not? I'll be seeing you," answered Halondra with a smile as she went away with her guards and her new clothes.

Billy followed her with his eyes until she was far. He then turned to Edison.

"It's time for you to do your part of the deal."

"What deal is that? I don't remember any deal." They looked at Edison with annoyance but he just raised his eyebrows and smiled mockingly.

Chapter 12

AN UNFORTUNATE ACCIDENT

The Esmeraland Fair was almost empty now. There were only a few vehicles and visitors around. They got on Edison's *Loader Vargas* and were ready to go. "Start the *Loader Vargas*, and let's go!" cried Maggie.

"Take it easy."

"Hey, you have company," cried Billy as they saw someone approaching the driver's window menacingly.

"Can I help you?" asked Edison.

"No, I just want you to make my Soltem."

Edison looked at him fiercely. "I don't have any rutters or even tongs left."

"I'm sure you have something, unless, of course, you want to die here and now."

"Are you threatening me?" cried Edison as he surreptitiously maneuvered something in the driving wheel.

"Yes, I am threatening you. Now, give me something." Maggie, Denise and Billy just watched what was going on. "Well, as I just told you, I don't have…"

Suddenly, the crook bent down covering his face with his hands, cursing and crying in pain. "Better luck next time," cried Edison, starting the *Loader Vargas* once again.

"That was a rough guy," said Billy.

"We have a lot of those around here. They take advantage of the fact that, once the fair is over the supreme guards go away leaving this place unattended."

"You got rid of him without causing him much harm. You are a good person, I mean galactic creature, after all."

Edison didn't answer at once, he just smiled at Denise's words. After a moment he spoke. "Yes, I'm a good creature but, as my mother used to say, talking with the truth, I really didn't wish to spend my *Loader* energy on that idiot."

"Well, then I withdraw my comment," replied Denise with an angry voice.

"Forget about it. For a moment I really thought you wouldn't keep your part of the deal," commented Billy.

"It's okay. It was just a joke. Of course I was going to keep my word. We just had to wait until it was dark again."

"I'm so uncomfortable sitting on the floor. Can you do something about it?"

"Of course I can, Maggie. Just keep still. You too, Denise." He pushed a button by his side and at once another row of seats appeared making the trunk a little smaller but widening the sitting space.

"Well, this is much better," cried Denise.

"Are you comfortable now?"

"Yes, I am. Thank you," replied Denise.

"Where does that smell come from?" asked Maggie making a face.

"Yes, it's quite strong. I can smell it too," exclaimed Billy.

"It must be one of the reagents they use at the laboratory."

"Do you sell those too?" asked Denise.

"Yes. The tongs are not so profitable and I'm not sure yet whether the grease for the lijas is working like it should. That's why I'm always trying to find new ways to make rutters. As I told Mary, where there are rutters there's Edison."

"Everything is rutters to you," commented Billy. "I guess you don't sell yourself because nobody would buy you."

Edison smiled and began to drive. As he drove away he insisted, "Remember, guys, the deal was just to take you there. I'm not getting involved in the rescue."

"We know that. We'll say we come from the Hantyl Protectorate and that we're going to work in the laboratories."

"If that's all you could figure out as a plan I wonder how you are still alive here," replied Edison, nodding his head in disapproval.

"It's not such a bad idea. My sister, Mary, saw a creature which came from that place when she found out the secret passage at the Multipower Center. She said he looked a bit like us."

"If you say so. However, I'll drop you near the fortress. If you go in by yourselves you might use…"

Billy asked, "What's that blue light in your panel?"

"This one?"

"Yes, what does it mean?"

"It means that I have to slow down, we are in a kind of ramp."

Denise said, "So we have to hold tight, don't we?"

Suddenly, they heard gunshots around them. "What was that?" cried Billy.

"Those are the Amarphy forces chasing someone."

Maggie shouted, "Can you avoid them before one of those shots gets us?"

Edison looked around and answered with a grin. "I don't think so. We are right in the middle of this fuss."

"Why are they chasing someone?"

"I don't know, but I suppose the fugitives must belong to the Liberator's Army."

Denise cried, "Look at that. I've never seen so many flying motorcycles together before."

"They are called Alphavisors. The fugitive must be an important leader of that terrorist group." The confusion was huge and the visibility was almost impossible due to the dust raised by the land vehicles running after the fugitives.

From the air the persecution was supported by the Alphavisors, the flying motorcycles, which fired their barrels in all directions trying to shoot a small land vehicle which tried to get away, The persecuted vehicle shook violently.

"That was a close shot," cried Billy.

"The Ulphavisors and Alphavisors are quite powerful," explained Edison. "I can't see very well but I guess there must be a lot of them in the persecution."

"What do we do now?" asked Maggie with a terrified voice.

"Calm down," replied Edison soothingly.

"Can you see anything? It's all covered with dust," cried Denise.

"I can see something..."

"Can't this piece of junk go a little bit faster?"

Billy shouted, "This is the *Loader Vargas*. It is not the *Speedy Gonzales*, Maggie."

"What did you say?"

"There comes one curve," cried Denise.

"I saw it. Hold on."

"And another one," advised Denise. The *Loader Vargas* was ready to make the turn when a sudden and strong impact shook the vehicle again. Everything got blurred and they all lost consciousness.

A little far from there at the Atilkawa Fortress, the other Aceiters were in their cells.

"What a nasty sound," cried Nailbytes inside his cell with his hands on his ears.

Mary did the same thing exclaiming, "I can hear a siren."

"It's time to go to the quarries," announced Master Cantelot.

Bruce replied, "But, Master Cantelot, we've just arrived here."

"That doesn't matter," replied Eshtor.

A group of armed soldiers appeared in front of them. One of them shouted, "All of you, get out and go to work." The cells opened automatically. Mary, Nailbytes and Bruce went out along with most of the prisoners. A multitude of creatures walked up the ramp towards the door.

"I don't like this at all," cried Bruce.

"You don't have to like it. Just walk. We're going to the stone fields."

"Do as Master Cantelot tells you. We have a lot of work today," said Eshtor.

"Look, they have the same weapons as the guards at the Multipower Center," remarked Nailbytes. Mary and Bruce looked at the weapons in silence.

The gates which led to a courtyard opened to let them leave the building and continue their way to the quarries. "What's in that courtyard?" asked Nailbytes.

"There's where we have our meals," explained Baldon.

After a while they passed under a stone arch and arrived to the quarries.

They could see a big and deep cliff. It looked like a grand canyon. "There are some creatures down there already," said Mary. "They got here before us. They come from another pavilion," explained Baldon.

"We share this working field with the prisoners from the Blissay pavilion," added Master Cantelot.

"And now what?" asked Nailbytes. The group went down followed by fully-armed guards and a lot of other galactic creatures. Once there, down deep into what looked like a canyon, Nailbytes spoke with a worried voice. "From what I can see here, I assume we have to use these peaks to break this huge white rock into pieces."

Bruce cried, "What a genius you are!"

"I know. But it would have been difficult that after spending so much time with you I would remain smart, wouldn't it?" Bruce raised his peak pretending that he was going to hit his friend.

"We'd better start working, guys," advised Mary.

Bruce turned to look around him. "Where are our new companions?"

Nailbytes answered, "If you mean Master Cantelot, Eshtor and Baldon, they are over there."

"And where is Burna?"

Bruce replied, "She is over there too, I can see from here. She seems to be measuring something."

"Silence! Go on with your work," said Mary starting to break stones. After a while they began to feel the Iriaje and the heat struck them hard.

Mary stopped for a moment and tried to wipe her brow. "We are watched closely."

"I can see that. There're a lot of those flying motorcycles as the one that Bruce drove at the square in Esmeraland."

"And a lot of guards with those strange weapons," added Bruce cleaning his face with his sleeve and looking around him.

"We must take a good look at everything considering that we have to plan our escape from here."

"Please, Mary, this is not a movie. We really are in another planet and in a huge problem," replied Nailbytes.

"Well, even if it's not a movie we must look for a way to get out of here," said Mary.

Bruce continued using his peak on the stone but, after a moment, he stopped, wiped the sweat from his brow and said, "If we plan something it must be awfully good. This won't be easy at all."

"There are all kind of creatures in here," said Mary, looking around her.

"We're in an intergalactic prison so there must be creatures from all those planets around this one," commented Nailbytes.

Master Cantelot, who had heard this, came near his friends. "Don't talk so much, guys, just keep your minds on your work."

Bruce was about to take his peak when he heard, "Hey, that peak is mine!"

"No! This is mine!"

"Stay away from me, you jerk," said one the creatures pushing Bruce abruptly.

Bruce answered pulling his arm, "That's enough. There's another peak over there." Bruce looked at it and exclaimed, "But the edge is dull."

"Fix it, stupid."

"Who are you calling stupid?" shouted Bruce. "Who?" The argument was getting hot.

Mary and Nailbytes, along with Master Cantelot, came near them. "Let him go," suggested Mary.

"No! That peak is mine!"

"But..."

At that moment they all heard a shout. "Sithel Isban!"

"Be careful, Bruce."

Mary threw herself over Bruce and both fell on the ground. The creature that had started the quarrel also fell down. "We won't miss the next time. You both will die!" shouted one of the guards. "No more fights. Is it clear?" Things calmed down and the prisoners resumed their work.

Nailbytes commented, "That shot was almost your death."

Mary said, "I wonder. From what I remember back at the Multipower Center, the shot that came from the same weapon didn't seem so powerful."

"Those weapons must have a sort of system which graduates the power of the impact."

"As always, Nailbytes is trying to find an explanation for everything."

"I was just wondering, Bruce," sighed Nailbytes.

Suddenly, a creature with a peak in his hands approached them. "My name is Segund Froter, I am the brigadier of this pavilion. You'd better work hard and make me happy, otherwise I'll make you very unhappy." He walked away laughing.

"Okay, keep quiet and go on with your work," said Mary.

"It's that skinny rhinoceros again."

Mary said in a low voice, "Keep quiet, Bruce."

"Haven't you heard me? Shut up!" shouted Segund, not too far from them. "You don't seem to understand, do you?"

"Sorry, we are working," cried Mary.

"One of you take that trolley and carry those blocks of stone upward." Mary and Nailbytes looked at each other and then both looked at Bruce. He walked towards the trolley and carried away the heavy stone blocks.

The work in the quarries continued under the fiery Iriaje of Esmadis. The Aceiters went on breaking stones, wondering what they could do to get out of this terrible situation. They didn't have the smallest hint about how they could get out of this galactic prison, let alone how to get back home.

Chapter 13

THE SECRET OF SATHAYE

"I'm so tired," commented Bruce.
"The work at the quarries is exhausting," exclaimed Mary. "I can't believe we're already back in our cells."
"It was tough. But I don't know exactly why it didn't seem so long to me."
"Bruce is right. I can hardly feel my arms due to all the stones I carried, but for some reason the day wasn't so long."
"Only your arms are dumb?" asked Mary. "What about your legs? Climbing up that canyon was a real torture."
Nailbytes said, "But what I didn't understand is why that guard took something like a picture of each of us."
"You will know that later," replied Master Cantelot.
"And what do you think about the time perception? Don't you feel there's something odd about it? Something strange is going on here. I noticed it since we got to this place," commented Nailbytes.
Bruce replied, "We don't have time for your theories."
"They're not just theories, Bruce. It's..."
Mary whispered, "Silence! Something is approaching."
"Are you sure?" asked Bruce, getting closer to the bars.
"Yes, I am. Can't you hear a kind of whisper?"
At that moment, in spite of the poor visibility, they could see that some guards walked by, dragging a creature along their cells. "What's that?"
Master Cantelot came near the bars in his cell. "I'm afraid they are bringing back a prisoner from the punishment cells."
"Poor creature," exclaimed Nailbytes, deeply moved at the sight.
"Now what is that noise?" asked Bruce.

"It's the other bell that announces that food is coming now."

Nailbytes commented, "But it hasn't been long since we arrived from the quarries."

"Well, it's alright for me. I'm hungry."

"You could eat all day long, Bruce."

"Calm down, boys," asked Mary. "How considerate of them to announce that the meal will be served. Do they do that with every meal served during the day, Master Cantelot?"

From her cell Burna cried, "Every meal? My dear, we only get one meal a day. And it's not so good either. The idea is to keep you hungry and weak."

Nailbytes asked, "Isn't there any other way to get more food?"

"Yes, there is. You can bribe a guard to get him to give you more. There's a lot of corruption here."

A large group of armed guards arrived. A few remained at the cells and the others continued their way down. "Okay, those talkers, you'll end up without any food if you don't hurry and come out quickly," said one of the guards. The cells opened automatically and the prisoners started to go out. One of them was held behind by a guard.

"Hey, you know you're punished. There's no food for you."

Eshtor shouted, "But I have already done my penance. Please, I'm so hungry."

"I told you to stay inside," insisted the guard, pointing his Isban at him and pushing him back into his cell.

"Look how I am!" exclaimed Eshtor lifting his tong over his stomach. Mary turned to him. It was terrible. All his bones were in sight. Anyone could see he had not eaten for a long time.

"What are you looking at? Get out and go, or do you want to look like that too?" said one of the guards who was watching the prisoners from behind. Mary didn't answer him. They all went out of their cells. They met other creatures who were going up surrounded by guards armed with Isbans watching over the prisoners. There wasn't much noise, only some murmurs could be heard. The darkness and the irregular soil made it difficult for the prisoners to walk. It didn't take too long for the Aceiters and the other creatures to arrive to a stone wall illuminated by a light coming from the outside.

They saw that the multitude walking in front of them turned to the left. At that moment they heard a noise. Master Cantelot said, "Those are the doors that lead to the back yard. They are opened automatically." They turned to the left with the others. There was much more light in there, and due to the darkness in which they had been in before they had to close their eyes so that the strong light wouldn't hurt them.

They gathered outside with all the strange creatures around. It was an abrupt change. The sensation of cold air was replaced by a suffocating heat.

The prisoners followed the guards to the courtyard where the food was being served to all the pavilions that shared this yard. Mary remarked, "I have noticed that our cell is two rings away from this courtyard."

Nailbytes added, "Yes, we had to go through two cell rings before we got here."

"If we think about escaping we wouldn't be too far from the exit."

"Low your voice, Mary," advised Master Cantelot. "But it's true, we are at the second ring."

"How many rings are there?" asked Mary.

"In our pavilion I think there are seven," answered Baldon who walked behind them.

From the corner of one of the dining courts a guard shouted, "Hurry up or you'll have no food at all!"

Master Cantelot advised, "Stick together, try not to wander around by yourselves."

"There are all kinds of creatures here as well."

"Yes, Bruce, they come from all the galaxies around and further away. If you pay attention to them you'll see they are the same ones we saw at the quarries," said Burna.

"Well, let's get on the line."

"Here we go, Baldon," said Master Cantelot.

They could see that each of these kind of dining rooms had six separate points where the prisoners waited in a row for their food to be served. There were all sorts of intergalactic creatures with different appearances and sizes, and many armed guards walking around watching over the prisoners. Master Cantelot, Burna and Nailbytes came to one of the queues followed by Bruce, Mary and Baldon. A few seconds later one of the guards shouted, "This queue is very long!" Looking towards the end of the queue, the guard put his arm just behind Bruce's back. "Okay, all of you behind him go to the other queue." Baldon went to find another line. Mary did the same.

The whole place was filled up with prisoners. The lines moved very slowly.

It seemed almost impossible for the guards to keep control due to the amount of creatures around the place. After a while Mary heard something. "Don't turn around."

She jumped in fear and asked without turning her head, "What do you want from me?"

"I have been watching you and your blond-haired friend when we were coming up the ramp."

"You mean Bruce?" asked Mary with an unfriendly tone. "And what do you want from us?"

"You are not from this galaxy. Where are you from?"

"We come from many Xfays away."

"That means a lot." Armed guards passed near them. It was too noisy.

Mary turned around very fast. "You are the Mayelli from the Esmeraland square."

"Yes, I am. My name is Atilio Mayelli, but I don't have much time. I am under surveillance and my execution has already been ordered."

"And how could I help you?"

"I have to save the Sathaye."

"And what's that?"

"There's no time for explanations. This will help you identify the Seven Demons of Shigahell."

"So it has to do with the prophecies…"

"Shut up! You must not let it fall into the hands of Lonar Mayer."

"Why? What is her…"

Suddenly someone shouted. "Okay, you two, what are you mumbling about? You know very well, Mayelli, that you're not allowed to speak with anyone."

Mary replied, "We're sorry, guard, we were just talking about how good the food looks from here."

"Well, you certainly have very good eyes, you're too far to see anything yet," said the guard holding his Isban. "I'm watching you closely."

Atilio Mayelli intervened, addressing the guard, "Just leave. You are still on time. You should…"

"Oh, please. Those Mayelli speeches," exclaimed the guard as he hurried away from them.

When the guard was far enough and looked distracted the Mayelli spoke. "Put your hand at your back, carefully."

Mary asked confuse, "Why do you trust me?"

"Because I don't have anyone else to trust, and, what's more, because I can feel that your presence, as well as your friend's, transmits something special. It's like…"

"Okay, walk apart, you two," shouted the same guard, pointing at them with his Isban. "You, go to that other line immediately!" Atilio Mayelli obeyed at once.

When Mary saw him walking away she stood still, confused, looking at her hand. "What is this supposed to be?" she asked herself. Atilio had succeeded in passing her a small object. It was the Sathaye. Mary looked at it discreetly. It was a small medal with a very thin chain. It was emerald green and steel blue and almost the size of a big coin. Taking advantage of the crowded surroundings, Mary put it on as carefully as she could so that it would be concealed under her tong.

Meanwhile, Bruce and others were trying to look for Mary, but it was almost impossible due to the multitude of creatures waiting for food. No one knew exactly what order the queues were following. Guards were everywhere with their Isbans trying to keep it organized, but it was almost impossible. Bruce was still looking for his friends when someone addressed him. "Hey, Canuto!"

The voice came from behind and Bruce flipped forward crying, "What do you want? Who is Canuto?"

"Do you have the list?"

"What are you talking about?"

"The list of the items we asked you to bring, Canuto."

"I'm not Canuto, idiot."

"Who are you calling idiot?"

"Wait!" cried Burna, who was very close to them. "You're confused, this is not Canuto Salgueiro, his name is Bruce and he´s not from this galaxy." The prisoner said no more and went to another queue. "So he mistook you for that scoundrel," commented Burna. Bruce just raised his eyebrows. The queue was moving forward at last. Burna spoke to Master Cantelot who was a little upward. "If you take a good look at him he does look a bit like that crook."

Bruce replied angrily, "Forget it!"

Very near there in another line, Mary still did not come out of her astonishment and curiosity about what had just happened. She kept putting her hand at her chest to feel the Medallion of Sathaye. But why had that Mayelli given it to her? She felt someone touching her shoulder and turned around frightened.

"You see, you scared her."

"It wasn´t me, it was you, Tina."

"But I didn´t do anything."

"Then who was it? Don´t tell me it was Ria, she´s busy looking herself at the mirror, as always."

"Look, Ber, that´s none of your business. It isn´t my fault that your face isn´t as pretty as mine."

Mary was astounded at what she saw. It was a creature with three heads, which, according to the make-up of the three faces and the clothes it was wearing, appeared to be a female creature. "What is your name, dear?"

"Always wishing to socialize, isn´t Tina?" commented Ber. "You´d better let her move on with the queue."

"My name is Mary. And yours? I mean your names... I really don´t know how to ask."

"Don't worry, dear. Look, the one with the beret is Ber, the one with the mirror and the bow on her hair, of course, is Ria and I am Tina. But, since we have to stick together, and I think that's the right word for our situation, don't you think so? I must admit that our real name is Tiberia."

Once she could recover from the shock Mary smiled and answered in a friendly voice, "And why are you here?"

"Scam. It was because of Ber."

"That's not true, Tina. Do not make me a bad name," replied Ber. "If Ria wasn't between us, I would give you what you deserve."

"Okay, that's enough. Stop fighting, you two," exclaimed Ria, taking her eyes from the mirror to look at them. "We are almost about to get our food."

"And you, Mary..."

At that moment a creature called from behind. Mary looked in front of her. She was already almost reaching the counter where food was being served. A few feet away she took a bowl, and when she was ready to receive her food she was pushed aside by a newcomer who shouted at her, "I'm first!"

"But I was here before you," replied Mary.

"I couldn't care less. If you don't like it that's your problem."

"That's not fair."

"Shut up and don't bother!"

"Leave her alone, you idiot!" cried Bruce, coming near her friend.

The creature walked towards Bruce with a small knife in his hands. "You'll pay for your words."

The guards just stood quiet, watching the scene with a mocking smile. "Be careful," cried Baldon, pushing Bruce away.

"Leave them alone, Tomaso. I assure you they won't give you any problems," said Master Cantelot standing in front of his friends. Tomaso just smiled and walked away looking back at Bruce and Mary with a harsh expression on his face.

The guard in charge was serving food into the prisoners' mugs but, just before it was their turn, he pointed at them with a sort of laser light and, as a consequence, he served them a smaller portion. He also gave them half an Ace capsule, not one like the others. "Now you understand why that guard took each of you a picture like you called it," commented Master Cantelot.

Baldon added, "That thing displays how much work you accomplished in this brightness. According to it they'll give you a portion of food."

Mary said, "The more you work the more food you receive?"

"Exactly," replied Master Cantelot.

"Who was that idiot, the one that wanted to take Mary's turn?"

"That's Tomaso Stapler, one of the most dangerous Umbulay Hawer in this place. It's better not to confront him."

"He looks like a big, fat rat," said Bruce.

"It doesn't matter what you think. Just listen to Master Cantelot."

"Relax, Nailbytes. I will."

One of the guards shouted at them. "You have to move or you will lose your place."

"We should look for a place to sit down now."

"That's a good idea, Baldon. Look, there's a free table and some seats over there," replied Nailbytes.

"Okay, let's go," said Mary.

They walked hurriedly to one of the twelve long stone tables with stone benches where there still seemed to be some empty places and sat down to eat their meal. The noise around made it difficult for them to hear one another but, at the same time, it was convenient because the armed guards who walked around weren't able to hear them. Nailbytes commented, "This looks like a bowl of cereal, but it is made from stone."

"We call them bowlags. They serve our only meal in them," explained Master Cantelot.

"And could someone tell me what this food is?" asked Bruce.

"It is like porridge, isn't it?" said Mary.

"I advise you not to ask. I don't think we'll like the answer."

"Nailbytes is right, let's just eat. I'm so hungry."

"Well said, Mary," said Baldon. "We call it Averridge."

"This brightness food is not bad. This time we have planton flavor Averridge," commented Baldon.

"What does it mean?"

"I think it tastes like banana," explained Nailbytes.

"Last brightness we had ornela."
"That tastes like orange," said Nailbytes.
Bruce commented, "You've learned all the flavors."
"It's not that. It's…" replied Nailbytes at the point of taking the first spoon to his mouth. He stopped and said, "I hope it doesn't have nuts."
Bruce replied without looking at him, "We would be lucky if it did."
"I was just wondering."
"Take it easy, boys," intervened Mary, "it's because of his allergy."
"Exactly, that's why I asked," cried Nailbytes.
"Hey, Bruce, there are two of those things that look like water cycles parked up there. Just like the ones back at the quarries." Bruce looked up to where Mary was pointing at.
Baldon explained, "Those are called Alphavisors. They are used to patrol the city and the roads. Here they use them to watch over the whole fortress."
"They look like the jet skies we have back home," said Nailbytes.
"I'm sure they do. They are very fast and powerful vehicles. They can elevate higher than a common vehicle," said Master Cantelot.
"Why are there more guards and Alphavisors at those dining rooms over there?"
"Bruce is right. There is twice the surveillance we have here," cried Mary, turning her head to see what they were talking about.
Baldon said, "It's because that's the pavilion for the highly dangerous prisoners. They sure need more surveillance."
"If political prisoners are Opasays, thieves and others minor are Blissays, what is the name for high dangerous prisoners?" asked Nailbytes.
"They are Wessays," answered Baldon. "In this dining room there are three kinds of prisoners."
Mary said, "Three kinds? Which other pavilions have their meals in this…"
An unpleasant noise interrupted her. In a nearby table a creature with a big trunk had swallowed in one bite all the food from his bowlag.

"Don't look at him like that, Nailbytes," Master Cantelot advised him in a low voice. "That's the way that creature eats."

However, that wasn't the only strange and grotesque event they could witness in the dining room. On their right a creature without arms ate putting his huge face into the bowlag. A little further, Bruce saw the two heads of one creature fighting over how much had each of them eaten. On the other hand, on their table, there was a creature with a tiny head who was satisfied after eating only one spoonful. Tiberia, the creature Mary had just met, sat a little far from them but seemed to be enjoying the food and a chat among her three heads.

Nailbytes suddenly remembered something. "Do any of you know..." He was interrupted once more by a loud suction noise. The wrinkled face of something like a snake, whose body was seated two tables away at the same table as the dangerous Umbulay Hawer Tomaso Stapler, had stretched all the way to Burna's bowlag and tried to eat his food.

"Hey, Ancog, you have your own food, leave mine alone. Go away!" claimed Burna.

In a hoarse voice, Ancog replied, "They gave me too little. What am I supposed to do?"

Once the incident was settled Naibytes spoke. "I was about to ask you before but with all these problems here I hadn't the chance to do it. Do any of you know where Esther is? I'm not even sure about the moment she disappeared, but I'm glad she did. They would know who she was in no time."

"Be quiet. Nobody knows anything at all."

"Don't be mad, Baldon, they are not aware of how things are here yet," said Master Cantelot.

Turning to Naibytes who sat eating his food next to Bruce and Mary, Baldon added, "She will be okay, but don't ask any questions." He sounded as if he wanted them to forget about the subject. Apparently, Esther had escaped during the previous darkness, though nobody seemed to know how she had done it.

After a little time they were all eating. "What are you doing now, Master Cantelot?" asked Nailbytes when he saw Master Cantelot standing up and looking around him.

"Don't you start with that now," cried Baldon. "Sit down before time runs out."

"Let me alone."

"You always do the same," claimed Baldon. "Every time we have our meals you start looking everywhere."

"Let me. I'm just looking for Camila and Toby."

"Doldo told you they are okay, Master, probably right now they are at the other courtyard."

Master Cantelot seemed to be pouting. "I can't be sure of that."

The guys looked around discreetly following the other prisoners with their eyes as they passed in front of them. They felt sorry for Master Cantelot. Trying to change the subject, Nailbytes spoke. "Some of those creatures don't look so mild, Baldon."

"You're right. For example, that creature over there is known as The Baron. He controlled the raw materials for medicines, but Ultro the Yagoon got tired of him and caught him with a false accusation."

"And how do they manage to be held in this pavilion?" asked Mary.

"I'm sure they pay for it. I know Tomaso Stapler paid to be here. However, in his case, Lonar Mayer uses him to get rid of political opponents pretending they were killed in fights between prisoners."

"Do you think they will want us to disappear that way too?" asked Nailbytes.

"I don't think so. You have just arrived here and, believe it or not, Esther did you a big favor disappearing as she did and leaving you behind. In this way they will think you don't..."

Suddenly everybody looked at Mary. She was taking a tissue from her pocket and wrapping some food in it. Bruce asked, "What are you doing? Are you saving some food so you can eat it later?"

"It's not for me. It's for Eshtor."

Baldon said, "Well, Mary, here we all see for ourselves. Each of us has to worry about staying alive first, and then we can start thinking about others."

"I'm sorry, but back in my planet there's something called compassion." Baldon kept quiet at Mary's answer while Master Cantelot looked at her with a bewildered expression on his face.

"Okay, eating time is over. Stand up, all of you, and pick up your waste."

"Who is that nice fellow?"

"I'm a collector, and who are you? Where do you come from? You don't seem to be from around here."

"His name is Bruce, Joel," answered Burna. "Please, Joel, just take the dishes and go away."

"Just a moment," interrupted Master Cantelot, "wasn't the Stinker supposed to be here on the earlier shift?"

"Yes, that's true, but the Stinker that was supposed to come had an accident and they send us here again. We were noticed just before this brightness. The Stinker will come back at the next brightness as usual."

Baldon asked, "What kind of accident was that?"

"I don't know. They didn't give us any details. We just know that we have more work to do. We're going to the Imhamway Space Station now."

"Hey, you over there, hurry up and get going. How many times have I told you not to chat with the prisoners!" shouted a guard from the back of the courtyard walking towards him.

"You'd better go or you'll be in trouble," advised the Master, and Joel hurried away.

A guard approached Joel before he had gone too far from them. "Don't forget to go to the fortress energy reactor BB Down. There's a lot of trash there, the guys from the other Stinker always forget to pick it up."

Joel asked, "And where is that reactor?"

The guard seemed annoyed with the question. "It's where the main energy duct ends. You'll see it when you go out. There's a surveillance booth next to it."

"I hope I'll find it."

"You are so useless, all of you. Get going." Joel obeyed in silence.

Sometime later, "What a terrible noise," said Bruce with his hands over his ears.

Nailbytes added, "It's a loud siren."

"Yes, it is. That siren means that the meal is over and that we should get up and go back to our cells."

"Come on, do as Master Cantelot tells you," added Baldon.

Hundreds of prisoners returned to their pavilions, oversaw by the armed guards and the flying Alphavisors. Mary kept a little behind looking around her until something called her attention. In the dining room in which they had their food, a creature seemed to have fallen asleep, with his head and arms on a table. She walked slowly to see what the problem was, but then she saw something terrible. It was Atilio Mayelli who was lying on the table, mortally wounded. Mary ran to him. "What happened?"

In agony, Atilio spoke feebly. "Prevent the alignment of... the Se... ven De... mons."

Mary asked nervously, "What are you saying?"

"Please look... af... ter the Sathaye. You must... must not let it fall into the hands of Luren... Perkol. It would be the... end."

"Luren Perkol? But earlier you spoke of Lonar Mayer," asked Mary.

"Just fight for our... dream... Stelars."

He spoke no more.

A group of guards came and one of them pushed Mary out of the dining room. Then, they just dragged him away in silence. "That was I," said Master Cantelot in a low voice standing behind her. "That's why that Umbulay Hawer ate with us here. This poor man was his next victim." Mary just turned her head and put it between her hands. The guards hurried them away to their cells.

Mary walked to her pavilion full of doubts and fears. Why had the Mayelli spoken at first of Lonar Mayer and then mentioned someone else called Luren Perkol? Was it just a simple confusion of names due to the pain, or was there something more to it? What exactly was the Sathaye? She looked at it cautiously. What power could it have? These questions seemed to have no answer.

When Bruce and Nailbytes were entering their pavilion something terrible appeared in front of them "What is this horrible image?" asked Nailbytes.

"Take it easy. Her name was Olaya Tewary, a highly dangerous prisoner, always trying to escape. She was caught and executed and they put that image for everyone to see so that we will think very well before trying to do the same."

Burna said, "But it wasn't there when we went to eat, Master, so they put it a very short time ago when we were eating."

"That's for sure."

"Okay, guys, let's go before the guards come," advised Master Cantelot.

They continued their way down to the cells along with the other creatures of the pavilion. When they arrived the doors were wide opened.

"Get in quickly. If they close and leave you outside you will be punished," advised Baldon. They all did so, and in a few seconds the doors closed.

Mary started to take out something from her pocket. "Wait, don't take anything out yet. The inspection will have place any time now," cried Master Cantelot. A group of well-armed guards were already approaching, watching over the prisoners to make sure they were all inside their cells. Once they went away the Master spoke to Mary from his cell. "Now you can take out what you want."

Mary took the tissue with the food she had brought along with her and went towards the loose brick on the wall. She took it away and called, "Eshtor, I have something for you."

Eshtor approached the hole with a curious look in his face. "Well, thank you so much for this. I'm really so, so hungry." He took the food and ate it in a hurry.

A little later Master Cantelot advised, "We'd better go to sleep before the guards and their prepotent commander Talmey come here and start shouting at us."

"That's a good idea," replied Nailbytes.

"Where are the beds?"

Looking around her, Mary said, "Maybe there's a kind of mechanism which will activate them." Bruce was also looking for something which would make the beds to appear. Mary spoke as she patted the cell wall searching for a switch, "Since we are in a far planet there must be something we have to push or pull and presto, we'll have our beds in front of us."

"No, my dear, I'm afraid nothing like that will happen. Just take those sleeping bags on the floor and use them," said Master Cantelot from his cell.

"What bags are you talking about, Master?" asked Nailbytes. "I can only see some old, dirty sacks."

Master Cantelot smiled at Nailbytes' words. "Those are the ones."

Mary took one exclaiming with disgust, "They smell horribly."

"I feel nauseous again," commented Nailbytes.

"I'm afraid they are all the same. Grab one."

"They are terrible," exclaimed Bruce, picking one and introducing himself into it with a grin. "I'll never believe in science fiction films again. They all say that everything in these far away galaxies is supposed to be very sophisticated."

Lying in her sack on the floor, Mary added, "Bullshit!"

Nailbytes spoke in an angry voice, "I hope that this nightmare will come to an end very soon." However, the emotions of the day and the tremendous fatigue overcame our friends and they slept tight until the next brightness.

Chapter 14

CRUEL PUNISHMENTS

Brightness came and along with it came the siren calling them to work. Some of them prepared to stand up from their sacks. "Ouch! My back is killing me!" cried Nailbytes.

"Mine too," commented Mary. "Sleeping on this irregular floor can break any person´s back."

All the prisoners were ready to go out but something happened. Fully-armed guards arrived to the cells of the Aceiters. One of the guards came near them. "Hey you, the one with the yellow hair, come here."

"I think they are calling you, Bruce," said Nailbytes.

"What do you want from me?"

"That attitude won't last for long when the scientists start to make their tests. Ha ha ha," exclaimed one of the guards.

"Where are you taking him?" asked Mary, deeply worried at the situation.

"That's none of your business. You'll know when your turn comes."

One guard waited outside and the other entered the Aceiters' cell as soon as it was opened. "Cover me if any of them tries something foolish. You know what to do. Just Sithel Isban." He pointed to Bruce a device that looked like a TV remote control.

"I can't move my hands, they feel like if they were tied up again."

"Okay, move!"

They took Bruce away to the fortress laboratory. "What can we do?" sobbed Mary in distress.

"I'm afraid there's nothing we can do," answered Baldon.

A little later the guards and Bruce arrived to the laboratory which wasn´t too far from the cells. They went in and pushed him to a metal chair. He almost fell but managed to sit down. "What are you going to do with me?"

"Just wait until the scientists are here." Some noises came from the outside. "Where do those noises come from?"

One of the guardians went to a window. "Oh no, it's Elisa." The other guard made a gesture of annoyance.

At that moment a creature dressed up as a doctor entered the room. "So this is the specimen that we have to investigate?"

"Yes, Dr Sulton, but Elisa has just arrived and it's for sure that she will want to know at once what jewels and garments we have here for her."

"Elisa always takes away our precious time. The only thing she cares for is to get hold of the executed prisoners' belongings. I think I'll have a chat with Ultro. Every time she comes we end up being late in our work."

"I don't know why, but I reckon I do like her," hissed Bruce.

"Don't try to be funny. Wait until I make the tests, you won't be so happy then. Certainly you will not be so eager to make jokes for quite a while," said Dr Sulton looking at Bruce.

Bruce was about to answer when someone knocked at the door. "It must be her," said one of the guards.

"Just smile and make all the reverences you can."

"We always do that, Dr Sulton," answered the guard.

One of them went to open the door and made a reverence to Elisa as she came in the room with arrogance. Bruce could see that she was very alike most of the creatures in Esmadis, something like a rhinoceros and quite a big one too.

"Welcome, Your Majesty. My heart beats with joy and my eyes are full with your beauty which is impossible to be found in any other living creature."

"That's alright, but the reason that I'm here is to see if you have already executed the Velsan prisoner."

"Let me see the registry, Your Excellence," asked one of the guards hurrying to a stone desk.

"How was your trip, Your Excellence?" asked Dr Sulton politely.

"As always, full of dust and Iriaje. How do you think it could be?"

"I'm so sorry," replied Dr, Sulton

"Yes... Here it is. She's been already turned to dust."

"Was it a quick death or did she suffer?"

"If you wanted her to have a particularly painful death, Your Excellence, you just had to say so. You know that your wishes are orders to us."

"No, I really didn't have anything special in mind for her, I just wanted to get rid of her because she was known to be more beautiful than I."

"No problem, Your Excellence, you can give us a list of all the ones arriving to this place and we will see the way to kill them. We'll find whatever charges are needed for that."

"Okay, I'll tell you which to kill. They will be the ones prettier than I. I mean those who think they are prettier."

"Fine. They will be killed without mercy no doubt?"

"Well, in that case you will have to get a massive destruction bomb or something like that," commented Bruce almost to himself.

Elisa frowned at the sound of a strange voice and, pointing to Bruce, she shouted, "Who is this imbecile?"

"He comes from a far away galaxy we think. We must do some tests on him to determine that." Elisa looked at him with despise and, suddenly, she approached him. She slapped him, making his face to turn abruptly to one side. Bruce looked back with a mark on his cheek. Elisa said, "Just kill this idiot at once. You don't need any tests. And make it painful. Let me know because I want to be present."

"We'll do so, Your Excellence." Elisa left the room.

The guard approached Bruce. "Well, you sure earned it. You'll die."

Somewhere else in another room at the infirmary. "Mum... Dad, please don't go, we need you..."

"It is okay, Denise, everything is okay."

"It is my entire fault. They died because of me," cried Denise, moving over on the stretcher with her eyes closed.

"Okay, just try to sleep."

"What's going on?" cried Denise again, rising half her body from the stretcher. She lied down and stared to the person in front of her. "Who are you? Where am I?"

"It's me, Esther. Try to get some rest."

Denise spoke with some difficulty, a little confused because of a commotion due to the accident. "Esther? I thought you had been captured."

"I was but I managed to escape. I hid in the infirmary and was lucky because the doctor was expecting some new nurses to help here and I told him I was one of them. Fortunately, I do have some nursing knowledge. I was here when they brought in the injured from the accident."

Denise said confused, "Okay, I remember something now."

"I could never imagine they would be you guys. I identified Maggie because of her red hair. I heard the guards talking about the accident and I assumed that you and Billy were there too."

"It was horrible, everything went blurred."

"It was quite hard. You're lucky to be alive," said Esther, putting a compress on her forehead. "Maggie and Billy were very lucky too. They almost didn't get hurt at all."

"And what about Edison? Incredibly, he accepted to drive us here complying with a deal Billy made with him," asked Denise.

"I don´t know about that Edison. I suppose he got away before the guards could get him."

"Well, I guess he did. Where are Maggie and Billy?"

"They are fine and were sent to work in the kitchen."

"Oh, no, what do we do now?"

"That isn´t so bad, they will be fine. There are a lot of creatures working there so it will be easier for them to go unnoticed."

Denise made a gesture of reluctance and asked, "Last night I think I heard someone talking in his sleep."

"You mean the last darkness? Yes, so did I. I think Billy didn't have a good darkness. He had nightmares and talked in his sleep, but I couldn´t understand what he was saying."

"This place sure affects everybody," replied Denise. "What will happen to me?"

"I advise you to pretend to be ill so that you won't be taken to another pavilion."

"Are they always so considerate with the ill?"

"Not really. They are just afraid of having any kind of epidemics among the prisoners. The guards could get ill too and that would be a great problem for them."

"But for how long will I be able to pretend? Once I am examined it will be obvious to them that I am not ill."

"I think I've taken care of that for now. I took off the energy cartridges from this Exems so it won´t work. They´ll have to get new ones."

"What are those Exems supposed to be?"

Esther answered with a smile. "We don't have time to explain it now."

"And where are my sister, Bruce and Nailbytes? Have you seen them? Are they alright?"

"They are fine at the moment but we must try to get in touch with Mary to tell her that you're okay. She might hear about the accident and she might freak out and do something crazy out of fear."

"That's true, but how can we do that?" asked Denise, becoming more conscious every minute.

"I don't know how we can send a message to her or to any of the others."

Denise shrugged her shoulders. At that moment a creature dressed as a doctor came in.

"Talking to the patients is good, Bolda, but there are a lot more to look after."

"Yes, Doctor, you're right."

"I need this stretcher for another patient, so get her out of it immediately."

"But, Dr Drusco, this patient just had a…"

Dr Drusco interrupted her abruptly. "I don´t care! Just move her away."

"I will, Doctor."

A nurse with a reptile face poked her head at the door. "You've a call, Dr Drusco."

"I'll take it, Nurse Tristal." The doctor went to the next room to answer the call.

Denise advised, "You'd better go. The doctor might get suspicious."

"Sure. But there's something bothering me. Why all the insistence in moving you away from here? This is very strange." Denise made a gesture as if she was feeling a very unpleasant smell "What's the matter?" asked Esther.

Denise answered tapping her nose with her hand. "It's that horrible smell, what is it?"

"Look, there's something under that small table with wheels."

"It's a vent. Where does it open to?"

Esther went to the table and bent her head. "Wow! It's terrible. Those seem to be the cleaning rooms down there. Those are the most stinking places in the whole galaxy. And imagine, they are just under the infirmary."

Dr Drusco came into the room again. "So what is this nurse waiting for to empty this stretcher? Do you want me to send you to prison so that you can learn to obey orders?"

Esther doubted for a second before answering, "I'm just making her walk a little so that she can recover sooner, Dr Drisco."

"I already told you that I don't care a bit about that. Just get her out." Dr Drusco left the room in a hurry.

Esther and Denise followed him with their eyes, and as soon as they considered he was far enough Esther spoke. "Definitively there's something going on with that stretcher."

"And how can we find out what can it be?" asked Denise.

"When the next darkness comes we'll take a good look at it."

Esther took Denise to the next room. "Look at that door."

"Speak low," replied Esther holding Denise's arm as they walked. "They can hear you."

They heard something outside the door. "Let's go to see what that is," said Denise.

"Okay, but follow me in what I'll say now," replied Esther in a low voice. Raising it she continued, "Let's walk to the door. A little fresh air will do you right."

When they got there someone very known to them was passing by. "Hey, that's Bruce," said Esther. "Where are those guards taking him to?" They saw their friend and the guards going down the ramp.

"Walk, you idiot!" shouted one of the guards, pushing the prisoner down the ramp.

"I think you will be Josela's next meal," replied the other guard, laughing.

Bruce didn't talk, he just walked, too frightened by what was ahead of him. They passed by what seemed to be a bathroom. A creature popped a head out of the door. "Where are you taking that poor creature? Hey, it's you, Bruce."

"Shut up, Baldon, go on with your cleaning," answered one of the guards.

Bruce kept walking with his captors while Baldon stood at the door staring at them. One of the guards turned back to him. "By the way, before I forget keep the cleaning protectors with you and take them back to the cells. There will be no one to open the storeroom at the next brightness, so you better take them with you. The guard of the next shift knows about it." They continued to push Bruce down the ramp.

The guards and Bruce arrived to the cells where his friends were waiting anxiously after getting back from the quarries. "Your friend is lucky. The powerful Elisa has condemned him to death," exclaimed one of the guards smiling broadly.

Mary and Nailbytes hurried to the door of their cell to meet Bruce, who had a terrified expression. "What happened to you? What's that mark on your face?" asked Mary.

"Elisa hit me."

"Silence!" shouted one of the guards who had Bruce.

"That damned creature, merciless as always."

"Take it easy, Master Cantelot, or you'll be the next," advised the guards.

"Let's go and see if Josela is hungry. Ha ha ha," exclaimed one of the guards.

"Yes, it's Josela's turn now because the lijas have already eaten an opponent. Ha ha ha," laughed the other.

Nailbytes pleaded, "Please, wait. We are here by accident."

"That doesn't matter now. This is the end of your friend," replied Eshtor.

"Don't say that. We have to think about something," cried Mary going back into her cell.

"Wait! Aren't you forgetting something? You must do everything according to the rules or you'll have problems with Lonar Mayer." Both guards stopped with Bruce. "What are you talking about, Master Cantelot?"

"When you execute a creature there must be witnesses present so that it will be a lesson for them. Isn't it so?"

"The Master is right," replied one of the guards.

The two of them came back with Bruce to see who they would take as witnesses. "I think it's obvious. You, your name is Mary, isn't it?" Turning to Nailbytes the guard spoke again. "You too. Come with us."

"Vildan, open the cell, it's the 312," ordered one of the guards speaking through some sort of microphone or Isikul.

The cell opened and Mary came out followed by Nailbytes. She looked at Master Cantelot who nodded his head, crossing his fingers. It was a last, desperate act hoping that they could find a way to save Bruce. The guard withdrew a device from his pocket and directed it to their hands so that they would be tied up. "These invisible cuffs again," said Nailbytes.

"Don't complain. I have them on for a while now. My hands are numb," replied Bruce.

"Okay, start walking now."

The three friends began to walk slowly followed by the guards, who kept at a certain distance to prevent the prisoners for trying to escape in any way. They came down the spiral ramp looking at the creatures inside the cells, most of which seemed at the verge of unconsciousness due to malnutrition. Mary cried, "How terrible! Look at that!"

"What?" asked Nailbytes.

"Shut up and hurry!" yelled one of the guards.

"Please, keep quiet," asked Bruce.

"What did you want us to look at?" asked Nailbytes keeping his voice low.

"Right there, inside those cells. The guards are piling them up like packages. That's inhuman."

"Do you think so? Of course those creatures aren't human but, unfortunately, we have been aware of that for a long time now," commented Bruce.

"I'm not talking about their appearance, I'm talking about their lack of
compassion for the prisoners. They don't care a bit about their suffering."

"I can see that. All this is a huge nightmare from which I wish I could wake up soon enough," said Nalbytes.

"We all want that. But the only real thing we have right now is this terrible situation," sighed Mary. "We have to be optimistic, though…"

A voice came from the cells. "Hey, isn´t it time for our meal? Hey, you, it´s time for our meal, isn´t it?" The poor visibility didn´t allow them to see who was shouting.

One of the guards laughed. "There will be no meal in this brightness, the supplies haven´t arrived today."

Mary replied, "That´s inhuman. You can let all these creatures die of hunger. You can´t do that."

"Shut up!" shouted one of the guards. "I can kill you right now!"

"You´d better keep quiet, Mary," advised Nailbytes.

Watched by the armed supreme guards they continued descending the spiral ramp. A faint, greenish light came from some tubes which ran along the corners of the ceiling. One by one, they descended along the rings of the pavilion.

However, a terrible scene interrupted their walk. "Don't take my mum away. Mum, what's happening to you?"

"Your mum is dead, cant you see? Get in your cell at once and shut up!"

"That's not true, she's just asleep."

"If you say so. Get back, I said," insisted a guard, pushing back what looked like a child of some strange kind of creature.

"What kind of planet is this?" cried Mary. She couldn't stand it anymore and ran to the child who was crying for his mum. One of the guards was ready to shoot her with his Isban but another one stopped him with a sign.

Mary embraced the sobbing creature who stood by his cell's door hugging something that looked like a teddy bear. "Don't cry, dear, your mum will always be at your side and she will take care of you, no matter where she might be."

The little one hugged her and kept crying on her shoulder. "I´m all alone. My dad died some time ago and now my mummy is dead too."

"You know, my parents died in an accident back at the planet I come from. It's only my sister and I now, but I don't know where she is. I hope she's okay. What's your name? Mine is Mary."

"My name is Emi. My brothers and my parents have all died in this place."

"I'm so sorry, dear. From what I've seen until now, this Eliom and Lonar Mayer certainly are not good for this planet."

"But it's not only Eliom. There's the Liberator's Army. They too kidnap people they think are collaborators of the government, and they can be even crueler than the supreme guards."

"This war should come to an end."

"I hope it does. I already lost all my family because of it."

"Someone has to do something about it."

"I've been listening to that for a long time."

One of the guards shouted, "Well, that's enough! You have an execution to attend."

"Take care, dear," exclaimed Mary, waving her hand to the small creature.

"Are they going to disintegrate you, Mary?" asked Emi, wiping the tears from his eyes.

"No, it's my friend Bruce they are taking to Josela," answered Mary, walking towards her friends and wiping some tears from her face herself.

The guards and the prisoners continued their walk. After a while, they arrived to the end of the spiral ramp. There was a hall with three hexagon doors.

Mary said, "Look at all those rooms. I wonder what's inside them."

"You'll know it very soon. At least what's in one of them. Ha ha ha," laughed one of the guards.

"Get into this room, all of you!" commanded one of the guards, opening the door on the right side using what seemed to be a key which shot a green light towards the lock.

Inside the dark, dirty room the guard looked uncertain. "Okay, how does it go now?" he whispered to himself.

"You always forget about everything, don't you? We've done this a dozen times. When will you learn at last?" answered the other one. "Put the condemned in this circle and the witnesses in one of those around it."

"Oh, yes, now I remember."

"Stay there," said one guard walking to a control panel on a wall. "Wait until the prisoner is untied so that he can fight back and make this more amusing." The guard smiled and freed Bruce's hands. Bruce tried to hit the guard but he was stronger than him and he was thrown on the floor.

"Are you okay?" asked Mary.

"Yes. I think I am," answered Bruce, rubbing his head with his hands.

"I hope Josela will chew you really slow," said the guard who had hit him.

"Okay, here we go," exclaimed the other guard as he pushed a handle. Before he left he untied the other prisoners with an ironic smile. "There's no need for you to have your hands tied in here."

The center circle had a sort of a slide going down to a room with stone walls.

The other ones went down below the room they had been in before, and they could see Bruce standing in front of them in a sort of cage which allowed them to see whatever would go on inside. From the upper room the guards could also see everything through a glass floor. Suddenly, they heard a ring. "Who can that be? Go and tell whoever it is that we are in the middle of an execution."

One guard went to what seemed to be a phone. "Hello? Who is calling?"

The guard who stayed on the glass floor kept looking from the prisoners to his companion who spoke on the phone. "Yes, we are making an execution ordered by Elisa."

In the room below our friends spoke in a low, terrified voice. "What do we do?" asked Nailbytes.

"I don´t know," answered Mary, sobbing in desperation.

"Let's see if I can twist this rail," cried Bruce but his intents were useless. It was a strong rail.

The guard hung up and told his companion, "Lonar Mayer is coming. He has just known that Esther has escaped and is supposed to be hiding somewhere around here."

"Damn! How did she find out?"

"I don't know, but we have to go upstairs at once. If we are not present they will blame us that's for sure. You know how mean Ultro the Yagoon can be."

"Yes, I do. He'll give in anybody to safe himself."

"What do we do with these idiots?"

"That's easy, just open the door and let Josela in."

"Yes, but we'll miss the fun."

"We'll have plenty of other executions. Don't worry."

"Okay, let´s go upstairs before Lonar Mayer gets there."

Before leaving the room one of them raised a handle and then closed the door behind them. Mary and Nailbytes stood helpless, waiting to see what was going to happen to their friend and not knowing what to do to prevent it. A big door opened wide. Mary and Nailbytes looked at it in terror. "And now what?" stammered Nailbytes.

"What's that noise," exclaimed Mary putting her hands to her head.

"It sounds like a growl," cried Nailbytes. They stood appalled, looking at what was coming out of that door.

Mary asked, "What kind of beast is that?"

"It looks like a dragon," replied Nailbytes. The beast threw fire out of its enormous mouth.

"It looks terrible," said Mary, walking around with her hands on her head in despair.

"This is his end," cried Nailbytes.

At that moment Bruce saw a stick on the floor. He took it and pointed it to the monster. "Don't you dare to get nearer," he tried to threaten the monster. The monster stopped, looking even bigger and terrifying. Mary and Nailbytes thought it was the end of their friend.

Chapter 15

AN INCREDIBLE DRAGON

The dragon stopped growling and spoke with a heavy Spanish Accent, "Why do we have to start with offenses, my son?"

Bruce couldn't believe his own ears. Let alone hearing a dragon talking to him, it was doing it softly, almost in a fatherly way. He was so surprised he could hardly speak. "What are you talking about?"

The dragon replied, "Well, I haven´t offended you, have I?" Mary and Nailbytes were as astonished as Bruce. The beast managed to sit down with his legs crossed and his chin resting on his right hand, if a dragon has a hand that is.

"That's the big problem. They all think I'm the worst ever but that's not true. Why do they think only bad things about me?" Bruce was still staring at the dragon who continued talking with a sad voice. "It's not easy to live with this terrible reputation, you know."

Bruce was, at last, starting to recover from shock. "And what's your name, dragon? Mine is Bruce."

"I like this politeness above all, but please don't call me dragon. My name is Jose Latorre, but they call me Josela."

"So you are the horrible monster, Josela?"

"By any chance do you have a mirror, my son? Why horrible monster? Of course I admit I wouldn't win any intergalactic beauty contest, but I'm sure I'm not that ugly."

"Well, that's the reputation they have made up for you."

"I guess I have to look very mean. If I don't I'll lose my job. Do you know how difficult it is to find a job nowadays? Especially for creatures like me."

Bruce lowered the stake and leaned against it. "You should look for something different anyway."

"I did so, a few Soltens ago. I gave out some papers offering my services for house cleaning, pet caring and even babysitting, but I can't understand why nobody called me. I even attached my photo on the flyers, but nothing." Bruce didn't answer, he just made a face. "I also offered myself for ironing in a laundry but nothing happened."

"This planet will never stop surprising me," commented Bruce with a half smile. "What will happen to me now?"

"Well, we will do the same thing we always do. I'll take you to my inner cage where nobody can see us. You will shout really loud and terribly, I'll do my share of growling and then it will be over. You'll hide until you can escape from here. That's what I've done to all the others."

"Wow! Thank you so much."

"You're welcome, my son."

Nailbytes and Mary watched from their place. "We'll tell them that Josela ate Bruce so that they won't look for him," said Mary.

"Then let's get out before the guards come back," said Nailbytes. He then added, "We must put on a sad face so that they will believe us. Come here, Bruce."

He approached them while the dragon waved goodbye and began to file his nails. "Stay in the dragon's cage," said Mary.

When he heard her the dragon lifted his head and spoke patiently, "Josela, please, my dear girl, Josela."

Mary replied with a smile, "Okay, Josela. Stay here with Josela until we can find a way to take you out."

Bruce began to yell and Josela growled as loudly as he could for a while.

After that Mary and Nailbytes spoke to each other. "Let's go now before those guards are back."

They went out of the room and met the guards. "Hi, how was it? Did your friend suffer a lot?" asked one of them with a wicked smile on his face.

"It was horrible. Please don't make me talk about it," answered Mary, pretending to be crying.

She looked at Nailbytes and saw that he stood quiet at her side. She gave him a pat on his head forcing him to bend it down and exclaimed, still sobbing, "We are both shocked."

"Well, it's a pity but that's the way things are around here. We'll go to Josela's cage later to pick up whatever is left of your friend, if there's anything left of course. Usually, we don't find anything at all. It seems that Josela has a very huge appetite."

"You must go back to your cells now," said the other guard pushing them towards the ascending ramp.

A little later, exhausted after walking up the long ramp, they saw all their fellow prisoners standing close to their cell's doors wanting to hear about the execution. "What are you looking at? Hey, Vildan, open the cell, it's the 312," commanded the guard. The door opened and Mary and Naibytes were pushed into their cell. Once the door was closed behind them the guards went away.

When he could see that the guards were already away from them, Master Cantelot approached them and spoke softly, "Poor, you, it must have been terrible to watch your friend die and in that horrible way."

Mary and Naibytes looked at each other for a minute and then Mary asked in a calm voice, "Master, have any of you ever been present at an execution? I mean, with Josela eating up a prisoner?"

"The truth is I haven't, my dear. I couldn't bear looking at that monster while he eats a friend of mine. I always try to cover my eyes the best way I can, but of course I hear the terrible screams. It is a horrible experience. As some other prisoners told me, the monster usually takes the victim into his cage. They only get to hear the screams but don't really see that dreadful scene."

Mary said, "In that case, Master, the only thing I can tell you is that Bruce didn't suffer a bit, and that he will be much better that any of us."

"What do you mean? And you say that the creatures in this planet don't have any feelings?"

Mary was about to answer when Eshtor interrupted, talking from his cell. "Wait, Master, I've heard something about Josela not being as terrible as he is supposed to be. There are certain rumors about creatures who managed to escape from him."

"I've never heard about that," cried Burna.

Before anyone could say anything more they heard a loud voice coming from the corridor. "Okay, where's the poor idiot that's going to die now?"

"What is he talking about?" asked Naibytes in a low voice.

"I don't know," answered Mary with fear.

"That's the one over there, Tunner, the one next to the cell of the Master."

"Oh, it's you, Burna. Come out, it is your turn now."

"Please no! I don't want to die!"

"Save your prayers for your executioner before he shoots you with his disintegrating rays."

The guards came near Burna's cell. "Vildan, open cell number 313," said one of them, talking to the Isikul. The door opened and the guards went in to get Burna.

"Have you seen that? They always tell Vildan to open the cell doors. He's the one in control," commented Nailbytes.

"Lower your voice. Yes, I've noticed it. They talk to him through that speaker and Vildan obeys without even looking at them. That's giving me an idea," replied Mary.

"And what's that?"

"It might help us to escape."

"Hey, you, keep quiet or Burna might not die alone."

"Okay, Tunner, we have to choose a witness now."

"What do you think? Could it be Master Cantelot?"

"I think that would be fine."

"It's so painful to see someone being killed because of his ideas."

"Stop that political chat, Master. Just walk out and come with us."

One of the guards approached the Isikul again. "Vildan, open cell number 315."

In spite of her attempts to fight the guards, Burna was taken to her execution. "Poor Burna, this is the end."

"Isn't there anything we can do to help her, Eshtor?" asked Mary.

"The only thing we can do is to wait and hope we are not the next ones to go."

"How terrible having to live this way. Always thinking that the next brightness might be the last one you will ever see."

"That's exactly how life in the Atilkawa Fortress is."

At that moment, Doldo, the guard that the prisoners bribed almost every brightness, came near the cells holding something that looked like a handkerchief to his mouth. "How disgusting. No matter how many times I have to go into those cleaning rooms I'll always get nauseous. That poor creature doesn't know what's ahead of him. And how are you? I'm bringing you the latest news," he said cheerfully. Pointing at the Aceiters he continued, "It seems that these strange creatures are really very lucky. The scientists are too busy now making new biological weapons in order to suffocate the revolution at the Caution Rai colony."

"What's happening over there?" asked Eshtor.

"I don't know exactly what's going on, but it seems there has been some kind of mutiny. They say that the miners want better working conditions, but of course Lonar Mayer and his generals won't give them anything at all, they will just kill them. That's why the scientists are quite busy now and that certainly makes you very lucky guys."

"If you can say we're lucky to be in this place," commented Mary with a sad voice.

"Well, you and your friends are very lucky, believe me. Well, at least not like those others who look just like you and were taken to the infirmary after that terrible accident at the Lonely Curve on the road."

"What are you talking about? There has been an accident?"

"Don't you know about it? A Stinker crushed into a cargo vehicle. One so-called Edison was driving and they say there were other three creatures just like you with him."

As soon as Mary heard the terrible news she came near them exclaiming with a worried voice, "I'm sure Denise is among the wounded. Billy and Maggie, too. Who else could they be?" exclaimed Mary.

Eshtor said, "Calm down. Did you hear if they are alive?"

"Nobody died but they are seriously wounded."

"Look, the energy has gone down a little. That means they've just used the disintegration cannons. Burna wasn't as lucky as your friends, Mary," said Eshtor.

"I feel very sorry for Burna, but at this moment I'm too worried about my sister and my friends. What else do you know about them? Where and how wounded are they, Boldo?"

"I told you already, I don't know much about it. If you want I can go and ask around, but it'll cost you more of course."

"Let him go," cried Nailbytes.

"Wait," replied Mary.

"Yes, wait a little until this nice creature makes me a good offer."

"I'm not making you any offer, I couldn't pay you, but I could give you a few mint candies which will help you endure the stench at the cleaning rooms."

The guard grinned and replied in a harsh tone, "I'm sorry then. There's no more information for free. However, if you give me those candies as you call them, I might let you use my Isikul for a while so that you can hear about the Nwephe-Shake games. Nobody works for nothing around here."

"Where have I heard those words before?"

"It was Edison, Nailbytes. But please wait!" Mary shouted to the guard who was walking away from them.

Eshtor stopped her. "Don't call him anymore. Let him go. That creature doesn't think about anything but the way to get more rutters from us."

"But I need to know how my sister is."

"I have a question, Eshtor. The guard said that he would lend us his Isikul. What did he mean by that?"

"I don´t know what that is," replied Eshtor.

Baldon was back followed by two guards. "Okay, Mary, you are going to help me clean the Nasty Rooms."

"What are you talking about? Those are the bathrooms. You said they were terribly filthy, that the smell was unbearable," replied Mary. "And we are in full darkness now. It´s time to rest."

"Shut up and walk!" shouted Baldon. "Open the door, Vildan, it's cell number 312."

Mary went out quietly, glancing at Nailbytes with a bewildered look, and followed Baldon. When the guards were out of his sight

Nailbytes turned to Eshtor and spoke sadly. "I thought that Baldon was our friend, but I see now that I was wrong."

"You never know who your real friends are."

Mary and Baldon went up the ring-like, dark ramps which led to the cleaning rooms. When they got to the Nasty Rooms Baldon turned to the guards. "Are you coming in with us?"

"Are you crazy? It's horrible in there. You and that strange creature can go inside and we will stay here and keep an eye on you. Don't try anything foolish, you know we'll shoot you at once," said one of the guards looking at Mary.

"We know that. I just want her to help me clean up all this mess. You know how disgusting it can be. Ha ha ha," replied Baldon.

The guards laughed at Baldon's mean comment. Baldon took Mary's arm and pushed her into the room, handing her a bucket with what looked as cleansing utensils. The smell of the cleaning room was unbearable. Mary put her hand on her nose with a nauseous expression. It was a small room with four small individual compartments. All the doors were dirty and some of them hang down at the point of falling on the floor. Each one of the compartments had a small dirty toilet. Above them there was a vent which ran along the room. It was impossible to see what was on the other side. "Take this and clean the holes thoroughly. The edges and the lower parts too. And don't forget to use that green spray. Of course, considering that you're so dumb, read the instructions so that you'll know how to use it correctly."

"I thought you were my friend," said Mary in a low voice, on the verge of tears.

"Shut up! Just do as I'm ordering you!" replied Baldon and walked away to clean the floor.

With resignation and a cloth in her hands, Mary went to the closed compartments and, with a sad face, bent down in order to begin her terrible work.

She started with the upper part but Baldon shouted at her, "I told you to clean the inside edges, you idiot!"

"How I hate him. This is horrible, Baldon. I want to puke."

"Just go on with it."

"Well done. Make her do the dirty work for you," laughed the guards listening to Baldon's orders from outside the door. Mary started to obey with a nauseous expression. Making a big effort to control her disgust, she bent down to clean up what seemed to be the toilets, considering that those boxes could deserve that name. At that moment, she felt something strange with her fingers. There was something on the edge, right under the ring.

Chapter 16

SECRET MESSAGES

Mary looked around to see if there was anyone near her. When she realized there was no one in sight she began to feel under the ring with her fingers, trying once more to overcome her nausea. She felt like letters written in some kind of protruding paint. Why would anyone write something in here? she thought. As she continued running her fingers over the protuberance something came to her mind as a sudden flash: "Hey, these are letters in my language." A big surprised smile came over her face when she could read what was written: Deni okay, spray.

She looked around her again and then took a good look at the spray in her hand. She turned it over until she could see that the label was a little detached from the tin. She pulled it to take it off completely and, turning it over, she read, Everyone's okay. Plan escape here. Mary put back the label and tried her best to finish her task. She then approached Baldon who was waiting for her at the door. "Forgive me, Baldon, and thank you."

Baldon smiled but one of the guards asked fiercely, "What are you thanking him for? Answer me at once, you idiot!"

Mary spoke with sarcasm. "What do you think it is for? For making me do this horrible job, that's why."

"Okay, shut up! If she's over with her work I'd better take her back to her cell."

"Yes, do that. She is a bother here," replied Baldon.

The guards took Mary back to her cell. Nailbytes asked her, "Are you okay? Mary didn't answer until the guards went away. Nailbytes insisted, "Well, what's the reason for that half smile?" Mary told him what had happened at the cleaning rooms. "It's incredible. How clever of them to use bread, or Berma, as they call it here, to write the message," said Nailbytes. "They took the idea from Yami, she used it to make figures at home."

"We must save some Berma or anything else that will help us write an answer as soon as possible," said Mary. "That will keep us in touch with Esther, Billy, Maggie and Denise, but how can we make contact with Bruce?"

"Well, you'd have to clean Josela's bathroom," replied Nailbytes with irony.

"That's it!" shouted Mary.

"Keep your voice low. What is it?"

"I must find a way to make Baldon send me to clean any bathroom near Josela's cage."

"But it had to be used by Bruce or someone who could give him the messages," commented Nailbytes. "And that might be dangerous. Someone unfriendly could see the messages and accuse us."

"You're right, but once I'm there I might think about something else."

"How will you manage to get them to send you over there?"

"I don't know. I have to think about something, some kind of excuse," replied Mary. "What's that noise? Are you playing with your Transler?"

Holding his Transler in his hands, Nailbytes answered, "I'm not playing. It seems that this device also works as a recorder."

Mary looked thoughtful for a moment and then spoke with enthusiasm. "I have it." She added, "If it could record the order to open the cell door, then the only thing we might need now is to get a speaker, or Isikul, and try to get out of here."

Nailbytes asked, "And where do we get an Isikul?"

"From Doldo, he has one."

"And how do we get him to give it to us?"

"Well, that's a good question."

"And one more thing, how do we get him to come to us?"

"I don't know, but we must think of something," answered Mary. "But let's talk in a very low voice, we're supposed to be asleep."

Meanwhile, at the infirmary of the Atilkawa Fortress, some patients were not sleeping at all. "Don't tell me that this kitchen uniform doesn't become you," commented Billy.

Maggie replied harshly, "Shut up! Stop teasing me! I look horrible, this brown overall does not fit anyone." Maggie and Billy had managed to be taken for prison kitchen employees.

"Keep your voice down, someone can hear you," said Esther. She then looked at Billy. "Was everything all right? Did you have any problems when you brought the food?"

"No problem. We could bring two trays," replied Billy holding two trays with some bowlags on them.

Maggie said, "But you have to hurry. The guards will come if you take so long."

"We told them that we would bring back the dirty bowls from the infirmary so it would give us a little time to be here," explained Billy. Then he continued, "So you think that Dr Drusco insisted on Denise leaving that stretcher because there's something hidden in it, Esther?"

"Yes I do. We must take advantage of the darkness to take a good look at it right now."

The Aceiters and Esther began to examine the stretcher's top carefully and ended up turning it over. Suddenly, Denise exclaimed, "Look, there's a kind of drawer on the floor."

"Pull it!" cried Billy.

Denise obeyed.

"What's that?"

"It looks like a secret entry to the floor downstairs. Where does it lead to?"

Denise poked her face through the hole and made a grin. There was a strange smell. "It's like the reagents we smelled on the *Loader Vargas*. I remember Edison telling us he was bringing them to the Spartack."

"Well, it means that the Spartack is here at the Atilkawa Fortress." They looked at each other in surprise.

"I think you may be right, Esther," exclaimed Billy, standing up with enthusiasm. "Help me move this bed."

"So the Intelligence Center of Esmadis, the Spartack is here," cried Esther

When they tried to move the stretcher they heard a metallic noise. "Where does that noise come from?" exclaimed Esther, leaning down and putting her hand all over under the stretcher until she found something. She grabbed it carefully and showed it to her friends.

"What the hell is that?" asked Billy.

"It looks like a strange Isban," replied Esther. "Though it looks more like a small barrel. Wait a moment, there's something written on it." She approached it to her eyes a little. "I can't believe it, it's a disintegrator."

"This means that there's not only another entrance to the Spartack, but also that those crooks hide things to sell them clandestinely," said Billy.

"It certainly looks so," exclaimed Esther.

At that moment Maggie, who had kept a little far from them until then, came near and asked, "What did you find here?"

"We just found a secret entry to the Spartack. It'll be easier for us to go there."

"And who is going down?"

"You and I are."

"Where are we going? What are you talking about?"

"You can complain afterwards, Maggie. Now we have to go down," said Billy. "We do need a rope though."

"I saw something like that near the vent," said Denise.

"Please, go and get it," replied Billy. "Esther, did you leave another message for Mary? I suppose that Baldon has managed to give her the first one already."

"Yes I did."

"It was quite ingenious to leave messages using the Berna. I would have never thought about it but we must hurry up. They won't take long to find out that we are not in the kitchen yet," commented Billy.

"Please hurry," cried Denise.

Before they went down Billy asked, "Meanwhile, please look for anything dirty for us to take back to the kitchen, bowlags or something. That way we'll have something in our hands when we get back."

"Okay, as soon as you go down we'll look around the infirmary for anything you can take back to the kitchen," said Esther.

Maggie and Billy went down the rope through the hole under the stretcher to the floor below them.

"Good luck," cried Esther from above. "Denise, help me raise the rope now and return it to the drawer."

"I can barely see anything here, and I've been looking around for a while now. What exactly do you expect to find here?" mumbled Maggie.

"Keep quiet," said Billy, "and look over there carefully."

"What's that? Is that the main office?"

"Yes, it is. We're getting to know more about this horrible place."

"It's frightening but what exactly are we looking for? I don't get it."

"We're looking for any clue we can find, Maggie. We have to take advantage of the present darkness. If there's nothing here we'll go on looking everywhere we can."

Walking carefully they arrived to a better lit place. "I can't see much here either."

"But it's better than the last one, Maggie."

"There are a lot of glass cases. What are they displaying in there?"

"I don't know. We just have to look for anything that might give us a clue about how they are planning the invasion of the Earth. What are you looking at so attentively?"

Maggie cried, "This looks like something in a city back in our planet. It's the Eiffel Tower in Paris!"

Billy hurried to where she stood. "You're right, and isn't that the Tower of London?"

Maggie remarked, "If it's not it really looks a lot like it. Why do they have these scale models here?"

"Look, this one looks like the Roman coliseum," said Billy. He then turned to another glass case. "This looks like a city in China due to the kind of buildings."

"That's Beijing."

"Don't shout, but yes, it is."

"Oh, oh, I understand now. They have scale models of the cities they are planning to attack. These cities will be the first targets of the bacteriologic attack."

"Oh no!" cried Maggie. "Look at those boxes over there. They are just like those we saw on the spaceship." Both went to where the boxes were. "I do not dare to open them," said Maggie.

Billy looked at her and then looked at the boxes. "Me either. Imagine what they might contain."

"What could be in that room?"

Billy asked, "Which room?"

"That one at your right."

Billy turned around. "Let's go and see." They both got to the reddish stone door. It had a semicircle shape.

"And now how do we get in?"

"I don´t know," replied Billy. "There must be a button or something to open it."

"Well, you´d better hurry to find it before someone comes in."

Billy looked all over the door and around it and Maggie watched the main door in case someone would come. "Here it is." The door opened letting out a white smoke.

"Well done."

Once the smoke was cleared they entered the room. Maggie cried, "Wow! It is very big."

"There´s not much light in here but, if you compare it to the other premises we have seen in this fortress, it sure looks huge."

"Yes, the infirmary looks big but it´s really made of a lot of small rooms put together."

"It´s not just the size, it´s…"

"What?" asked Maggie.

"It´s that it looks like the control room of the Nasa Space Center. I saw it on TV. Long tables full of computers in rows, and look there."

Billy was impressed at the sight before his eyes. Big screens occupied the front wall and the whole scenery around them. "It´s so strange. All this is made of a reddish stone, isn´t it?"

Billy commented, "That´s the least important thing about it."

"What do we do now?"

"I really don't know but…" replied Billy with a worried frown." Let me see if I can enter the systems."

"Shall I put the lights on?"

"Wait a moment, let me take a look first. Even with the lights off I can get to see something. There are a lot of computers but the front screen above seems to be the one which monitors all the others."

"Have you noticed this? There are many papers near the computers but they all look like papyrus."

"You surprise me," cried Billy. "What a difficult word, 'papyrus'. Do you know what it means?"

"Of course I do. It's a very fashionable kind of paper they used tons of years ago. My grandmother told me that. She is so cult, and elegant too."

Billy smiled at his friend's words. "Now we must see what these papyrus, as you call them, can tell us."

"Simple. Just use the Transler Mary used in Edison's vehicle, remember?"

"It is true, I remember that."

He took his device from his ear. "I'll use it as a Transler so I'll be able to read all this."

"Look up there. That's exactly what I deserve, a throne just like that one."

"What are you talking about, Maggie?"

"Up there. Look again."

Billy turned his eyes to the upper part of one of the walls in the big room.

"It's a very elegant chair. It seems comfortable, all in velvet. That's what I should use."

"Silence!" replied Billy. "I suppose those rails under it can take it over the whole room so whoever sits there can supervise the work."

"And the rails have a semicircle shape."

"Just as this room. Look at it."

Billy continued examining the papyrus with his Transler.

"Who do you thinks sits there?"

Without taking off his eyes from the papers, Billy answered, "I don't know, but I guess it could be that condor woman, Lonar Mayer."

After a while Billy exclaimed, "Oh, no, this is exactly what I was afraid of."

"What do they say?"

"These machines seem to contain all the information about the great invasion of the Earth. We have to do something about it."

Maggie replied with a grin, "I have the feeling that I won't be on time to train for my riding competence next week, will I?"

"Forget about that. I want to see if I can do something about this."

"Something like what?"

"I don't know. Maybe I can reset it." Billy started to manipulate the machines, but after a while he exclaimed, "I can't understand most of these codes. We have to come back here with Nailbytes."

"Look!" shouted Maggie. "This icon looks like the one we use for Internet."

"Try to get in and see what happens."

She did so. "Hey, this looks like our Facebook."

"And how useful could that be right now?" asked Billy.

"I don't know but I want to see something." From time to time Billy looked at the door in case someone would show up. Suddenly, she exclaimed, "Oh, no, this is terrible."

"What is it?" asked Billy. "What's so terrible?"

"This is the end."

"Talk to me. What are you reading there?"

"She's gone too far."

"You're talking about Lonar Mayer, aren't you? What did she do now?"

"Who's talking about that horrible creature. Rose Wilson bought a jacket just like mine. Look."

Billy couldn't believe his ears. "You better shut up! Let's get out of here."

"Don't shout. They might hear us."

"Well, if they do, at least I wouldn't have to hear all your nonsense."

"I'm sorry, but it makes me furious that Rose is always a copycat."

"I can think about so many things to make us mad at this moment. Let's go back before the night guard comes."

They started to go out when Billy stopped abruptly and put his hands to his head. "What's the matter?" asked Maggie.

"You make me so mad I can hardly think right. But you have the courage to ask what's the matter? I just realized you said you entered Facebook and you didn't think about sending a message to our parents?"

"I wasn't able to write anything, I could only read. You think that if I could have written I wouldn't have sent a message to Rose in the terms she certainly deserved?"

Billy didn't answer her. He just shook his head. "What's on that table at the corner? I didn't see it before." Billy approached the table. "Look, these bags have some objects that look like those whistles used to call dogs."

"But with what can they use them here? I haven't seen anything close to pets."

"I don't know, but the bags have some instructions or whatever written on the tags."

Billy took the Transler and passed it over a tag. "I have it. These whistles are used to control the panthers accompanying the guards. They are going to use them today."

Maggie took one in her hand. "What's this switch for? It has three levels."

"It must be for something of course," said Billy as he went on reading the tag. "It says here that it shouldn't be used on the higher level because the panther will become useless. It seems that it has happened before."

"What does useless mean for a panther?"

"I don't know but let's take some and put them on the highest level. It will sure be of help if we have to face those animals."

"I hope you're right and that this will help us to get away from here."

"So do I," replied Billy.

"Quiet, someone's coming." Both hurried away. They ran to the hall where the secret door on the roof was.

"You go first. We must hurry," cried Billy.

The rope was waiting for them and they climbed up without any problem.

Denise and Esther were waiting for them upstairs. "We heard you coming and had the rope ready in case you were running away from someone."

Esther asked, "Did you find anything?"

"Yes, too much, but we must do something fast. Please tell Baldon to take Mary to clean the kitchen."

"Alright."

"What do we do now?" asked Maggie.

"We're going back to the kitchen. I hope the guards haven't noticed our delay. We've been here for too long," said Billy.

"Hurry up!" cried Esther.

"Beware! It is very cold out there at the courtyard."

"That's no problem, Denise. We came by a corridor under the courtyard," explained Billy

"Okay, let's go, guys," cried Esther again.

Maggie and Billy went back to the underground corridor to cross over to the kitchen. It was very dark, the only light was the greenish one from the tubes on the ceilings. It didn't take long for them to arrive at the ramp which took them to the prison's main kitchen. When they reached the ramp Maggie asked, "Hey, where is the guard?"

"I do not know. Let's go fast."

Little by little they started to feel the smell of burnt porridge emanating from the kitchen. They both reached a small spiral ramp leading to the hall. At their right they had the kitchen's cleaning room. In front of them, a little to the left, there was the kitchen's big opened door. On the other side, close to the door they were standing at, there was another big door leading to the main patio.

"That's why that fool was not in his place. Look!" exclaimed Maggie.

Billy directed his sight to where Maggie was pointing at. "That guard is certainly busy."

"So I see, Maggie. That's the reason he didn't notice that we weren't here," said Billy, when he saw a couple embracing near he door.

"She works in the kitchen too. She's one of the washing up team."

"How interesting knowing everyone's life," replied Billy. "Anyway, let's go."

They both went up the ramp and through a narrow corridor to the left, being careful not to get too close to the patio door because it would open just by stepping near it.

They finally arrived to their cells by the kitchen.

The rest of the darkness went by quietly. When brightness arrived the prisoners had to resume their daily routines. Time went by and Mary and Nailbytes were returning to their cells talking about the last events. "I'm dead. These quarries are really killing me," said Mary.

"It is exhausting. But unfortunately, I do not think we have the possibility of leaving these small cells yet," commented Nailbytes. "My back will collapse if I have to go on sleeping in these sort of bags through more darkness."

"Speak low. One of these creatures might hear you and it would be our end," replied Mary. "Now we must find Doldo as soon as possible."

"He's over there, at the door of Master Cantelot's cell."

They hurried to their cells. The guards let them in, closed the doors behind them and left. Doldo stayed silent until his companions were far from there. "Hey, you're lucky, it seems that the mutiny at the Caution Rai mines is getting out of control. The Liberation Army is behind it and Lonar Mayer and, of course, Ultro the Yagoon are both over there so we will have peace and quiet for a while here."

"So that's why there haven't been any executions lately."

"Yes, Master, they also have a riot at Pluternay, the factory protectorate. But, on the other hand, we have to put up with the terribly annoying Elisa moving around here."

"That's bad for them. The Isbans and all the other weapons used by the supreme guards and the Amarphy are made at that protectorate. But tell me, what is that despicable creature Elisa looking for in this place?"

"Master Cantelot, as always, Elisa is after the belongings of the executed prisoners."

Eshtor replied with a grin, "But aren't the creatures of the Liberator's Army aware that, in no time, they will be fighting against chemical weapons?"

"Well, that's true. Some weapons have been taken over there already, all the scientific force is working on that."

Nailbytes commented, "So they won't try to find out where we come from, at least not yet."

"But as soon as Lonar Mayer suffocates the rebellion, as she always does, and comes back, she'll take care of you and I assure you that she will have no pity."

Mary said, "I hope that we will not be here by then, Eshtor."

"What did you say, strange creature?" asked Doldo.

"I was just kidding."

"You'd better keep quiet. I'll go now but don't forget about my next payment if you want to have more news," said Doldo walking away. He turned around abruptly and added, "I have other news, very, very important ones, but it deserves a special payment."

"Just go," said Eshtor, going to the back of his cell.

"Why did you tell him to go? I had something to ask him."

Mary made a gesture to Nailbytes summoning him to keep calm. Nailbytes cried, "There's that terrible siren again."

"Relax, this is our only meal in this brightness," replied Eshtor.

Meanwhile, at the kitchen, "I am very tired, these trolleys weigh a ton."

"Do not complain, Maggie. They don't weigh at all, these trolleys float in the air, you only have to push them."

"But it's so hard having to wash all those bowls after the meals."

"Don't tell me about it," replied Billy. "Did you put the Berma baskets or bread in all tables at the dining room?"

"Yes, this time I remembered."

"Those two talkers, don't you have anything to do?"

Billy just smiled, then turned to Maggie and said through clenched teeth, "Monic is a tyranic creature."

Luckily for Billy Monic did not hear his comment due to the great noise in the kitchen. She went near them, wearing a bright green chef suit and a chef cap. "Well, did you leave the trolleys with Rojano Averridge and bowlags?"

"Yes, we did,"

"And the protion jugs? You forgot them on the last brightness."

Billy answered, "Yes, we did. We left six in each dining room, eighteen in all."

Monic turned to them and cried, "So go and wash the food tanks, now!"

Maggie and Billy went towards the big five food tanks in the kitchen, mingling among the multitude of galactic creatures who worked there going from one side to the other with various tools and kitchen utensils. Once they got to the tanks they went up to the second level by a ladder next to them where they worked pouring the ingredients into the tanks, mixing the food inside with huge ladles.

All the cooking work was overseen by armed guards, who did so from different corridors located on the top, spanning the entire kitchen. While using the big tools to help the team who was cleaning the huge tanks, Maggie asked Billy, "Do you think Esther could tell Baldon to bring Mary here?"

"I sure hope so, that's the only option we have now."

Maggie just stared with a look of concern, but she knew this was just the beginning. The fact of being communicated was good, but they knew that they needed much more than that if they wanted to leave Esmadis, let alone save their world.

Chapter 17

THINKING ABOUT A BETTER PLAN

Mary and Nailbytes were back from their meal. "I tell you, I'm sure I saw Maggie and Billy, they were going inside somewhere, Maggie's red hair is unmistakable."

"But where could they be going to?"

Mary was about to answer when they saw Baldon waiting next to their cell.

When he saw them he spoke loudly, "Okay, you are not bad cleaning up the clean rooms in the pavilion, and since I am the cleaning brigadier I'll send you to the kitchens. They sure need some cleaning over there." Luckily Mary caught Baldon's idea, but she couldn't figure out how cleaning the kitchen would be of help. Master Cantelot called Baldon and he went to his cell.

The guards that had come along with Baldon waited with their Isbans aiming at the cells. Nailbytes took advantage of the moment to whisper on Mary's ear, "Why did he tell you to clean the kitchen?"

"I don't know, but I feel there's something good behind it."

Nailbytes handed her some bread, "So do I."

Mary looked slyly to the bread he had just given her. "I was thinking that it might be convenient to leave something behind, a cleaning utensil or anything like that, so that you'll have a pretext to come back there."

Mary cried, "Well thought!"

Baldon came back from Master Cantelot's cell and made a sign to one of the guards who, through his Isikul, ordered to open Mary's cell. She just took her things, left the cell and began to walk behind him. Along with the guards who had come with him, Baldon and Mary went to the cleaning room.

Meanwhile, at the kitchen, things were not good for Maggie and Billy. As she always did, Monic was rushing them. "Hurry up or you will lose your meal."

"Okay, Monic, I will go faster," replied Billy by the washing machine. Maggie looked down from the staircase as she went down to the first level to take her meal. Billy took his food in a hurry and went to the cleaning room to see if he could meet Mary, or at least take a look to see if she had left a message for them.

The kitchen's door was opened so Billy went through it and came into the cleaning room. Once inside he could see that Mary was already gone but he went to what could be the silo and tried to see if there were any messages there. Plans escape?

Billy read and took a small piece of Berna from his overall pocket, always checking that no one came. He then wrote, Meet your clean room. After that he went out and back to the kitchen

Mary was back at the cells from her cleaning task and she and Nailbytes were trying something. "Hey, Doldo, can you come over here please?" asked Mary.

Doldo stopped talking to a companion and went towards them. "What do you want?"

"You must know that the semi-final game of the Nwephe-Shake is hot, so I was wondering..."

"Yes, the Tigers are unstoppable this season, though the Thengasy Pirates have this player, Tati Goizueta, she is the best Bular-Ufu that ever existed..."

Eshtor intervened, "Don't overdo. She is not the best ever. Tati Goizueta might be one of the best this season, but just as Ken Klupor or Ilse Banser..."

Doldo replied, "And what do you know? Have you considered how many times she went out in every game in the last three seasons?"

Mary said, "Okay, you got it. So I was wondering if you would be willing to make a deal. Of course, it is a very convenient deal for you…"

"Don't fuss with me. Just tell me what you want."

"Well, you know we are crazy about the Nwephe-Shake, and we won't mind losing anything if we could only follow the game through your speaker…"

Doldo interrupted her. "My what?"

"Sorry, your Isikul, and we can give you a lot of these useful mints to help you at the cleaning rooms."

"No, there's no deal."

Nailbytes made a grin and said, "Damn, we'll never leave this planet," and walked away from them.

Mary insisted, "Hey, these mints are such a relief for you. You shouldn't refuse this opportunity to make your hard job a lot easier."

"There's no deal. I'm not sure if it's worthwhile to put my job at risk for some mints."

Naibytes stood quietly looking at them, but then he put his hand in his pocket and felt something in it. "Okay, forgive me for my prior outburst. Look, here I have something delicious. These are multi flavors Liberator's ammunitions, and this is a succulent Escaper."

Mary smiled at Nailbytes' words and, changing her expression, she added,

"You see, on top of this my friend is offering you my wonderful Escaper. Hey, those are supposed to be mine."

"I know those delicacies. In that case…"

"I'm sorry, but I think Doldo deserves them more than you do."

"That's not true. Those are mine," insisted Mary.

"Well, if I don't get that Escaper there's no deal."

"Okay, you win, but I insist. It isn't fair."

"It might not be fair. That's what life is about. Here, take my Isikul, but you can only keep it until the next brightness, and I advise you that if the guards ask me about it I'll tell them that it has been stolen from me."

"We'll tell you about the game later," said Nailbytes.

"Never mind. I'll listen to it with the others guards."

"It is a deal. Take the mints."

"Yes, and the Escaper too," replied Doldo. "Yummy, yummy, I'll see you."

Once Doldo was out of sight, Master Cantelot replied with a smile, "I must say, Mary, you are a good actress and a bit psychologist too. By telling him that you didn't want to give him your Escaper you aroused his greed and that did it."

"I was hoping it would work," answered Mary.

"We have to use both the Transler and Doldo's Isikul," said Nailbytes. "Go to the clean room at the kitchen now. Tell the guards you forgot your cleaner there."

"Up to now the plan is coming out quite well."

"Yes, everything turned out well. Let me see now what we can do with this speaker," said Nailbytes, taking off the Transler from his ears. "I have to see if it has registered the voice of at least one of the guards." Mary looked attentively how her friend was manipulating the Transler. After a few minutes Nailbytes cried, "I have it!"

"You are a genius," cried Mary with a broad smile on her face.

"I know."

Along with Nailbytes they waited for the next darkness to come. As soon as it arrived, "Ready, put the Isikul next to the Transler and cross your fingers."

"Okay, one, two, three, go!"

Putting on the recording Nailbytes ordered, "Open the door now, Vildan. It's cell number 312."

While the other prisoners slept, the bars opened before Mary's, Nailbytes' and Master Cantelot's smiling faces. Mary and Nailbytes hurried out of their cell. She tried to push the trolley but it was too heavy for her. "Wait! You have to make it go up a little, just like every vehicle in this planet," explained Nailbytes.

"And how am I supposed to do that?"

Nailbytes came near and started to manipulate the handles. "Look, this is the way to do it. Just push these buttons and it will go up." Suddenly, the pushcart went up little above the ground. "Presto!" cried Nailbytes.

"Fine. I keep forgetting that we're stuck in this planet and that everything here is so queer," said Mary.

"Now get in."

She walked towards the cleaning rooms pushing her trolley up the ramp carrying Nailbytes inside it. When she arrived to her destiny she heard a harsh voice. "What are you doing here in plain darkness?"

"I'm sorry, guard, but I was sent to clean this room again. It seems that I didn't make a good job before. But I'm so tired, I sure didn't want to come."

"Shut up! You don't get to choose what to do over here. If you didn't do your job as you should have you'll have to finish it now, so go and do it."

"It still smells bad," replied another guard.

A third one said mockingly, "The next time you fail doing your job I'll see that you don't get your food on the next brightness. Okay?"

Mary entered the room pushing the cart. She went towards the silos, approached one of them and knelt looking for new messages. She searched with her hand until she could feel there was something there for her. "Wait." Nailbytes came out stretching his arms and legs. "It was quite crowded in there."

"Leave your complaints for another time. Now we have to wait."

"Wait for what?"

Suddenly, they heard a voice. "Hi, sis."

Mary looked up at the ventilation rail on the ceiling. "Denise!" she called when she saw her sister's face.

Nimbly her sister went down the vent to where Mary was.

"That's it, Denise." Mary was moved by her sister's presence.

Both sisters hugged each other for a moment. Denise spoke. "It's so good that you could come back quickly. That vent is very uncomfortable and the three of us had to come down through it at the same time. Can you imagine that? It was terrible."

"Where are Maggie and Billy?" asked Mary.

"They are upstairs in the infirmary with Esther," answered Denise. "As soon as there were no guards at the infirmary they moved to the next room with Esther."

"So she succeeded to get away from the cells. We were afraid she might have been caught again and probably killed. She certainly is a warrior."

"Yes, she somehow managed to end up in the infirmary passing as a nurse."

Denise looked at Nailbytes. "Billy asked me to show you this. It is a device used to manage the space panthers, the beasts used by the guards." Nailbytes took it in his hand and looked at it carefully. Denise went on, "According to Billy it has a sort of force regulators, can you see that? Here we can read something like slow force, then regular force, I can't figure out the other sign."

"Yes, it's kind of blurred," said Nailbytes.

"Anyway, Billy and Esther think that it might be useful to help us escape."

"What have you planned for our escape? Please tell me you have something. Don't forget we have to take Bruce out too."

"They all think it will be easier if we escape in groups. It would be much more difficult if we tried to do it together."

"They might be right about that," replied Mary with a frown.

"And how have you planned to form these teams?" asked Nailbytes.

"You, Billy and Maggie should go together. Billy needs you to help him destroy the invasion programs and the delivery truck might be here…"

Mary interrupted, "So you did find the Spartack Center?"

"Yes, we did. It's just below the infirmary, but as I was telling you Billy thinks that the delivery truck can be very useful."

"What do you mean by that?" asked Mary.

"They think they can take the place of the creatures which bring the supplies for the fortress."

"Wait, let me see if I understand it. Billy thinks you can go into the truck that brings the supplies to the prison?" asked Mary.

"Yes, that's it. But he says he has yet to define some details," said Denise.

"I can imagine that. It will not easy to escape from there," commented Nailbytes.

"He'll have to consider all the details so that the guards won't catch them," replied Mary.

"And that should not be so easy," commented Nailbytes.

"Anyway, I read Billy's message. How did it occur to him to use bread?"

"Wait, let me tell you everything. It was because of a strong stench that came from the ventilation duct that led to the bathrooms."

Denise started to tell them what had happened up in the infirmary. "Later, Esther saw Baldon making signs to her, telling her that she shouldn't speak to him, but asking her if she had a pencil or anything she could write with. She then had the good idea of leaving him messages using Berma. Esther thought we could do the same and put them under the bathroom rings so that no one would see them."

"Do you mean using bread?" asked Nailbytes.

"Exactly. Now, about the whistles, it was because..."

"Okay, we don't have much time. What have they planned for your escape?"

"Billy thinks that I should hide in the rubbish bins so that I can get away from here. I'm small so I'll fit in right. However, though I'm not at all like Maggie, I must say they are nasty and smell terribly."

"Unfortunately, sis, we don't have many options. They are right. We can't escape together so it will be really much better if we divide in groups, just as Esther and Billy have planned. That rubbish bin idea is good."

"And what about you and I going together in the dumpsters, Mary?"

"I'm afraid I'm too big to fit in there, they would find me at once. I'm sure, though, that you will go through unnoticed."

"Okay, you can catch up your talk later. Now, you'd better come up here and put these clothes on, Denise," said Billy from the vent above them. "Nailbytes, come up here quickly please."

Nailbytes obeyed. He went towards the wall under the vent and started to go up. Billy helped him because his friend had some difficulty due to his weight and then he went down carefully.

"Hi!" cried Mary.

"Hi!" replied Billy. "This is not going to be easy but we must try."

"Yes, I think so too."

Looking at Denise, Billy said, "You must go up. Esther is waiting for you there with some clothes."

"What clothes are you talking about?"

"Just go and see."

"I'm coming up," answered Denise.

"When you go out there will be a Stinker nearby. No matter how terrible it might smell, you have to get into it and wait until it's carried away to the Imhamway Station. We will all meet there and go together to the spaceship," explained Billy. "Now, go, hurry."

Mary repeated, "So our meeting point will be the Imhamway Space Station?"

Billy answered, "Yes, I think that's the most convenient. We'll meet as near to the *Iron Warrior* as we can."

Denise commented, "Esther told me you couldn't sleep well at the last darkness. Why is that?"

"I don't know, but in my dreams I saw somebody who told me her name was Lautana Martin. She asked me for help, and she always repeated Sise Lautana. I don't know what that means."

"Yes, neither do I," replied Mary, but the Mayelli gave me this…"

One guard shouted angrily from the outside, "Who are you talking to?"

"Hurry up or we will go in!" insisted another guard.

"I was singing, sorry," replied Mary. "You'd better go now."

"You are right," said Billy, but I think we shouldn't talk to Esther about this dream. I remember her reaction at her home when Centi mentioned that name."

"Yes, I remember too," said Mary. "This is increasingly confusing and complicated."

"Okay, let's go," cried Billy. "Denise, did you give them the whistle?"

"I forgot. Here it goes, sis."

"Do you think this whistle will be useful?" asked Mary looking at it in her hand.

"Well it seems that they control the panthers with it," replied Billy.

Denise asked, "What about you, Mary?"

"I'll try to get out of here too, dear, but…"

Billy said, "I'll leave you here for a while so you can talk a little, but please, Denise, hop in the dumpster as soon as possible." He went towards the vent and started to climb up.

"What do you mean by saying that you will try? You are going to do it, aren't you?"

"Of course I will, sis. But you know there's always a risk. If I can't do it…" answered Mary with wet eyes. She took something from her pocket and gave it to Denise, clutching her sister's hand over it. "I want you to have this."

Denise looked at it and sobbed, "But this is the last photo we have of all of us. Mum, Dad, you and me. You are the eldest, you are the one that's supposed to keep it." Mary had a sad expression on her face and remained silent. Denise sobbed, "I get it, you think you won't be able to get away, isn't it?"

"I'm not saying that, sis, don't worry."

"I can read it in your face. I'm not going away without you. I wouldn't know what do without you."

"Don't talk that way. But as I'm telling you, there's just a little possibility that I might not do it. Please you will have to look after Granny Vivi in the way she has been looking after us."

"You see. Then I will stay here with you."

"No you won't. Stop crying and go up there now." Denise wiped her tears while Mary kissed her on the forehead. Mary spoke again, making an effort to sound optimistic and almost happy. "Take good care of yourself, my little naughty girl."

Denise answered, sobbing, "It's been a long time since you called me that way." They hugged fiercely. A voice interrupted their farewell.

"You are taking too long. Hurry up or I'll carry you into it myself."

"I´m afraid, Mary."

Mary gave her sister a light push. "Don't say anything more. Just go."

"But, sis…"

"Just go! Billy's gone already. Hurry!" commanded Mary, trying once more to sound calmed and sure.

A voice came through Mary's Transler. "Mary? Can you hear me?"

"Yes, I can hear you," she answered, putting her hand on the Transler in order to change the frequency, trying to get a better communication.

"Go and look for Bruce. We'll wait here."

"No. You and Esther should get out now. I'll get Bruce and we'll go out together. Knowing him I'm sure that by now he has some ideas of how we can do it."

"But that's going to be too risky," replied Denise.

Some voices started to sound very near. "Again! Hey, you idiot, I told you to hurry. Wait until my companion comes back, I can't let the corridor alone."

Mary whispered, "Go! Go!"

"Okay, sis." Denise hurried up the duct and disappeared.

Mary looked at the door, thinking with a deep sigh, The important thing is that Denise gets out of this safe.

At that moment the door flew open and two guards entered the room. "Who were you talking to?"

Mary took a short breath and answered calmly, "I'm not talking to anyone, I told you, I'm just singing, it makes me company."

"This one is completely nuts. Okay, if you are over with the cleaning, get out of here now."

Mary went back to her cell. This scene had been witnessed by Denise. As soon as Mary had left the room she went out from the vent and saw her friends.

"Good luck, guys."

"Thanks. Good luck to you too. Here we go," said Nailbytes.

"Did you bring the food for the sick creatures from the kitchen?" asked Esther.

"Yes, that's the excuse to come here, but we must hurry before they found out it's a trick," explained Billy.

"What is this? It looks like rubber," asked Denise, looking up the vent to the garment Esther had in her hands.

Esther intervened, "Yes, it's something like that. Baldon uses it for protection when he is cleaning the bathrooms."

Billy smiled and said, "Anyway, it's a good idea to put it on, Denise. If the guards happen to pinch the trash, they won't hurt you because this rubber is quite thick."

"Okay."

Billy went to the stretcher and started to go down. "Hurry up, Nailbytes," he whispered from below.

"I'm going. Denise, go with Esther, she's waiting for you." Denise nodded her head and went away.

"Okay, let's go," exclaimed Billy. He then saw his friend standing near a stretcher. "What happened? What are you waiting for?"

"It is that creature on the stretcher. He looks like Master Cantelot."

"Who is that?" asked Billy. "Forget it, we don't have time. Hurry!"

"Just let me see the name at the bottom, Billy."

"We don´t have time for that. Hurry up!"

Nailbytes went down without reading the name of the patient. Denise put the drawer where it had been, under the stretcher, and went to the next room where Esther waited for her. As soon as she saw Denise, Esther said, "Put on the rubber clothes that Billy gave you. Now we have to wait for the next darkness," she continued, looking around her.

Under the infirmary, Billy said, "Let's go to the Spartack Center," walking along with Nailbytes to the next room.

"Wait, somebody is coming."

"Let's go to that dark room over there." They run fast trying not to make any noise.

"And now what?"

"Calm down, Billy. We´ll stay here in the dark for a while."

"Look, that´s the office door," whispered Nailbytes pointing to a door nearby where a guard was sitting on a chair. Billy nodded and they both looked towards it.

At that moment the guard at the door stood up from his chair and welcomed someone in. "Welcome, Your Majesty."

"Is that poor bastard dead?"

"Yes, Your Majesty, just like you ordered. You request is over there," answered the guard, pointing to a table nearby.

"Well, it was about time too," said Elisa, walking towards the table. She opened a box and took off something.

"This is a beauty. It certainly didn't look right on her fingers. It looks perfect in my hand."

"That ring fits you so well. And the pink tong you're wearing today enhances your beauty and elegance, Your Majesty."

Elisa smiled showing off her finger with pride. "That's right, there's nobody in this galaxy as elegant as I am."

"Please, Let me tell you that you are not only elegant, milady, you have many virtues no other creature has in our whole universe."

Elisa stopped staring at her ring and said, "You are so right. I'll talk to Eliom. I think you need a promotion."

The guard kneeled at her feet. "Thank you so much, Your Majesty. A promotion will be humbly received and loyally acknowledged."

Elisa was about to leave the room when she turned around and said, "I remember a nice black tong a companion of her was wearing. What happened to it?"

"A black tong? I don't know... Let me see if it is somewhere around here."

"Look for it. I'm sure I would look very well in it, really as in everything I wear."

"Whatever you say, Your Majesty." Elisa left the room and the guard remained alone in it.

"That woman looks like Maggie. She could be her sister; she's as arrogant and vain as she is."

"Low your voice," replied Nailbytes. "They'll hear us. And that is so silly..."

"But it's the truth. Anyone who hears her would think that she and Elisa are close relatives."

"Keep quiet, let's go before someone finds us here. We were lucky that nobody has come near us yet. I sure hope that Esther and Denise have already dropped down the rope. If they haven't, I don't know what we are going to do."

"If they haven't done so it will be because someone is near them. Let's hope that will not happen."

"You know listening to that mean woman as well as, I must admit, my silly words, has given me an idea but I'll have to think more about it."

"I hope it's a very good idea," said Nailbytes. "It's beginning to get clear again so brightness is coming. What are we going to do when the chefs come to work?"

"I don't know. We have to stay here. This looks like a storeroom. I just hope they won't need anything for a while."

Nailbytes bent his head with resignation but then he saw something. "What is this?" He walked towards a box, bending his head to prevent being seen by the guard. He took out a black tong.

Billy came near him. "This must be the one Elisa was asking for."

"But what is it doing here?"

"Maybe the guard kept it to sell it later," said Billy. "They are using that hole on the roof to take out this kind of things, don't you think so?"

"Maybe."

"Anyway, this can be useful to go ahead with my idea. Take it." Nailbytes took it without a word.

Billy went stealthily towards the door to see if the guard was gone. "Let's go in now. Hurry!" They hurried to the Spartack Center.

"Wow! Everything here is made of light red stone. Look at the wall."

"That's what Maggie said."

"You mean I am thinking just like Maggie?"

"Exactly."

"This planet is certainly not good for me."

They arrived to the main room and Billy, recalling where the doorknob was, opened it. "Hey, it's identical to the one at the Nasa Space Control Center," exclaimed Nailbytes.

"I had noticed it too, but all that matters now is to format the programs."

"We first have to see if there is a light switch."

"Maybe the lights come on as in Esther's house, on a voice order."

"I'll try that, but only on this computer at the center. It seems to be the main one." Billy nodded in agreement.

They went to the computer at the center of the room. "Central control lights."

"It worked!" cried Billy.

"Wow! Look at that!"

"It's impressive. It looks better with all those lights on. Now we have to see if we can do something with all this."

"I think it would be better to look for an emergency deleting program so that we could erase all those files."

"Well, then, look for it."

Nailbytes begun to manipulate what seemed to be the main computer. "I think I have an emergency delete program over here. My dad explained to me that when they put a computer on a spy plane, they put this program so that the pilot will be able to erase all the files before jumping out of the plane."

"Okay, hurry up," said Billy, walking to the door to take a look outside.

After a few minutes that seemed like hours, Billy made a gesture to Nailbytes from the door, asking if he had finished. His friend signed back shaking his head. Billy made a grin and went near him keeping his eyes on the door. "What are you waiting for? Why are you taking so long?"

"Wait a minute. I have a little more to go."

"What's up? What are you waiting for?" asked Billy with an annoyed voice.

"I need more tools."

"Don't you have them there?"

"The problem is that I usually look for them in the Internet."

"Wait, someone is coming." Nailbytes turned off the machines and Billy put off the lights.

A guard came in along with another creature which walked slowly and looked a little old. "I'll leave you here. Finish up putting in all the information and call me."

"Okay, Tonlay, no problem. I don't think it will take too long." The guard nodded and left the room. The creature turned on the lights and started to work on one of the computers holding some papers in his hands.

Nailbytes and Billy, hiding from him, whispered to each other, "Now, what are we going to do with this one?"

"Let me think," answered Billy. Both started to look around them.

Soon one of them found something. "Look. Those are the controls of those handcuffs they put on us when they brought us here. A guard must have forgotten all these in here."

"How do they work, Nailbytes?"

"You just have to push this button and an invisible rope ties your hands up. Now we have to look for something to stop him from making any noise."

"We'll do that with this cloth," replied Billy.

"We'll have to be real fast," commented Nailbytes.

"Okay, let's get near him, and on the count of three…" said Billy.

They carefully approached the creature which was concentrated in his work.

Billy made a gesture with his hand lifting one, two, three fingers… "Now!" In a few seconds the creature was immobilized, with hands and feet tied up with the cuffs and a cloth in his mouth. Billy and Nailbytes took him to a small wardrobe where he could hardly move at all.

They went to the computer the creature had been working on. Billy said in a low voice, "Maggie found something like Internet in here. She could even look at her Facebook. However, if we are…"

Nailbytes interrupted, "There's probably some kind of satellite which captures the communications from the Earth, and that's how they know about us. How much water, or Ace, as they call it, we have."

"Anyway, if she could do that I'm sure you'll find what you need."

Billy saw a worried expression on Nailbytes' face. "What is it?"

"It's just that this center and all these systems are a tremendous sign of updated science."

"Yes, I agree. In some subjects they seem to be quite ahead of us."

"They sure are. Don't you feel deeply appalled of what this means? They are by far more than just some kind of elementary creatures as we thought they were. They have great scientific knowledge and they are going to use it against the Earth."

After some minutes in silence, Nailbytes spoke. "Look, Billy, this is very interesting."

"What have you found there?"

"The Spartack Center controls the military forces. Here are the details of
all the weapons they make at Pluternay."

"Excellent! That could be of help to us."

"I think so too. For example, here we have how to use the fuel, or energy as they call it. It says that it's necessary to be careful not to mix this element with something called Donsel, which might damage the spaceships' systems or even make them explode. And for what I can read they are referring to the ships they'll use in the invasion."

"Just destroy the files, Nailbytes, there's no time for analysis."

"As always you and everyone else trying to make me hurry. What do you think if I change the words, 'Do not mix' with 'Mix' so they will damage their ships themselves? I can do the same with some other words so they will do everything wrong."

Billy raised his eyebrows in surprise. "That's a very good idea. You're brilliant."

"I know."

"Okay, genius, go ahead but hurry up. Someone might come any time now."

Nailbytes resumed his search of the tools he needed in order to fulfill his task and Billy stood at his place near the door. After a little time Nailbytes exclaimed, "Okay, I think it's all ready."

"Well done. Let's get out of here."

"But... Wait."

"What happened now?"

Nailbytes took a few seconds to answer. "This is creepy."

"What is?"

"There are some humans captives somewhere in this galaxy."

"What are you saying?" asked Billy.

"They're being used. I don't know for what."

"Did the computer tell you that?" asked Billy again.

"Yes, it did."

"I do not know, but…"

"Hurry, someone's coming!" cried Nailbytes. "We have to take these cuffs, they might be quite useful later, don't you think?" They hurried to hide themselves but Billy stumbled over something and made a noise.

"Who's there?" asked one of the guards, coming into the room with his Isban on his hand.

"I'm sure there's someone in here," added the other guard, coming in behind his partner, also with his Isban.

Chapter 18

SOMETIMES IT'S BETTER NOT TO KNOW

Nailbytes and Billy could hear quite clearly what was going on. One of the guards turned around and spoke to the others. "Listen up. Stay watching the output, the order is Sithel Isban."

"Where's Dr Horkey? I left him working here," asked Tonlay, one of the guards

"Do you see? That's what comes from going away. We should have stayed at the door watching over this room."

"Leave your lectures for another moment. Let's see if there are any intruders in here."

The guards entered the room looking around them. One of them exclaimed, "Look at that in the middle. That machine is showing a sign saying that…"

"Saying what?" asked the other guard. They approached the main computer.

Tonlay exclaimed, "I don't know much about these machines, but I think that the files have been erased."

"What are you saying?" said the second guard as he came near.

"I mean exactly what you just heard. I think someone has erased some information on these machines."

"What do you mean by some?" asked the second guard.

"Don't you see that this is our death sentence?" asked Tonlay. "We'll be disintegrated. Ultro the Yagoon advised us that we should protect this room with our lives if we had to, remember?"

"What do we do now?"

Tonlay replied, "I don't know, but right now we have to keep quiet about it. We must think well before we say anything or we will be disintegrated at once."

A third guard came near them. "Sooner or later they will know about it and they will kill us. What if we run away?"

"Don't talk so much nonsense. Let me think for a moment," said Tonlay.

Billy and Nailbytes thought it would be a good time to run away. The three guards were in the center of the room and had left the exit free. But they were wrong. One of guards saw them and yelled, "Hey! You two!"

The others turned around and took off their Isbans. Tonlay shouted, "Sithel Isban." They came near pointing their Isbans to them. "Walk out!" shouted Tonlay.

Billy and Nailbytes went out from the Spartack watched closely by the guards. Once on the outside, Tonlay looked for the commands to close the door.

"Watch them carefully, Murtel." One of them just nodded his head. At last Tonlay was able to close the door. He then asked, "Who are you?"

Murtel replied, "They must be the ones who erased the information."

"But why would anyone want to erase part of the information about an invasion to that far away planet, the Ace planet?" asked Tonlay.

He and Murtel suddenly looked at each other. "So you come from that planet, don't you? The Ace planet did send a special force after all."

"Okay, come with us now," demanded Murtel.

The Aceiters began to walk slowly towards the exit. Billy took a deep breath and spoke with a solemn voice. "Well, you caught us. We knew we would fall into the hands of a superior race like yours." Nailbytes looked at Billy, a little confused at his friend's words. Billy put on a mean face and spoke with a fake voice. "But you will pay for it. We'll use our magic powers on you. Did you, by any chance, think that the Aceiters would send plain creatures on this dangerous mission?"

Nailbytes looked at Billy, hoping he really knew what he was doing, and whispered to him, "What powers are you talking about?" Billy hit him hard on the stomach with the elbow of his free arm. "Oh, I see. These powers," said Nailbytes rubbing his stomach.

Billy continued, "Okay, let us go or I'll turn you into terrible monsters."

"And what is a monster?" asked Murtel.

"Something very alike what you already are. You won't change much," muttered Nailbytes.

"Silence! I have to concentrate," shouted Billy with the same fake voice.

Closing his eyes and putting his fingers on his head, he added, "Put your Isbans on the floor, slowly." The guards stared at him for a moment, not too sure of what they should do with this menacing creature. They finally made up their minds to obey the shouting monster. Billy continued, "Now on your knees, all of you. Put your heads down. Don't you dare look at me." When all of them, including Nailbytes, were on their knees, Billy grabbed Nailbytes' arm and he cried, "Let´s go!"

They ran away as fast as they could, back to where they had come from.

Fortunately, the rope was in place so they were able to go up, pull it quickly and close the entrance to the second floor. "Couldn't you take a little longer?" asked a mocking voice.

Billy replied, "I'm sorry, Maggie, we were saving the Earth, you know, the planet we live in."

Nailbytes added, "Yes, the place where you go with your parents every Sunday to ride your horses, remember?"

"Don't be sarcastic. And you, I sure hope they will give us a gold medal for saving the planet." Making a small pause, she added, "Or even better, they could give us a prize in cash."

"Why are you always complaining so much?"

"Because I had to hide in this ventilation grille and it's quite uncomfortable."

"Well, it comes with the job."

"Yes, look at me, I'm covered with dust. It's so disgusting," replied Maggie, shaking off her tong.

"Now we just have to wait for the next brightness. As soon as it arrives we'll go on with our plan. I hope nobody comes in."

"And what is that plan if I may ask?" asked Maggie.

"You'll know it when the time comes," replied Billy.

Meanwhile, Mary had managed to get away from the guards thanks to the poor lighting at the ramps, had arrived to the cells and was now talking to her fellow prisoner. "You didn't answer me, Master, who is, or was, Lautana Martin?"

Master Cantelot and Eshtor looked at each other and said nothing. "Was she, or he, somebody you knew?" insisted Mary.

"Sometimes it's better not to know. It is safer for you," replied Master Cantelot.

"Listen to Master Cantelot, Mary," said Eshtor. "Knowing too much about the Seven Devils of Shigabell could be very dangerous for you."

"Then it has to do something with the seven devils," insisted Mary.

"Please, Mary, leave it there," cried Master Cantelot.

Mary kept silent for a moment and then she spoke. "Anyway, I'll go with Bruce now. I hope everything goes okay."

"Well, you haven't done so bad until now."

"Baldon," shouted Mary.

"Low your voice," advised Master Cantelot.

Baldon came near them. "Hello."

"Thanks for helping us."

"It's okay. I'll do anything to prevent those bastards from getting away with their crimes."

"Why don't you run away with us?" asked Mary.

Baldon answered sadly, "As I told you before, I'd rather not leave. I'm sure those beasts will go after my wife and children. I'll stay here although I don't know for how long."

"Your family must miss you a lot."

"And I sure miss them too. You can't imagine how much. But I wouldn't forgive myself if something would happen to them because of me."

"Okay, go now before they find you," spoke Master Cantelot.

"Master, wouldn't you come with us? You'll be safe there."

"Thank you, but just as Baldon I'm afraid for my daughter Camila and my grandson Toby. I'd put them in great danger. I'm sure those creeps will kill them. If I stay I can still hope that I will find them some day and, somehow, we'll be able to go away together."

"Okay, Master, I hope we will see you again some day."

"So do I. Please be careful. If you succeed in keeping Lonar Mayer from invading the Earth be sure to do it for good. She knows that's the only place in which she can find the Ace we need, and she won't stop at anything in order to get it."

"We will, Master Cantelot. I have to go now, I must take advantage of this darkness. I'll leave this trolley here."

Baldon opened the cell door for her and Mary started to walk down the ramp into the darkness, holding her arms in front of her to avoid stumbling with anything on her way. The cleaning gear she carried tied to her body with a belt made a little noise as they knocked with one another. Mary kept walking towards the deepest place of the prison. As she used to do when she walked through the woods back at home, her thoughts kept her company. It looks so creepy down here, but I guess it is better this way. I can't see an inch from my nose and I don't have a torch. I can't make any noise or I'll wake up someone." But something happened.

She heard a voice saying, "Sise Lautana."

"Who said that?" she asked herself. She looked around but she couldn't see anything. Fear gripped her. "Is this trip driving me crazy for real?" She went on listening to strange voices around her. She remembered that it was like the dream Billiy had told her about. But she was not dreaming.

"Sise Lautana."

Now it had been clear. "Something is moving". Fear almost paralyzed her.

She saw a somewhat confusing, far image. Making her best effort to control her fear, she followed down the spiral ramp of the Opasays' pavilion. At last she arrived to the deepest part of the fortress.

In the darkness someone spoke. "What are you doing down here?"

Mary jumped at the sound of that voice but made a big effort to stay calm.

It was a guard.

After a small pause she took a deep breath and answered, "I came to pick up some cleaning products and take a look to the cleaning room. Baldon sent me."

"Okay, let's go inside," said another guard.

Passing by Josela's cage she commented, "Oh, dear, this cage looks terribly filthy. You poor guys have to clean it up."

The guards looked at each other with an angry expression that changed into a mocking smile. One of them answered at once. "That's what you think, you idiot. You'll clean this filthy cage, as you call it, and right now too."

Mary spoke with a pleading voice, "But I was sent to clean only the cleaning room."

"Shut up and do as I say!" replied the guard triumphantly.

The other one took off his Isban and pointed it to Mary. "Do it or you'll die."

Mary made a grin and went to the cage entrance. The guards opened it carefully and closed it fast as soon as she was inside. She started to clean the cage's floor.

The guard continued with his orders, "When you're finished there, go into Josela's cage."

Mary thought it would be a good idea to go to the cage so she could look for Bruce. However, to avoid arousing any suspicions, she went on pretending. "But something terrible might happen to me in there."

"You are a whining creature. Go there as soon as you finish the outside."

"Okay, I'll go in there when I'm finished here," she answered with a sobbing voice. Mary glanced furtively to the room where Josela was supposed to be and waited until the guards went away. She hurried to clean up the front cage and went carefully into Josela's inner cage. As soon as she was inside she went towards to the big gate. It had a door through which Josela used to come out. When she peeked in she saw Bruce. "Hello."

"Hello, Mary. Our staying here is sure improving our acting skills, don't you think?"

Mary smiled at her friend's words and asked him, "Are you okay?"

"Yes, I am. Come in so they won't see you."

Mary went in taking care not to be seen by the guards and asked, "Did you figure out a way to get away from here?"

"Something like that. Now don't ask me why just now, but I must cut the wires of the communication device."

"What do you mean?" asked Mary. "Is it the one on that stone table? Why do you have to do that?"

"I told you not to ask, remember? I'll explain it to you later."

"Okay, but I suppose it's so that they won't be able to communicate and ask for reinforcements, isn't it?"

"Exactly."

"Do you think you can catch the attention of the guards so that I can go out for a moment and cut the wires?"

"Sure I can. No girl likes rats. Or lijas, as they are called here."

Bruce went to hide himself from the guards and Mary went to the cleaning room outside the cage. She waited for a moment and started to scream. "Help me! There's a horrible lija in here!"

"What's the matter with you? If there's a lija in there it must be a very small one. Kill it. A real grown-up lija would have killed you in a second. Ha ha ha!" yelled one of the guards from the outside.

"Please, you kill it," cried Mary from the inside.

Four guards walked to the room with a grin of disgust. When Bruce saw them walking to the cleaning room he hurried out of the cage, ran to the communication device and cut the wires. He also took a couple of Isikuls as fast as he could and ran back to the cage.

Inside the cleaning room, the guards spoke angrily to Mary, "Where's that terrible lija?"

"It came out of that hole in there and made 'grrrrrr'."

"It made what?"

"It growled to me. It was horrible."

The guards shook their heads and went out. "Maybe some lijas have made small holes in the ducts and are coming up through them. It seems that only small ones can come out, but imagine if the big ones get to do the same. We should tell the engineer in charge about this as soon as the next brightness comes."

"Hey, what am I supposed to do if it comes back?" asked Mary with a worried voice.

"Just kill it and go on with your work, okay?" answered the guard as he went out, closing the door behind him.

Mary followed him with her eyes and when she was alone made a grin to him and went on with the cleaning. Once she was finished she went out with her cleaning articles. She met the guards. "Okay, I'm over. See you at the next brightness."

"Just go. You are a fussy creature."

"Sorry. Goodbye."

It was all very dark on her way. Even the small light that the tubes on the ceiling used to provide were out. I can't see a thing. I wonder where Bruce is, thought Mary as she walked slowly using her hands to avoid any obstacles.

Suddenly she heard a voice. "Hello."

She almost cried but Bruce put his hand on her mouth just in time. "You frightened me. I could have had a heart attack."

"I'm sorry," answered Bruce taking his hand off her mouth and pointing out to a door nearby. "Let's go to that room now."

The two friends walked to the room. Bruce opened the door carefully in case someone was inside it. Once they went in Bruce said, "Here's Edison's grease, they left it right by the entrance to the duct so that the next shift can use it."

"What do you mean?" asked Mary.

"It's very simple. Do you remember when Edison told us that he had a kind of grease which kept the lijas away from the energy ducts? Well, I heard some guards talking about the BB Reactor..."

Mary interrupted him abruptly. "You just said the BB Down Reactor? Where have I heard that name before?"

"I don't know but let me go on. The guards that watch over that duct are going to disconnect the power in this darkness until the next one so that they can get in and rub the grease over the duct walls.

This means that the energy will not run through the duct for a while and considering, as the guard at the meals courtyard said, that these ducts go all through the fortress, this could be our way to escape. We'll go in there and look for a way out."

"Yes, I remember now. Well thought," said Mary.

"And how did you get to know all that?"

"Well, it seems that many guards like to gather outside the door of Josela's cage in their free time or whatever. Maybe their commander doesn't come down here often and the guards feel free to talk. Anyway, I heard a lot of conversations among them and I also could get hold of a grease pot." She kept silent for a moment and then continued but with a worried tone. "But how will we keep from running into the guards who are working inside the ducts?"

"Those are the three idiots who were at Josela's cage."

"Okay, but how are we going to avoid them?"

"We'll do it. If we hurry we won't run into them. And it will be only four of them because they won't be able to ask for reinforcements. I cut their communication wires and took their Isikuls, remember?"

"Yes, but they can kill us right there in a minute. And we don't really know the way out, do we?" insisted Mary. "Moreover, if we stay too long here the next brightness will come and they will activate the energy and that would be our end."

Bruce just made a grin and shrugged his shoulders.

Mary was looking around her when Bruce asked, "There's something written here."

She turned to him. "Where?"

"In that paper next to the duct access."

Mary said, "I can't understand it, it's written in their language but... Wait."

"Don't shout. Someone could hear us."

"I'm sorry. I just remembered that the Transler RX7 can also read texts."

"That's right. What are we waiting for?"

Mary took out the device from her ear and passed it over the paper like a scanner. "It says the days in which they will apply Edison's grease on the ducts."

"And when will that be?"

"It says... third and fourth darkness in this Soltem."

"Soltem is 'week' in their language," said Bruce.

"Yes, I know that. We just have to cross out this and put instead fourth and fifth darkness so that they will be doing it later and we won't come across them. They won't be able to ask anybody about it because they will be cut off from their companions."

"That's a very good idea, but there's a kind of diagram there too."

Mary passed her Transler over it to see what it was about. "It's the route of this energy duct."

"Excellent. It will guide us to the exit."

"Exactly," exclaimed Mary, using her device on order to scan the map.

"It shows here that this duct leads to the BB Down Reactor." After a small pause she continued with enthusiasm, "I remember now. The BB Down Reactor is outside the fortress. I heard that from that crook I came across the day I ran away from the Multipower Center after I got myself into... Never mind, now we have to change the numbers of the darkness, but how are we going to do that?" Mary looked around her, searching for something that could help them. "Don't you have something in your pockets we could write with?"

"No, I only have the whistle. Denise gave it to me but we can't write with it."

Suddenly, Bruce exclaimed, "This will do it. It's a small piece of coal."

Mary took a look at it and smiled as she saw something else which would be of great help too. "Hand me that stone, we can use it to get a fine point on this coal and use it as a pencil."

Bruce handed her the stone and stood watching Mary as she managed to sharpen the piece of coal, then, with great care, using her Transler she started to change the words written on the sign. "Okay, it's ready. I hope it works."

"We must have faith, Mary. If it doesn't we will be either disintegrated or become the lunch of those horrible giant galactic rats. Let's go now."

They suddenly heard steps coming towards the room.

Chapter 19

DEEP INTO DANGER

"We must go!" cried Bruce.

"I'll follow you." They opened the duct's entrance and went into it. "We can't see much in here."

"But it's enough to see where we are going," replied Bruce, crawling slowly through the duct.

"Auch!" cried Mary.

"It's not too high and quite narrow in here. We have to move crawling."

"So I gather," said Mary, rubbing her head. She added, "It stinks."

"Just walk and stop thinking about it."

Leading the way through the duct, Mary asked, "How did you think about this duct?"

"I made a little searching around. Josela told me that people thought they could escape going through the lijas burrows but they all ended up being eaten. I went near one of those but then I saw these big ducts on the walls and thought that we might use them to escape. They seem big enough for us to go through up to the exit of this fortress."

"And why didn't anybody think about that before?"

"I suppose they didn't think it would be possible because of the energy which circulates through the ducts. They didn't know the energy had to be disconnected from time to time to put Edison's grease. Remember that when he took us to Esmeraland, when Billy came out of the *Louder Vargas* and dropped down a bottle, Edison told us that it was something new he was bringing to the fortress, something that hadn't been used for long."

"Yes, I remember that. And how can the lijas get into the ducts?"

"I don't know. I guess they make some holes on them."

The two of them kept crawling through the duct. The visibility was scarce, they could hardly see what was just in front of them as they went forward. "Look, the duct climbs up over there."

"Well, we'll have to climb up too."

"Are you wearing your tennis?" asked Bruce.

"Of course I am. What else would I be wearing to go off in a caravan?"

Bruce sighed deeply. "To think that all this started with a simple and pleasant trip in Billy's caravan."

"Forget about it. We'd better hurry up and try to climb this duct as soon as possible. I hope we won't get exhausted too soon. It's been a while since we ate as we used to."

"Do you want me to go first?"

Mary replied, "Yes please. I think the duct won't be so smooth now. The energy must have put it out of shape, at least a little."

"Yes, look at my hands, they're already full of calluses."

"You can complain after we get out. You sound just like Maggie." Bruce grinned and went on climbing up the duct. "It's a bit high and it sure is tiring," said Mary sounding short of breath.

"Come on. You can do it."

"But don't go too fast."

"I'm not going so fast, it's you who is going too slowly."

"I am doing my best."

Suddenly, Bruce exclaimed, "Ouch! Damn it."

"What's the matter?"

"I just felt something in my leg…"

Mary yelled, "Be careful, it's a lija! That's his muzzle showing out of that hole."

"His what? Ouch, it's bitten my pants and is holding it in its teeth."

"Try to get rid of it!" shouted Mary.

"I'm trying, but it sure has a strong bite," shouted Bruce, shaking his leg in an attempt to get away from the lija.

"Don't let it pull your leg through the hole."

"I won't. But it's not easy," cried Bruce, grappling with the lija, trying not to fall down.

"I'm going to help you," said Mary as she hurried up the duct to where Bruce was fighting with the creature.

Once she was near her friend, Mary started to look for something to use against the lija which continued trying to pull Bruce's leg into the hole. All of a sudden, the lija cried in pain and released Bruce's leg as Mary hit its muzzle with all her strength. "That sure was a strong lash."

"My belt was the only thing I had to hit it with. It was almost getting your leg into the hole and that would have been your death," said Mary with a trembling voice.

"Thank you. I was lucky to be wearing these jeans, the lija couldn't tear it up much."

"We must go on and be very careful," said Mary, putting her belt back on and taking good care not to fall down the duct. They kept on climbing up until Mary stopped and said, "I'm exhausted. If we don't take a small rest I'll will faint."

"But where can we stop to take a rest?"

"Keep moving forward, I can see a light a little further away."

Bruce said, "Be careful. Maybe it's a hole with another lija trying to get us."

"Let's see where that light comes from."

They went on until they were near a hole through which the light came into the duct. "It seems like some sort of cave. We can stay there and rest a little."

"Let's do that, Mary, you look very tired."

They sat down at the entrance of the cave to rest, at least for a moment.

Bruce saw that Mary was manipulating an Isikul. "What's going on?"

"That's what I'm trying to find out," replied Mary still managing the device. "I heard they have given the order to get us."

"But how do they know that we escaped?"

"I do not know. Maybe one of our pavilion companions has betrayed us," Bruce exclaimed. "Then let's hurry."

"Wait. Let me see if I can hear more, it could help us to know what's going on over there."

"We must go on," insisted Bruce. Mary made a grin but stood up and climbed up along with her friend. The small rest had given them a little more energy and they went up the duct eagerly. "I can already see the end a little further," commented Bruce.

"Let me see." Bruce moved to one side so that Mary could take a look to the duct before her. "Oh, that's so good. I was really exhausted."

"Yes, I can see it on your face." Mary shrugged her shoulders and kept crawling up. "We are at the top at last," exclaimed Bruce.

"Let me get up there too."

Bruce got to the top and sat waiting for Mary. "Wow! We still have to go on a bit more."

"Yes, I can't see the exit now."

"We just have to crawl on but it seems to be going down. It will be easier than climbing up as we have done until now."

"Wait, Bruce," cried Mary, "I can't go as fast as you do."

Suddenly, a loud noise frightened them. "What was that?"

"I don't know, Bruce, but something like a door just closed behind me. Maybe I pushed something when I was crawling." Bruce didn't answer and they kept on through the duct. Suddenly, something horrible came out from a hole.

"It's a lija!"

Bruce turned around to see what was happening but Mary stood still, lying on her elbows. The lija grunted, showing its enormous teeth. Bruce said in low voice, "Very slowly take out Edison's grease from your pocket." Mary obeyed as the beast walked slowly towards her. Bruce kept quiet because if the lija heard him it would come for him and he didn't have any grease with him.

Mary opened the bottle and a strong smell started to expand in the duct. "It seems to be working. The lija is going back a little. I'll put some grease on my arms and legs." The lija grunted fiercely but started to walk away. As soon as the creature disappeared Mary spoke. "I'd better go in front. That way they will smell the grease and won't get near us."

"Yes, you will leave that smell behind you as you crawl." Mary started to crawl immediately and Bruce followed her.

"I hope we'll find the exit soon, it won't take too long for them to realize that the ducts were our only way out from here," said Bruce.

"I know that, and the only thing they have to do is to put on the energy and it would be our death."

Mary turned back to him with a grin. "Thanks for reminding me of that."

"You're welcome but... Just a moment, are you feeling a cold wind in our back?"

Mary answered without turning around, "No, I don't feel anything."

"Then why do I feel it close behind me?" replied Bruce, looking back. "Oh oh."

"What's the matter?" asked Mary, keeping her eyes on the duct before her. "Hey, why don't you answer me?" she insisted, turning around to look at her friend.

When she saw what was happening she hurried back to him. "I guess I wasn't leaving any grease behind me anymore."

Bruce, keeping completely still, just nodded in agreement. A huge lija was standing right behind Bruce, ready to devour him. In spite of her desperation, Mary could see that Bruce was a few millimeters from one of the duct's bonds. This gave her an idea. "We don't have much time, at least not enough to take out the grease from my pocket. The lija will jump as soon as we make a movement." Bruce didn't say anything, he just looked at her and at the lija who was growling, trying to tear up his pants. "Listen carefully. We'll count to three, I'll pull you in my direction and you will throw yourself backwards pushing that small lever at your left. Can you see it?" Bruce looked around him and saw what she was pointing out to him. Mary crawled slowly towards him and spoke in a very low voice, "On the count of three: One, two, three…"

Bruce moved backwards at the same time that Mary pulled him as hard as she could, managing to push the lever at the same time. The lija jumped to get him but was smashed by the heavy door which had fallen just over it. "Oh, it looks terrible," said Mary.

"Don't look at it. We were close. How did you realize that the small lever activated that door?"

"Remember a little way back? I unintentionally pushed one of those and the door almost closed over me."

"Thanks. We have to go on now."

"I hope we can get out of here quickly. We don't have much grease anymore." They went on crawling as fast as they could through the duct until one of them found something.

"What's the matter? Why did you stop?"

Bruce replied, "Because of that. Look." There were letters written on the duct wall. Something very strange about it caught Mary's attention. Bruce read it with difficulty. "It says that the Earth is in a big danger because of the Seven Devils of Shigahell."

"Exactly."

"And so what? We've heard that before."

"You didn't need the Transler to read it."

"Yes, but the writing is not very clear and…" replied Bruce. Suddenly, he realized what his friend was sayin. "Wait, it's written in our language." Mary nodded her head with fear and sadness on her face. Bruce mumbled, "It means that an Aceiter has been here before us."

"Yes, and the writing is not so clear which might mean that it was written with difficulty."

"What are you talking about?"

"This is what I'm talking about. These stains look like blood. They cover what's written in the lower part…"

Bruce looked at what Mary was pointing to.

"It's true. Maybe a lija ate the poor Aceiter."

"I wonder if this will have anything to do with Sise Lautana."

"What did you say?"

Mary took her face with both hands, crying, "What is going on in this planet?"

"I do not know. We'd better go now if we do not want to end like that person."

They continued crawling for a few minutes more until, "We can't go on. Look at all this dust, it's blocking the way."

"What's that supposed to be?"

"I think this dust comes from the lijas which were disintegrated when the energy went on. Probably the guards didn't bother to sweep it away and left it all here."

"Look, there's a door over there. We might be near the exit."

As they hurried to the door, Bruce advised, "Use your Transler to see where this door opens to."

Mary passed the Transler over the label on the door. "What does it say?"

"We could say that we are, at last, out of the fortress. This is where they get in to clean the ducts."

"Excellent! And now, what?" exclaimed Bruce, seating down behind Mary.

"I guess we use the speaker or Isikul to ask the guard outside to open the door. We can't open it from this side."

"We'll have to try. First we'll write down the code," said Mary as she picked up a small stone and used it to write the numbers on the floor. "Here I go. Let's keep our fingers crossed. Hey, Vildan, open the exit door WR4."

Bruce and Mary waited for a few seconds, keeping their breath nervously.

"Door WR4? Who are you?"

Mary didn't know what to say. Bruce took the Isikul off her hands and spoke with a grave voice. "Hey, you idiot, we've been cleaning this duct for a long time now, just open this door at once."

Mary was frightened and spoke very low. "Do you think they will be so foolish as to believe that…?" At that moment the door opened wide in front of them.

"What were you saying?""

"Correction, they are very foolish." They went out, looking around them carefully.

"We have to see what's around us," said Bruce. "It's cold out here. And the next brightness is almost here. We came out just in time."

"There's something like a sand hill over there."

"Maybe we can get near it and look what's on the other side."

"Wait, someone might see us." Mary and Bruce climbed over the dune and came down on the other side. They kept down on the sand.

"There are armed guards over there and they have their trained panthers with them. I can't see well but the animals seem to be wearing some kind of collars around their necks with iron leashes. The guards are holding the leashes but they also hold something else in their hands."

"I think those are the whistles they use to control the panthers. Billy told me about it and I happen to have one of those with me."

"Mary Ann Wright, I sure bless now your marvelous habit of keeping everything you can find. I hope this whistle will be of help to us."

Mary didn't answer, she was paying attention to something she had just seen. "Look at that surveillance cabin. There are a couple of Alphavisors on the right, just like the one you used to help Billy, remember?"

"That's true, but the problem will be to get near them."

Mary thought for a few seconds. "This cabin doesn't have any windows on the back, so if we go near, carefully, one by one, they won't see us. We won't have much time to take those Alphavisors, or galactic motorcycles as they look to me, though."

"It's the only thing we can try. Who goes first?"

Mary cried, "You go first."

"Here I go." Bruce walked slowly on the sand until he got to the back of the cabin. He made a sign to Mary. She followed him carefully.

"Well, now what do we do?"

"We have to wait for a chance to take those Alphavisors."

The guards walked from one place to another holding the huge panthers. Mary and Bruce kept quiet and still, waiting. Suddenly, Bruce spoke in a low but nervous voice. "It's now or never. They have stopped to chat at the other side."

Mary made a sign with her fingers, "One, two... Now! Let's go!"

They both ran towards the galactic motorcycles but, when they tried to turn them on, something didn't work.

"What's the matter with this piece of junk?"

"I don't know. They seem to have a safety device."

The guards had heard the noises but couldn't see what was going on. They went towards the Alphavisors led by the panthers.

"We'd better run." Mary and Bruce started to run followed by the guards and the animals. There were several dunes around them but they were not high enough to hide them from their persecutors.

"Release the panthers, they will get the intruders," shouted a guard and the rest of them obeyed. The animals could run much faster now.

Mary and Bruce were exhausted, they felt they couldn't run any longer and the panthers were coming after them. "Go away!" shouted Bruce.

"I won't go without you."

An enormous panther had seen them on the dunes and started to approach slowly, showing its big teeth. Mary and Bruce walked back, terrified. "Go, please, I'll see what I can do."

Mary replied, "No way. We're together in this." Suddenly, another panther jumped, pushing both to the ground. Another two animals came near them. All the beasts growled at their next victims. The guards arrived. The Aceiters, paralyzed by fear, looked how the beasts were getting closer to them, showing their terrible fangs. Fighting against her terror, Mary reacted, "The whistle."

"What whi… Oh, I see. I hope it works." Bruce blew with all his strength but no sound seemed to come out of the whistle. However, something incredible happened. "What's going on here?" asked Bruce.

"I don't know. I think I have gone crazy: The panthers are dancing."

"What kind of dance is that?" asked Bruce again.

"I certainly don't intend to ask them."

"Hey, are you crazy? You're supposed to attack not have a good time," exclaimed one of the guards as one panther danced around him and another beast did the same around the other guard, holding a rose in its jaw.

"This looks like a dance contest. Should we applaud?" commented Bruce, still surprised at the view of those terrible beasts dancing happily as if they were waltzing in a wedding.

"Just run. Let's get out of here."

In spite of what was going on, other guards were still going after them.

"Run fast!"

"That's what I'm doing."

"Let's go up that dune," shouted Bruce.

They climbed over the sand dune but the sound of a shot from an Alphavisor nearby forced them to lie on the ground. After a few seconds they crawled to the top. "What's that noise?" asked Mary.

Bruce listened for a minute and cried, "Come on! Hurry!"

"Where are you going?"

Bruce replied, "A vehicle is approaching, it will be arriving to this curve soon."

The guards were getting closer every minute. A shot from other Alphavisor almost got them again. "That was close," cried Bruce. "The only thing we can do is jump over the vehicle as soon as it diminishes the speed as it takes the curve."

Mary ran behind him until they got to the verge of the dune over the road.

"Ready to jump?"

"To jump where?"

Bruce cried, "Here it comes, jump now." They both jumped to the roof of the vehicle passing just under them the minute that an Alphavisor had them on its view.

It was a strong blow but not as hard as they had expected. They got hold of some objects tied to the roof of the vehicle to keep from falling. When they were a little further, and felt a bit safer, they saw that the objects on the roof were, in fact, weapons. Mary commented, "This looks familiar somehow, don't you think?"

"Maybe because it's a violet van?"

"A violet van? It can't be true."

"What is it?"

"Yes, Mary, what is it?"

"Who said that?"

"I did," replied a voice coming from beneath. "Creatures of the universe, will I ever get rid of you? Though I reckon my trip will be much more fun now."

"Don't tell me it's…" whispered Bruce.

Mary just nodded her head. Then Mary and Bruce spoke at once. "Hello, Edison."

Mary added in a low voice, "I don't know if I should laugh or cry."

Chapter 20

A CRAZY ESCAPE PLAN

"What do we do now?" asked Denise.

"Let's go. The Stinker will be here soon and we have to get to the back entrance where they leave all the dumpsters," replied Esther.

"And where's that door supposed to be?"

"It's quite near. Let's go before the next brightness comes."

They walked through a dark corridor, passing by a few doors on their way.

Denise walked with certain difficulty not only because of the rocky ground but also due to the thick rubber attire she was wearing. They kept looking around, taking good care not to be seen. At last they arrived to a big metallic door. Esther opened it carefully in case someone was outside, but they were lucky. There weren't many guards at the backyard at that time. They didn't see anyone near them.

"Look behind you to see if someone is coming," whispered Esther. They went out and Esther closed the door slowly. The bins were side by side in a row in front of the door. This would help them not being seen. Esther pushed Denise down.

"What is it?"

"There are four guards making their rounds at least. That's what I can see from here."

"What do we do now?" asked Denise, crouched down and trying to keep her balance.

"We'll wait until the Stinker comes up. As far as I remember it will be here in no time now. We have to pay attention to it because we won't have much time. As soon as it enters the backyard we have to seize the opportunity to put you inside one of the bins."

In front of them they saw a backyard not so different from the ones they were familiar with, not too big, surrounded by huge stone walls. All of them dirty, messy and with lots of old items piled everywhere. Some vehicles which looked like hoists moved around floating a little above the ground, taking merchandise from one place to another.

"I hope that Stinker comes in soon," said Denise. "We can't stay here too long."

"I know. We have to be very careful. Being in this high level doesn't help us much. It's good because they don't have to lift the bins up to the truck, but it also makes us more visible from below."

"And what is going to happen to you? How will you manage to escape?"

"I must find a way. It won't be long before they find out who I really am."

"Listen, can you hear that noise?" asked Denise.

"That must be the Stinker. Be ready to go into a bin. Try not to make too much noise."

The Stinker came into the backyard, floating above the ground as all the others. It stopped for a moment and then went in reverse towards the bins. It stopped again very near them. A creature came out of it and started to take the bins. "They sure make a lot of noise," commented Denise.

"Now jump in."

Denise managed to get into one without being seen. The creature took off the lid from the first bin and looked inside. He put the lid back and pushed it into the Stinker. When he was about to open a second bin, a guard, who was watching from below, shouted, "Hey, Woldun, that way you won't be able to find out if there are any runaways in those bins. Do your work right." Turning to another guard he continued, "Hey, Tental, bring me the big fork. We have to teach these creatures how to do their work."

His companion approached with a strange tool that looked like a big, menacing fork. "Let's see now," he said, walking towards the bins.

Staring at him, Woldun took off his mask and cap and shouted, "What do you think you're doing? I don't have time for this. I can't search each bin, Oltar. Don't forget that we are working in double shift, the other Stinker is still out of work because of the accident."

Oltar came near the creature with a fierce expression on his face. "Work is work. Do you want me to tell Ultro the Yagoon that we are not doing our job as we should? Anyway, you can choose at random, you don't have to look into all of them. Let's pick the one you just lifted."

The guard walked to the back of the Stinker with the big fork in his hands.

"Hurry, open the lid." Woldun obeyed.

"This is the way to do it," cried the guard as he shoved the fork into the bin trying to get to the bottom of it. "You see now? There's sure nobody here."

"But you have to do the same with most of the bins. You never know whether there's someone inside."

"Okay, I'll bring you the second one."

"No, you'd better bring the third one. Put this one in."

Woldun brought the second bin at the row and put it directly into the truck.

Smiling sarcastically to Oltar, he went for the third one. "Let's see if we can find anything in here," he said, as he pricked the interior fiercely.

Suddenly, they heard a cry. "Ouch! Bastards!" Both Woldun and Oltar withdrew their Isbans. Oltar called the other guards while Woldun started to search into the bin, looking for the owner of the cries. Four more guards came by with their Isbans and stood at the door behind the Stinker. A few minutes later, taking someone out of a bin, Woldun shouted with a jeering, "Well, well, well, look who we have here."

Oltar cried, "I know this prisoner, he's Telwar, from the high danger pavilion. He must have taken advantage of the lack of guards in order to get away."

"Okay, come out, quickly," said Woldun, pulling the poor creature out of the bin.

"Please don't. It hurts." Woldun and Oltar threw him on the floor behind the Stinker. Unable to stand up, with a bleeding leg, Telwar begged them, "What will you do you with me? Please, have mercy."

"Of course we will, poor bastard," answered Oltar. He turned to one of the other guards. "Take him to the lijas. With all this blood they will eat him in no time. Take some prisoners with you so that they will see what happens to those to try to escape."

"No, please, don't do that." The two guards carried him away.

"It's late. Am I supposed to stay here until the next brightness?"

"I'll just check out this bin and you will be free to go."

"But that's the last one. There's no place for more." Woldun brought the fourth bin. Oltar pricked the interior fiercely with the fork.

"Nobody's here. You've made me lose a lot of time already. Bye."

"You can go now but I can see that you do have room for more bins," replied Oltar, getting out of the Stinker.

Woldun shouted at him, "I do, but I have to save some place for the bins of the other places I'm going to now. Don't forget they haven't repaired the other Stinker yet."

Oltar made a gesture with his hand and went into the building, and Woldun started to accommodate the bins, one close to the other on the truck. "You're so mean with the members from the Liberation Army."

Without turning around, Woltan answered, "And what do you care about it?"

On second thought he turned over to see who was talking but felt a hard blow on the head.

When she heard the noise Denise put her head out of the bin. Esther was about to shoot the guard with her disintegrator but when she saw the terror in Denise's face she didn't do it. She put the weapon away and pushed Oltar's body away from the Stinker so it wouldn't be seen. "Thank you."

"Shh, don't speak, dear."

"What are you doing with those clothes and that breathing device?" insisted Denise when she saw the strange clothes on her friend.

"I've just put them on. They use these to work on the Stinkers."

At that moment they heard a voice calling, "Hey, Woldun, what's taking you so long? Just tie up those bins and let's go. It's late."

"That must be the driver," whispered Esther, and then, speaking with a harsh tone, she answered, "Let's go. Hey, pana, those ropes are not too tight so I'd better stay back here to keep the bins from rolling over."

"Okay, you stay there if that's what you want."

The Stinker started to move and after a few minutes it was out of the fortress. Denise, with her head out of the bin once again, asked, "What does 'pana' mean?"

"It's a sort of a local word for friend."

"I thought they were going to find me. I felt that big fork on my arm but it didn't hurt."

"Billy's idea of wearing these clothes was really bright. It's a pity that Telwar didn't have our luck."

"Did you know him?"

"Not much. He was an active member of the Liberation Army." Esther sounded sad and she changed the subject. "We have to find out how long will we take to get to the Imhamway Station."

Denise kept silent just looking around her. She saw something and pointed it to Esther. "Look over there, there's a sign. Maybe it will tell us where we are."

Esther looked at the sign by the road and told Denise, "We will not have to wait too long. One or two stops more and we will be there."

"That's good news," replied Denise. "Do you think you can communicate with Billy through your Transler?"

"I'll try. The Transler doesn't have much scope as a communications device." Esther withdrew the device from her ear and started to push some small buttons on it. "Billy, do you copy me? I'm Esther, on frequency 36X."

"Esther, Esther, I can't hear you very well."

"Well, I can't scream either," said Esther in a low voice. "We are on our way to the Imhamway Station."

"Imhamway, you said?"

"Yes, we're going there."

"Good for you, Esther. Things seem to be a bit more complicated for us. Brightness is almost here. I have to go now," replied Billy.

"So Esther and Denise have escaped and are on their way to the meeting point."

"That's wonderful. It's our turn now," replied Nailbytes.

"We've lost too much time already. Let's go before the guards are back," said Billy.

"Yes. We have to go to the next step of our plan," said Nailbytes.

"And what step is that?" asked Maggie.

The boys exchanged glances with a smile and Billy hurried to the other room. "Wait a minute."

"Where's he going to?" asked Maggie, intrigued at her friend's silence.

"He'll be back in no time. I hope all this works."

"How did it go with Denise and Esther? I heard they escaped."

"I think they are trying to escape as we speak. I just hope they will be able to get to…"

"Here I am."

"What's that mud in your hands for?" asked Maggie. "Where did you get it from?"

"We saw it in the other room. It seems to be used in healing bruises or something like that."

"And why would we need that for?" insisted Maggie.

"It's part of the plan. You'll see," replied Nailbytes.

"What on earth does that mud have to do with our escape from this terrible place?"

"It's simple. Just rub it on your face," said Billy.

"Are you crazy? My beautiful face covered by mud."

Nailbytes spoke with a harsh voice. "Look, we are in serious problems. This is not the time to…"

Billy interrupted him, kicking him with his elbow, "He is right, but you know this mud is what they use around here to protect their complexion from the heat, the Iriaje, as they call it."

"This is such a silly trick, I won't fall for it. Do you think I'm a fool?" Nailbytes nodded his head in agreement with a broad smile. "I won't put anything on my face."

"But…"

Billy cried, "Keep quiet, both of you. Someone is coming."

"Hurry, to the grille." The three friends ran to hide.

"Wait here, guards," Elisa said, entering the room. "I hope Lonar Mayer will be able to suffocate this rebellion once and for all."

"Yes, Your Majesty. We're sure that it will be so. Our best warriors are already on their way."

"Of course they are, but remember that this doesn't mean that the executions will stop. And also, remember that you must go on giving me all the valuable belongings of the executed."

"Of course, Your Majesty."

"By the way, what happened to that foolish creature who dared to say those foolish things to me, remember?"

"He's inside Josela's belly now, just as you ordered."

"They told me that he had some companions. Did he?"

"Yes, Your Majesty, so I heard."

Elisa seemed to be thinking about something with her hand on her chin. "I was thinking about those bastards. They should be used for the experiments at the lab, but only the boys. I'd like something different for the girls."

"What would that be, Your Majesty?"

"I couldn't help noticing their beautiful fair skin. It would make a gorgeous coat."

"I'm sure it would be very becoming, Your Majesty."

"Then do it. I want their skin. I'll talk to Lonar Mayer as soon as she's back. I suppose the rebellion must be over by now."

"We hope so too, Your Majesty."

"I have to go now."

"Do you want us to prepare your transporter, Your Majesty?"

"Yes, and do it quickly. The sooner the better," she said as she left the room.

"Follow me, guards."

Two of the guards went after her while the others stayed at the room. One of them used his Isikul. "Security, do you copy me?"

"Yes, what's up?"

"Prepare Elisa's transporter, she's on her way."

From the other end of the Isikul came a strange question. "Do you know anything about the Spartack Center guards? I didn't get their last report."

The guard made a grin and answered, leaving the room, "That's strange. I'll go down there and take a look. I hope they haven't been fooling around. If they did they will be punished." He went to the door and shouted, "Follow me!" The guards followed him out of the room.

The Aceiters came out of the grille. "We're running against time now. When that Esmiro gets to the Spartack he'll see that something is wrong," commented Nailbytes.

"I know," replied Billy.

Turning to Maggie he said, "Will you put that mud on your face or do you prefer to end up as a nice coat for that terrible creature?"

Maggie remained silent as she started to rub the mud on her face. "Now tell me what this is for."

"Well done. You also have to put on the black tong we took, remember?" said Billy.

"Yes, I left it in the other room. I'll bring it right now." She hurried to the room and came back putting on the clothes. "And now let's go before they find us."

"Do you think it will work?" asked Nailbytes.

"I don't know. We have to cross our fingers, that's all we can do."

The three friends left the room with Maggie still complaining about the mud. "You haven't told me yet what this is for."

"Wait a little. We will tell you," replied Nailbytes.

"Just a moment, that's Esmiro. He's going into that door," interrupted Billy. "That must be the Spartack Center."

"We'd better hurry," cried Nailbytes. "We should go, one by one, to the door where Elisa's transporter is waiting for her."

"That could be a good idea. We have to be very careful. We'll go to that room over there, the one with the withdrawn door," said Billy.

"Yes, I can see it from here. We have to walk carefully, it would be easy to stumble on this stone floor."

"We're not blind, Nailbytes. I'll be the first one," said Maggie.

Billy and Nailbytes exchanged glances, smiling at their friend's words. "You go first but, please, listen to Nailbytes and be careful." She started to walk towards the door, bending her body trying not to be seen. She had no problems and stood at the door, waiting for the boys.

"She did it. It's our turn... Wait, that door is opening." They hurried to hide in the little darkness that still existed. Billy tried to stick his head out a little to see what was going on.

"Security, answer, you idiots."

"Who is it? Can you see anything?" whispered Nailbytes.

"It's Esmiro, talking on his Isikul. I think he already knows everything."

"Who has gone out over the last hour?" asked Esmiro.

The answer came at once. "Just Elisa."

"Okay, but we have to check any departing transporter. We are looking for fugitives. Put on full alert."

"We're dead!" cried Nailbytes.

"I hope you are not right. If not..."

"Shut up! There he comes," said Nailbytes. "What are we going to do?"

"We will get hold of him when he comes into the room. Come here."

"The same way we did with that creature at the Spartack Center?"

Esmiro walked towards the infirmary with disgust. He entered the room but he fell down. "What's going on here?" he cried. Before he could stand on his feet again, Billy and Nailbytes were able to tie him down with the magnetic cuffs and took him into the room, putting a cloth in his big mouth. Unable to move or talk, Esmiro could only put an angry face to his captors.

"I hope this will keep him quiet until we can escape from here," said Billy.

"So do I. You can explain it to him later. Let's get out of here now." They ran out of the infirmary.

"Wait!" cried Billy, holding Nailbytes' arm.

"What is it?"

"Wait until those guards go away." They went into the infirmary as a group of armed guards walked by. "Now let's go before more intergalactic things come over, or someone comes out of the infirmary." They walked carefully towards the room where Maggie was waiting anxiously for them.

"What kept you so long?"

"Didn't you see what happened?" asked Nailbytes.

"No, I just bent down and heard someone cursing about something…"

"It's alright, Nailbytes, let's tell her what the plan is now."

Billy and Nailbytes hurried to explain their plan to Maggie. When they were finished, Billy asked, "Did you understand it?"

"It's a crazy idea, do you really think it will work?"

"I don't know but we have to go ahead," replied Billy.

Naibytes stuck his head out of the door to the corridor. Inside the room they were about to enter another conversation was taking place. "Shut up, Tempoy! If that's so it will be his end. I really don't know what's going on but the fact that he didn't want to talk about it means that something disastrous happened there and he's afraid of what Lonar Mayer will do to him."

"Brightness in, brightness out, we will soon find out what happened, Alther. At least Elisa has gone away already. She's the most annoying creature in this galax," commented Tempoy.

"Keep your voice low. Do you want someone to hear you?"

"She's gone now and there's no one from her entourage around here."

"You never know, Quinto, there can always be a snitch somewhere," replied Tempoy.

"Why don't you go and get something to eat? Brightness is almost here."

"Good idea, Alther. Go, Tempoy." Tempoy left the room in silence.

As soon as he saw that his companion had left the room, Quinto spoke in a low voice, "Do you think he might be one of Ultro the Yagoon's eyes and ears, as they call his spies?"

"I don't know but I don't trust him much. He might tell that idiot of Elisa everything we're talking about. Anyway, we'd better focus on…"

Maggie looked at Billy and Nailbytes, took a deep breath and entered the room speaking with a firm voice, "I hope that all those references to my dear Aunt Elisa are just my imagination, aren't they? For your own good, it better be that way."

"Who are you?" asked Quinto.

"I'm Auntie Elisa's and dear Uncle Elion's pet niece."

"A niece? I haven't heard anything about a niece coming to visit."

"Well, that's too much. So my dear and perfect aunt has to keep you informed about the whereabouts of her family? Please, it sounds offensive to me. But I'll tell them the terrible things you're talking about them."

"Please, sweetie, calm down," begged Quinto with a mellifluous smile.

"Of course, dear, we were joking," added Alther.

"I'll think about it, but now don´t tell me that you still haven't repaired my beautiful aunt's *Caribbean Star*. She's waiting for it to be ready for her banquet today and, of course, I need it to get out of here, I mean, to go to her party."

"Your Excellence, the problem is that the spare parts we asked for aren't here yet and we couldn´t do anything about it. That's why your dear aunt had to leave on another ship."

"Well, I can only tell you that I hope you'll enjoy your disintegration once my Uncle Eliom hears about all this."

"No, please, don't do that. We'll repair it at once or, even better, we'll find a way for you to meet with your precious Aunt Elisa."

"You'd better do so."

Nailbytes whispered in Billy's ear, "I must reckon that Maggie is doing a great job."

Billy smiled.

"If you're in such a hurry, we could take you on one of the Huntscapes so that you will be at Her Excellence's banquet on time."

"I think that will be fine. What are you waiting for? Prepare everything right now."

"Don't you worry," said Quinto hurrying to the window.

"Hey, you, prepare that Huntscape V for Her Excellence and tell Honlay that he's going to take some passengers immediately." He turned and asked gently, "Where exactly does he have to take you?"

"At the banquet..." Maggie started to answer when she felt a slight push on her back. "Wait a minute, I'm thinking I'd better go to Imhamway Space Station first so I can pick up some orders for my auntie."

"But, Your Excellence, if the banquet is in Esmeraland it would be better for you to go to…"

"Wait!" cried Alther. "I don't know if you really are Elisa´s relative."

The Aceiters kept silent. Billy looked at Nailbytes with a frightened face. Would this be the end of their strategy?

Chapter 21

PERSECUTION

Incredibly, Maggie reacted speaking loudly with a fierce tone of voice. "Don't you dare to speak to me like that. This could cost you your death, you should know that. I decide where I'm going. Is that clear?"

"I'm sorry, Your Majesty," replied Alther, bowing to Maggie.

The guard put his head out of the window and asked once more, "Is everything ready?"

They could see something like a huge parking lot full of all kind of spaceships, some of them lacking many parts and others fully operative. Groups of armed guards and other creatures walked around carrying tools and boxes. From the outside a voice answered, "It's all set."

"Please come with me, Your Majesty," said Quinto.

"At last. Let's go. These are my personal servants as every important person, I mean creature like me, should have."

"Of course, Your Majesty," answered Quinto.

As they went out to the parking lot Billy and Nailbytes tried to keep their faces low so that the guards wouldn't have a good look at them.

The Huntscape has the shape of a huge, black beetle. Quinto came near the vehicle whose height surpassed his head. When he pushed a button on the outside the side door opened upwards just like a racing car. Maggie went in first followed by Billy and Nailbytes. The vehicle was already floating over the ground and a creature was waiting inside. They went in and the door was closed. Alther spoke from the outside with a pleading voice, "I hope you will tell your

Aunt Elisa and of course your kind Uncle Eliom the way we have served Your Majesty, won't you?"

"I will but don't get too excited about it." Quinto kept silent but made a slight grin. "Let's go now. Hurry!" commanded Maggie.

"To the Imhamway Space Station, isn't it?" asked the driver.

"Yes, how many times do I have to repeat it?"

"I'm sorry, Your Majesty, I just wanted to be sure."

Billy said in a very low voice, "I knew the idea of being Elisa's niece could work…"

But suddenly, looking out of the window, Nailbytes replied in a low but firm voice, "Bend down, now!"

"What's the matter?" asked Maggie.

"Just keep your head down. He´s one of the guards from the laboratory."

They could see that right at the metallic door there were some armed guards which seemed to be looking for someone next to Talmey. When the driver saw that they were all crouched, he asked in a worried voice, "What are you doing? Are you hiding from someone?"

Maggie hurried to answer with a firm voice, "Oh, don´t talk so much nonsense. They are just cleaning up my feet and my shoes. I have to be fit for the banquet. That's what servants are for."

"They are doing what?"

Nudging Nailbytes without raising his head, Billy said, "We are serving our lady. We are cleaning her feet."

"It's incredible," muttered the driver. "Elisa and her family are quite special."

"Did you say anything?"

"No, Your Majesty, of course not. Have a good trip."

"We're going through the gates," whispered Nailbytes when they had passed by the door and could see the high stone walls from the outside.

"Free at last," replied Billy.

"What are you talking about?" asked the driver who had heard their voices.

"Don't pay any attention to these fools," replied Maggie at once. "It's a real problem to have silly servants. That's what I always complain to my Aunt Elisa but she won't change them. Can't this thing go faster?"

"I'm sorry, Your Majesty, I'll try to go faster."

"I hope we will get at Imhamway Station early enough."

"We all do," replied Billy in a very low voice.

"I'll like to know what's that thing over there, the one that shows those small green lights."

"It's a Life Radar. It detects any living creature around it. This is one of the most powerful ones in the whole galaxy. We can recapture fugitives in a very short time."

"This vehicle is very well equipped," commented Nailbytes in a very low voice looking around him.

"Well, considering we have a long drive ahead of us, I will tell you all about the wonderful trips I've made with my dear uncle and auntie. I remember once we went to a far away galaxy to do some shopping...

And I will tell my dear Uncle Eliom to give you a promotion. You really deserve it."

"Of course I do after having to listen to all this nonsense, I mean after all my hard work."

Maggie replied with an annoyed voice, "What did you say?"

"Nothing at all, Your Excellence. Please continue to tell me about all those marvelous trips."

Somewhere in the middle of the Esmeraland Desert, Mary and Bruce were seated inside the van and Edison went on with his chat: "I hope taking you to the Imhamway Station won't cause me any problems. All the guards must be looking for you. Anyway, you might as well give me your papers so I can adopt you once and for all."

"You don't have to exaggerate," replied Bruce. "And it is better if you tell us how did you escape at the time of the accident? You were supposed to be with my friends."

Edison sounded a little guilty at first. "Well, it wasn't so easy. I didn't get hurt, at least not much, and I had to tell some lies too. But the guards know me so they didn't waste their time on me. Anyway,

I'll take you to the Imhamway Station and… What happened with your face?"

"Elisa hit me."

"That creature is so bad, but anyway you have to arrive to the space station on your own, if not I'll…"

Mary interrupted with irony, "Yes, we know, we will be on our own from there on, isn't it?"

"Okay, guys, but I insist…"

Mary and Bruce spoke in unison, "Nobody does anything for nothing."

"Yes, but besides that, I sure hope just taking you there won't get me into trouble."

Mary looked at her Sathaye with a smile because the light didn't blink in Edison's presence. She commented, "Well at least we know that Edison is not one of the seven devils."

Bruce added, "This guy doesn't even get to be an ogre from a children fairy tales book." Edison smiled at them, wondering what they were talking about

Suddenly, they heard a loud voice. "*Loader Vargas*, stop at once or we'll start shooting."

"I think your hopes are dashed now."

"Keep on with your sarcasm. It might be useful for you to survive at the Atilkawa Fortress again," shouted Edison.

"Don't pay any attention to Bruce. Just try to go faster."

"I will. Hold on, guys."

Mary shouted as she looked backwards, "You'd better hurry. We have a lot of vehicles full of guards behind us."

"Why doesn't this thing go a little faster?" asked Bruce

"Calm down. But you're right, we are losing speed."

"I'm aware of that. It seems that the crash with the Stinker ruined the *Loader* more than I thought."

"But Benji repaired it, didn't he?" said Bruce.

"But it was just to allow it to get to the space station, not to help some strange creatures to escape from prison." At that moment they felt a strong impact

"Are they attacking the *Loader Vargas*?" asked Edison.

"Well, you are taking some creatures they want," replied Mary.

"Shut up! I knew this would bring me a huge problem. Hold on hard."

Bruce looked out of the window and cried, "There's an Alphavisor flying over your van and pointing it with a barrel."

Edison turned back for a second and looking forward again. He replied, "Those are the unipersonal vehicles of the Amarphy. They can fly at a very low altitude."

"It's just like the one we tried to take a while ago but we couldn't. At Esmeraland I did drive one of those," commented Bruce. A strong jolt shook the van.

Mary raised her eyebrows. "Are these things able to destroy the *Loader*?"

"No, I don't think so. This vehicle has a shield but I'm afraid it might not be enough against powerful weapons. Anyway, I hope this junk will resist."

They heard a noise at the engine as if it was going to stop. "I'm sorry, *Loader*, of course you are not junk," said Edison with a sweet voice, blowing a kiss at the air. Mary and Bruce looked at each other in silence. There was another blow but this time it seemed to have damaged the engine.

"Oh, no, this blow damaged the steering system."

"What are we going to do?" asked Bruce.

"That's a good question," shouted Edison.

"Be careful. It looks like this junk is going out of the road," shouted Bruce.

"More respect to the *Loader Vargas,* it might get offended again," replied Edison with a grin. "But I can't control it, hold tight, I'll try to stop." The *Loader Vargas* went from one side to the other, completely out of control.

"Such a hard work to escape from that hell to end up dying this way," exclaimed Bruce.

"Keep quiet!" I'm trying to stop it."

Fortunately, Edison succeeded to control the van until it stopped.

"What a relief," cried Mary.

"I'm afraid this relief won't last long. Look over there," replied Bruce.

"I see they are getting out of their vehicles. But these are not like the Roman soldiers, they have a different uniform, something black and green."

"They must belong to a special force, Bruce."

"They are coming…"

"Shut up, you two. I have a plan. Just follow me in anything I say, okay?" said Edison in a low voice.

"All of you, come out of the van with your hands up," demanded one of the guards armed with an Isban, as the others, also well armed, surrounded the *Loader Vargas*.

Before getting out Edison winked at Mary and spoke in a shrill voice, "Please, don´t kill me, it wasn't my fault."

Bruce looked at Edison in surprise and was starting to say something when Mary's expression silenced him. Standing besides the van the guards demanded, pointing to them with their Isbans, "Stay where you are with your hands up and don't you dare to move a muscle."

"So Edison has decided to join the Liberator's Army. How interesting."

"That's not true, Officer Major, these creatures kidnapped me. What could I do?"

"That poor creature is a coward. He has been crying all the way, begging for mercy, asking us not to kill him," replied Mary, following what Edison had told them to do.

"She is right, officer, he's just a frightened chicken," added Bruce.

"Taking hostages is so boring. They keep asking for pity," continued Mary with a smile.

The officer went to his vehicle to use the radio. Edison spoke to his friends in a low voice, "You didn't need to exaggerate so much you know."

One of the guards who had stayed near them spoke to his partner. "This persecution has mobilized half the Amarphy, but at last we got them."

Another one added, "Ultro the Yagoon will be so glad that we could recapture them."

A third guard said, "We'll take them to the fortress for interrogation so they will tell us everything we want to know."

"Okay, start walking," demanded a guard, pushing Bruce and forcing the others to follow him.

They came near one of the vehicles. "Go into this Ulphavisor, quickly."

Edison was about to do so but he stopped to say, "Please, don't put me with the yellow hair one. He is a complete savage."

The Officer Major looked at Edison, turned to look at Bruce and shook his head.

"Okay, Crybaby, you and his partner will go in the back seat and the yellow hair goes in front."

"Thank you," cried Edison.

The officer spoke to two of the guards as the rest of them started to walk back to their vehicles. "You go in the back seat with those two and you, Vultro, drive on. I'll follow you and call the Atilkawa Fortress so they will be expecting us."

The guards hurried to obey their orders and pushed the prisoners into the Ulphavisor.

The Aceiters couldn´t help thinking that the vehicle looked like the British taxis, even in the seats arrangement, as they had noticed some time ago. "What do we do now?" asked Mary from the back seat.

Bruce shrugged his shoulders.

"That's enough talking, you two. Shut up!" cried the guard seating in front of them at the back seats, pointing his Isban to them.

Bruce sat besides the guard who drove the vehicle.

"Hey, Yurhay, do you know the fastest way to get to the fortress?"

Yurhay answered with an annoyed expression, "Just follow the coordinates on the panel, Vultro."

"Where can I see that?"

Yurhay turned to his companion in the back seat and yelled at him, "Here, can't you see? It says road coordinates. Just type them down."

Edison looked at Mary, winkling an eye to her and, immediately after that, he threw himself on the guard, crying, "What are you doing, Mary?"

Due to Edison's strong push, the Ulphavisor's door opened and Edison and one of the guards fell on the ground. The driver turned around to see what was happening and Bruce, taking advantage of the situation, pushed him hard with his feet, throwing him out of the car. Mary closed the back door and cried, "Get this thing going! Hurry up!"

Bruce sat at the driver's seat and started the engine at once. This caused a cloud of dust behind them.

The Ulphavisor rose slightly over the road and Bruce accelerated as much as he could. Everything happened so fast that the other guards reacted when the fugitive's vehicle was already underway. "Wow! We were lucky," shouted Mary from the back seat.

Bruce kept quiet for a while looking at the rearview mirror. After a few seconds he answered, "That depends on what you call being lucky. Look back, we have a complete army behind us."

Suddenly, a whole contingent of guards on their vehicles had come out from the thick dust cloud and the persecution through the wide desert was on again. Mary turned back to take a look and grinned. "As always, I talk too much."

"I hope this thing can travel fast."

"Look at that front panel, maybe you can see what its maximum speed is."

"Unfortunately, I'm not Nailbytes, I don't get these electronic things. The only thing I can do is to drive as fast as I can."

A strong impact shook the Ulphavisor. Mary bent down her head, protecting it with her hands. "We have to see if this has a defensive device," she shouted.

"I saw a sort of barrel on the roof, maybe that's it."

A sudden maneuver forced her to fall on the seat.

"Well done. You avoided that shot."

"But I can't keep doing this forever. Sooner or later they'll get us." The vehicle shook again.

"I believe you!" she cried.

"Well, if you do, you'd better do something instead of just talking about it."

"I'll go up there. I suppose I have to go up these steps over here."

In spite of the dust cloud around Bruce could see that there were many vehicles chasing them. At their side some Alphavisors were waiting to shoot them while other Ulphavisors were coming close. Mary got to the top and seated at the barrel. The position had a kind of protection shield all around it. Suddenly, Bruce saw an Alphavisor just in front of him, ready to shoot. Thanks to a quick maneuver he was able to avoid it. Immediately another shot was about to hit the vehicle when Bruce managed to dodge the blow. Mary had to hold tight to the barrel to avoid falling off her seat.

"Hurry up to operate that barrel."

"I don't know, I can't move it, it's pointing straight forward. Maybe that's the only way it shoots."

The Ulphavisor kept avoiding most of the other vehicles' shots but some of them succeeded in causing some damage.

"If you keep talking we'll end up blowing into pieces."

"I am trying. Let's see what these levers are for." The barrel, along with the seat, started to go round.

"I'm getting dizzy!" cried Mary.

"Instead of playing with it do something before they disintegrate us."

A stronger blow shook them. Bruce looked out of his window and saw some smoke coming out from the Ulphavisor. He kept quiet but felt terrified.

At that moment, a hard explosion took place. "I hit it!" shouted Mary.

"Excellent. Keep on with that good aim."

However, the Ulphavisor was still being attacked by their persecutors.

"You have one at your right, just over our heads," shouted Bruce.

"I saw it. Get a little closer." Bruce turned sharply to avoid a shot. "I didn't get it."

"I'm sorry, I couldn't turn when you asked me to, that one was too close to us. But never mind, here comes another."

"You mean that one just behind us? Okay, aiming. One, two and... three."

Another loud explosion shook the air.

"Again, well done."

Meanwhile, at Imhamway Station, Esther and Denise were hiding behind a pile of boxes by the door that led to the parking lot of the landships. From there they could see what was going on at the take-off and landing platforms.

"How can we get on the *Iron Warrior*? The ship is heavily guarded."

"I don't know but we have to think about something quickly," answered Esther. "Maybe if we could distract the guards, but it won't be easy."

Denise remained silent but her face showed her concern.

"Hey, wait a moment," cried Esther, "that's the *Sinister Phantom*. What is it doing here?"

"To whom does it belong to?"

"To the almighty Lonar Mayer."

"Well, it must be heavily guarded too."

"Yes, I guess you're right. Wait, someone is calling," said Esther as she went a little further, trying to listen through her Transler.

Denise looked at her and turned her eyes to the platforms. She began to hear some voices. "You have to be more patient with the slovos. If they were brighter they wouldn't be slovos, they would be Eliom's generals, or maybe teachers."

"You are always defending them, Marton. I'm tired of your permanent justifications for their behavior."

"Hurry up, partner, we are late."

"It's not that I always defend them, Gornoy, it's just that the way you hit them seems too much to me."

"Yes, Gornoy, it was too much," said his partner, approaching him.

"Okay, leave it at that. After all, every creature treats them in that way, they must be used to it by now. I assure you I'm not the first and won't be the last one to give a slovo a good blow now and then. He'll end up learning not to charge more than he should."

"He was just asking you for a little more. The truth is that your spare parts are quite heavy."

"Forget about it, Lifam. Let's go. And you, Marton, go ahead and bring the vehicle here so that we can go at once."

"Where do you want it, Gornoy?"

"At the back parking lot."

Marton manipulated his bracelet to bring the vehicle. The three creatures walked away unaware of Denise's presence. Esther came near her. Looking at her friend's face, Denise asked, "What's wrong? Why do you have that expression in your face?"

"I just... you don't know what happened just now. That criminal Lonar Mayer doesn't have mercy."

"But what did she do now?"

"She ordered a chemical attack on the revolt of Caution Rai and Pluternay. There were thousands of dead, all poisoned."

Denise said nothing.

Esther covered her face with both hands. After a few seconds Esther calmed down and said, "Why don't you go and take a look to see if your friends are here already. Lonar Mayer will be here soon and it won't be long before the guards realize that they have escaped."

"I'll try to take a look."

"Be careful," said Esther. "There are guards everywhere."

Chapter 22

TRYING TO GET AWAY

Mixing up with other creatures and strange vehicles which went from one place to another on the station, Denise got to the main door and saw that her friends were not there yet. Looking around her she saw there were guards coming on strange trucks. She thought they must have found out about the escape and went to the parking lot to see if her friends had arrived there. Standing on it for a few minutes, she thought, From what I could see through the holes back in Edison's boxes I'm sure we have been here before. I hope all the others will be able to get here. There are no guards, at least for now." However, a little further, she could see some intergalactic ships parked and someone bending down near one of the ships. Who can that be? Maybe it is one of them. "It isn't any of my friends, it's a slovo," she muttered to herself when she approached the creature. She addressed him in a low voice. "Are you all right?" The slovo lifted his head to look at her. "My goodness, what happened with your face?" exclaimed Denise.

The slovo answered between sobs, "A customer just hit me."

"How mean. Nobody should hit you like that, no matter what your fault was."

The slovo rubbed his cheek which was a dark purple now. "I think I have an Ace pill here," said Denise, putting her hand in her pocket. "Now I need a piece of cloth."

"A piece of cloth? What for?"

"So that I can crush the pill and you can put it on your face to calm down the pain and the swelling."

"Thank you but you'll need that pill when you get thirsty. Ace is very rare around here."

"Never mind, you certainly need it much more than I do. At least it will calm your pain," answered Denise as she tore off a piece from her tong and put the cloth on the slovo's face.

He stood up and kissed Denise's hand. "Thank you so, so much," he mumbled and rushed away.

Esther was standing near her. "Okay, Denise, a bunch of your friends are about to arrive here. They are Billy and the ones who ran away with him. We have to wait for them in case they might need any help."

"How do you know that?"

"Nailbytes just spoke to me through the Transler. He said they are quite near."

"Maggie, Nailbytes and Billy are in that group. They were going to pretend that Maggie was Elisa's relative."

"I hope Billy's idea came out right. I had my doubts about it," commented Esther with a grin. "The guards are not too brilliant but they are not complete fools either."

"Wait. A vehicle is coming this way."

"Let's hide and wait for the inevitable."

A Hangescape stopped at the door that communicated the parking lot with the station hall.

Maggie came down with a huge smile on her face. "Thank you, but before you go let me tell you about my trip to the wonderful…"

"No, please, just get off, quickly. I have to get back right now," replied Selkun with a desperate tone of voice.

As soon as she had her feet on the ground, the driver started the car. Billy had to pull Nailbytes off the car before it went away in a big hurry. "Well, you sure fed him up."

"And us too," added Nailbytes.

"You told me to act like Elisa and that's exactly what I did."

"Yes, we must agree that you did well, but that poor Selkun was on the verge of madness."

"Hi, guys. How are you?" The newcomers turned around.

"Hello, Denise. It's so good to see you here," said Billy.

"It sure is nice to see you all again."

"Well, girls, I have to tell you that all went fine."

"Are you telling us that the crazy idea of making Maggie go as Elisa's relative went well?" asked Denise.

"Yes it did," replied Esther. "But I'm impressed. No one would think about such a crazy plan."

"Maggie is unique," cried Denise.

"That's true. We used her special personality to get away and it worked," remarked Billy.

"Well done. Now we just have to wait for Mary and Bruce," said Esther.

Denise's face brightened up at these words. "So my sister got away from that terrible place after all?"

"She was able to get away, but now let's hope they will get here safe," said Nailbytes.

"We all do. We'd better break up so that the guards won't see us together. Billy, Denise and I will wait here. Maggie and Nailbytes will wait at the main door. We'll use the Translers to be in touch and maybe one of us will be able to communicate with Mary or Bruce as soon as we can," proposed Esther.

"Let's go," cried Billy.

"I hope they will be here soon. The news about the escape won't take too long to spread over the place, and we'll have half of Lonar Mayer's army after us," commented Esther with a worried frown.

"We have to act fast then," said Billy. "Nailbytes, see if you can communicate with Mary and Bruce to know where they are now."

"That's a good idea," he replie. "Mary, Bruce, do you copy me? I'm Nailbytes, frequency 36X."

"Is that you, Billy? I'm Bruce. We are in the middle of a persecution."

"I can't hear you very well, Bruce," replied Nailbytes with his hand on his ear manipulating the Transler.

"How long will it take for you to get here?"

"How long? I will be happy if we get there alive, no matter when."

"I don't get you very well. We will wait for you. Goodbye."

"It was Nailbytes. He wanted to know when we would be there," said Bruce.

"How nice. Our genius friend. I just hope we will get there," cried Mary.

"That's exactly what I just told him," shouted Bruce. "You have another Alphavisor at the left."

"Wait till I can raise this thing a bit. I have it in sight now. Ready, go."

Nothing happened, though…

"What became of that perfect aim?" asked Bruce.

"It says here in this panel that I have to regulate it again. But how?"

Bruce had a scared expression. He said, "I think I was too optimistic." They both felt a strong impact which destroyed the back of the vehicle.

"Take it easy. That was only the trunk," shouted Mary.

"But my panel says there are some damages in the energy system."

"We must think about something quickly or it will be our end," said Mary from upstairs.

"I know that. But…" Bruce started to talk, but suddenly he slowed down.

"What's the matter? Where are you going?"

"I want them to follow me," replied Bruce.

"Well that's exactly what they are doing now." Recalling a recent experience, Bruce drove the Ulphavisor towards a sandy field. A strong impact shook them.

"That was tight. Why are you driving in circles?" asked Mary.

"Wait, I just wish the help will come soon."

"What do you mean?"

Suddenly, they began to hear some grunts nearby and something horrible came out of the depths. "What are those monsters?" cried Mary.

"They are scoorts."

"Whatever, they are horrible," shouted Mary.

But things didn't go as expected.

"What's that?"

"Oh oh, more scoorts," replied Bruce.

"What do we do now?"

"Try to avoid them, that's all we can do," answered Bruce, driving the vehicle from one side to another.

"There are four of them," said Mary.

"I can see them. I didn't know they were having a family party today."

"How can you make jokes at this moment? Let's get out of here," said Mary.

"I will do that."

Some explosions were heard.

"Hey, the scoorts have toppled some of our pursuers," said Mary.

"That was the idea."

"You have become an expert."

"I just found a button that says 'regulate'. And to think that my grandmother always complained when she saw me playing those war games," commented Mary.

"Push it and hope it works," shouted Bruce. The Ulphavisor went on avoiding some impacts.

"Drive carefully," asked Mary.

"I'm just trying to stop them until we can attack again."

"Wow! It says 'Barrel regulated'."

"What are you waiting for then? Shoot!" An explosion followed Bruce's words. Looking out of his window, Bruce smiled. "I don't know where you got that perfect aim from."

"While I try to go on attacking them, try to communicate with the others with the Transler."

Bruce turned his head up to Mary. "I can't do everything at once. And I don't even know how to use all this stuff. I never thought I could miss Nailbytes so much. I sure need him here."

"Well, never mind that now. There are more ships coming," said Mary.

"Take care of them."

They felt another blow on the back. "They are destroying this thing!"

"It will be enough if we can succeed to go on and get to the station," cried Mary from upstairs.

"I'm afraid that if this goes on we won't get out of here alive." One more blow shook the vehicle. "See what I mean?" asked Bruce.

"You just go on driving. I'm here waiting for you. Have some..."

A new impact came along with a noise of broken glass. "The back window is gone," announced Mary.

"We're still alive and that's all that really matters. Just go on shooting."

Another blow ripped off one of the back doors.

"That was near," exclaimed Mary. "No problem. I was lucky not to be seating over there anymore, and we still have another back door."

But at that exact moment another blow ripped it off.

"What were you saying?" asked Bruce.

"Forget it!"

"Yes, you'd better go on attacking our enemies."

"I'm on it. Come here, get a little closer," Mary spoke to the ship flying just over her head. "That's it. Take this!"

Bruce heard a loud explosion and he shouted, "Well done! I must say it again. You have become an expert."

"Thanks. What was that?"

"Sorry, I had to dodge another vehicle."

"Well drive carefully. And now what?"

"Look in front of you. That's a patrol. Shoot before they do."

"Okay."

Mary directed the barrel towards the patrol. The enemy saw it but didn't have much time to avoid it and the vehicle blew up in pieces.

"Well done!"

"Another one is coming close to us. I think we are entering an urban zone or something like that," said Bruce.

Through the dust they could see some stone buildings and a few vehicles going from one side to the other. "This means we are getting near to the Imhamway Station. Just drive along the dark path."

"The dark path you say? Okay, I see it."

However, a strong blow threw Mary down into the back seats. She sat down and cried, "I could jump on time. But the barrel is gone."

"I hope we are near the station," replied Bruce. "Oh oh, we are running out of energy. This thing is slowing down."

Mary came behind him to look at the road in front of them. "Just follow the dark path and try to keep close to the other passing vehicles."

"Yes, that will make some of them crush."

Bruce made a hard turn to the left which threw Mary to the other side. He looked back quickly to see if she was alright. She stood up feeling a little dizzy. "I'll hold tight from now on."

"Okay, here we go again."

"What are you waiting for?" shouted Mary. "Those guards are aiming at us."

"I did it on purpose," said Bruce.

The shot from one of the Alphavisors came but...

"Did you see? They hit the vehicle next to me."

"That was smart. Now drive between those cargo vehicles over there, we'll pass unnoticed among them."

"I'll do that. Hold tight!"

The Ulphavisor, almost completely destroyed, continued his way with difficulty towards the Imhamway Station.

"Sis, do you copy me? We are at the Imhamway Station."

"Denise?" cried Mary, deeply moved by her sister's voice.

At the station, Denise, along with the others, was bending on her knees. "We are trying to get out of here."

"We'll be there soon."

"You sure are very optimistic," cried Bruce. Denise didn't answer.

At her side Esther advised her, "Speak low or the guards will hear you. They already know about the escape."

"One of us should go to the entrance to alert Nailbytes and Maggie. If we use the Transler the guards might hear us," suggested Billy.

"You go," asked Esther. "The colors of your tong are very alike those used by almost all the merchants present at the fair. They'll think you are one of them."

Denise added, "That's true. The mean creature who hit the poor slovo wore one just like yours, green and blue."

"Okay, I'll go," replied Billy.

Billy hid among the vehicles and went to the main door.

As soon as she saw he had arrived there, Denise asked, "What are we going to do? We have to get out of here."

"Yes, you will, but back to the Atilkawa Fortress," shouted a guard pointing his Isban to them. He cried to his companions, "Hey, fellows, I have some of the fugitives here."

Other guards came by. "Well done. Now, start walking." They took the prisoners surrounded by all the guards to the take-off platforms. Esther and Denise, guarded by a group of guards, passed through the elevators and ramps. Some creatures watched what was going on, others simply followed their routine.

They arrived at the *Sinister Phantom* which was parked at the nearer platforms.

"We just have to wait for Lornar Mayer to get here," said one of them with a proud voice.

"What do you think we'll get for this?"

"Wait and see," answered enthusiastically another guard.

They all turned to another one who was running towards them. Short of breath due to the exercise, the new arrival said, "I've just spoken with Ultro, he says we should put the prisoners on the ship. They are on their way here."

One of the others replied, "Aren't we supposed to take them to the fortress?"

"I don't know. It seems that Lonar Mayer wants to use Esther in Caution Rai."

"Okay, you heard the orders. Get on the ship." Esther and Denise got on the *Sinister Phantom*.

Once inside and in spite of her fear, Denise exclaimed, "It's impressive."

"It sure is. It's one of the most powerful weapons in the galaxy," commented Esther surrounded by the guards.

"You can chat later," demanded one of the guards angrily.

At the door appeared a slovo asking, "Since you still have to wait for a while, why don't I take down all these boxes?"

The guards looked at him with a sneer look. "What for? Can't it wait?"

"I'm afraid not. Lonar Mayer wants all these down there as soon as possible. I wanted to do it before but I couldn't. There are not so many boxes but they're very heavy."

"Then call some more slovos to help you take them down."

"I wish I could but they are all busy."

"You have your pallet truck. Do it yourself then," replied a guard.

"Okay, it's down there. I'll bring it up."

When the slovo walked near Denise, she recognized him and was about to say something but he winked his eye to her and she kept silent.

"It's strange, I can't communicate with Esther and Denise," commented Billy.

"The Transler is not such a good device," said Nailbytes. "If they have already sent guards after us, I hope Mary and Bruce will be able to get here as quickly as possible."

"What on earth is that?" asked Maggie, pointing her finger to a seriously wrecked vehicle which was, apparently, coming towards them.

"It's an Amarphy vehicle, or what's left of it," replied Billy, trying to see who was driving it.

"It seems to have only the front wheels. I can't understand how it can go on like that. It sure comes from a rough battle."

"But have you seen who is driving it?" shouted Nailbytes. "It is Bruce!"

Inside the vehicle Bruce was trying hard to park it, but it was quite difficult considering its condition. "It goes from one side to the other, I can't control it anymore." Suddenly, it crashed with some parked vehicles.

"Here comes the *Landthunder*," cried Mary, a little bit shaken by the impact.

"Hurry! Jump out!" cried Bruce.

A strong explosion destroyed the Ulphavisor. "Mary, Bruce, run quickly, we're over here," cried Billy. They both ran among the other land vehicles that had stopped, startled by the gunfire and the explosion. Once gathered, they ran up the stone stairs and went quickly to the take-off platforms. They walked, mingling with the rest of the strange creatures who were still shaken by the last events.

On the *Sinister Phantom* Esther was looking out of a window. She saw that the *Iron Warrior* was nearby. Taking advantage of the fact that the guards were watching the slovo while he took down the boxes, she looked at Denise and made a sign to her. Suddenly, they heard screams and gunshots. The guards inside the *Sinister Phantom* looked out and saw some creatures running from the guards who were firing at them, in spite of the other creatures who tried to protect themselves every way they could. "Who are those creatures?" asked one of the guards looking through the window.

The other guard went to the window that was next to the entrance ramp of the ship. "What is it?" At that moment the slovo dropped one of the boxes and some Ace pills came out of it.

"That's Ace. Why would Lonar Mayer want to take it out of his ship?" exclaimed one of the guards with an annoyed face.

The other guard pointed his Isban to the slovo. "Just a moment, no one told you to bring down those boxes. What's happening here?"

The slovo replied, "Well, you know, one has to think in advance…" But in a quick move he threw a box to the guard making him fall down the ramp. Esther pushed the other over his companion but this last one shot the slovo before he fell on the ground below.

Esther sat at the driving seat and pushed the button to close the door. The slovo lay motionless on the floor of the ship.

Chapter 23

A DEADLY SPACE BATTLE

Esther sat on the pilot's seat and looked through the window at the Earthlings who had arrived at the take-off platforms. They were chased by many armed guards with Isbans which came from the higher levels running down the ramps. She quickly identified some basic weapons on the ship. She manipulated the controls and soon two small barrels came down from the bottom of the *Sinister Phantom*.

She began to shoot the guards who were chasing her friends and, at the other side, the ones guarding the *Iron Warrior*.

On the platform below Mary shouted, "On the floor!" They obeyed immediately, scared at the shooting around them. All the creatures on the level ran for refuge. Others, like the Aceiters, just fell on the ground, leaving their bundles anywhere around. It was a total chaos. They could hear the shooting and some screaming around them. Above their heads they saw some yellow lights. The ships coming in or out had a blue light around them.

"The shooting is coming from that ship," shouted Bruce, lifting his head a little.

"From here I think I can see a familiar face in there," said Billy also lifting his head a little.

"Get ready to go, guys, we must get to the *Iron Warrior* now," shouted Mary with her head up.

"But we don't know if it has been repaired. What if they catch us in there?" replied Billy.

"Just go!" shouted Mary.

They stood up and, still a little crouched, started to run towards the spaceship. Due to the shooting going back and forth, some creatures fell wounded on the ground. The guards had a problem shooting at the Aceiters because many creatures and their bundles came in their way and kept them from having a good view of the fugitives.

Esther went on shooting, trying to cover her friends, and Denise took care of the injured slovo. "Why did you do this, my friend?" asked Denise with a soft voice, bending over the creature,

The dying slovo answered in a frail voice, "You helped me. I'm Jerry."

"Yes, I recognized you. I was only trying to relieve a bit your pain and you have given your life for us."

"That's the real friendship, Denise."

On the outside, the others were arriving at the *Iron Warrior* platform already without surveillance since the guards had gone to respond to the sudden attack that came from the other spaceship. A small staircase led to the door of the ship and they went up in a hurry, covered by Esther's shooting. Bruce ran to the control panel.

Nailbytes sat down next to the computers and started the engine.

Mary saw a small label on one side and came close to it with her Transler.

A few seconds later she shouted, "Benji and Centi did it. They fixed it. It says here that the ship is in full capacity."

"That's wonderful! Give me five," cried Billy lifting his hand to his friend. Mary did so and they all laughed for a few seconds.

Inside the *Sinister Phantom* a sad event was going on. "How can I help you?" cried Denise, looking around her. Turning to Esther she asked, "Is there a first aid kit in this ship?"

"Just leave me here. It's too late for that. I'll fade away alone. That's the way with slovos."

"I can't do that, Jerry," replied a sobbing Denise.

"You've done very much already. You did something no one had ever done for me. Just stay a little away from me please, and take good care of yourself."

For a few seconds Denise resisted to obey him, but the pleading eyes of the slovo made her walk away. After a minute the slovo had disappeared. Denise turned to Esther and asked in a sad voice, "What do we do now?"

"I must get you out of here," answered Esther. "I'll try to communicate with the others. I think they are on the *Iron Warrior*. Mary, do you copy me?"

"Yes, Esther, I do. We are almost in front of you. I'm Bruce. We can hear you very well."

"Bruce, tell Mary to be very careful."

"Why, Esther?" It was Mary.

"There's a space battle taking place up there. It's too risky to take off right now."

"What are you talking about?"

"What you just heard. The Liberator's Army is fighting with the supreme forces. If we go up we will be in the middle of it."

Looking through a low window Denise saw something that made her shout,

"Those are supreme guards and they come with Lonar Mayer, the condor punk woman, as Bruce calls her."

Esther listened to Denise's words with a frown and then spoke to Mary. "We are in a crossroad. If we stay here we'll die but if we go to the space we'll be facing a huge battle and we'll probably end up the same way." They heard shooting and blows on the ship as if someone was trying to get into the *Sinister Phantom*. "Okay, Mary, there's only one wise decision to be taken. Let's take off," cried an excited Esther.

"Fine, we are ready. And Denise? What is going to happen to her?"

"Don't you worry about that, I'll get Denise out of here in due time."

"Okay, I trust you. Thank you. I just hope this will be our last battle before we can go back home."

"I wouldn't be too sure about that," answered Esther in a low voice.

Denise made no comment but looked at her with an intrigued expression on her face. Then she took a look at the window and cried, "Quickly, they are installing portable cannons. We must hurry!"

Suddenly, both spaceships were impacted with enemy bullets and they could hear loud screams all over the place.

Inside the *Sinister Phantom*, Denise asked, "What is all that yelling out there?" "That must be Lonar Mayer in desperation to see that we are taking away her beloved *Sinister Phantom*."

"What's that sign on the panel?"

"It's the beginning of the take-off cycle of the ship. Hold on."

Esther shouted to Mary, "We'll go first."

"Okay, we'll follow you," replied Bruce.

The *Sinister Phantom* took off from the Imhamway Station. Softly floating on the air, it went towards the station exit.

Meanwhile, on the *Iron Warrior,* they heard a strong noise. "I suppose one of us has to pilot the ship when we go out to space."

"Who can do that?" asked Maggie almost in a whisper.

Bruce spoke with a firm voice, "I sometimes borrow my dad's car so I think I may know something about this."

"Well, I think this machine was designed to be driven by any idiot," commented Nailbytes.

"So I guess Bruce could drive it."

"Shut up, Maggie!"

Mary intervened. "Ignore her, Bruce. Will you come here, please?"

Nailbytes replied, "Just come here, I've already began the take-off maneuver."

The *Iron Warrior* moved slowly towards the exit it had entered on arrival, but it kept receiving shotguns from the soldiers below it. Bruce approached his friend, sat next to him and said, "It doesn't look at all like a common wheel. It's more like an airplane one. It is a half wheel I think."

"Just pretend that you are driving your dad's car, Bruce. Pay attention to that small screen in front of you and I'll tell you what you have to do. I'm the only one fit to do this, don't you think so?"

"Shut up and just tell me what to do, Nailbytes. What do I do now?"

"It says here that we must take control, so, when I tell you, just grab the wheel firmly and stay calm."

"I have it."

"Fine, here we go. Initiating take-off..."

"We are shaking!" shouted Maggie.

"It is all right. Don't shout. Nothing is going to happen to us. Just pull the wheel a bit upwards, Bruce."

"Okay, it's done."

"Well done, Bruce. Now we are fine," commented Mary.

"That was Esther and Denise on the *Sinister Phantom*. It's our turn now. Are you ready, Bruce?" asked Nailbytes.

"Yes, I think I'm doing fine. Of course, if my father ever finds out about my driving his car he kills me."

"But your brother Alex takes it every time," commented Billy.

"But Alex has a driving license and I don't," replied Bruce.

"Hold tight, everyone."

"We're ready, Nailbytes," cried Billy.

"Initiate," said Bruce. The *Iron Warrior* took off from the station and began its ascent into space.

"Esther, do you copy me now?"

"Yes, I do, Bruce."

"We're on our way to the space."

"I'll adjust our coordinates to avoid colliding with you."

"Fine, Esther," replied Nailbytes.

A little time later, the spaceship was at the outer space. "We left Esmadis," cried Maggie.

"But look, ahead of us we have the battle Esther told us about."

"What are we going to do?" asked Maggie.

"Calm down," replied Mary. "Just go on, Bruce. You, Nailbytes, can you prepare the defensive and attack systems?"

"I'll switch on the systems," cried Nailbytes. "Wait a moment, what is this?"

"Nailbytes, please don't tell me more bad news?"

"No, Mary, on the contrary, the screen shows me it has a shield field and Benji increased its power. We are well protected."

"Good for Benji. I wish we could thank him," added Billy.

"And I think we'll need it right now. Careful, some ships are getting closer," cried Maggie.

"What are those things? They come from everywhere," asked Nailbytes with a frightened voice.

"I don't know, from here we can see that some have a diamond shape and others look like old plane models," commented Billy.

They saw that not far from them an intense battle was taking place. Spaceships were being persecuted and many of them exploded all around. "They seem to be coming towards us," Maggie spoke in a trembling voice.

"Can you maneuver this machine properly, Bruce?" asked Mary.

"I think I can."

"Well, then act fast. We will soon be attacked by those dreadful forces," cried again Maggie. They felt a strong impact. Through the window they could see that the diamond-shaped ships weren't too big but had two barrels on each side and another one on top which made them very dangerous. "They are attacking us!" shouted Maggie.

"Take it easy," replied Mary. "Bruce, call Esther and ask her who we are supposed to attack."

"I'll do that. Esther, do you copy me?"

"Yes, Bruce, I do. Tell me."

"We're in the middle of the battle but we don't know who we are supposed to fight against."

"The Diabolical Diamonds are our enemies and the Air Fs are the Liberator's Space Force. I'm trying to communicate with them."

Their ship had a sudden shudder.

"What are we going to do?" asked Maggie.

Mary cried, "Nailbytes, can you see if there are any weapons on this ship?"

Another strong shudder made them jump on their feet.

"And you'd better do it quickly," begged Maggie.

Nailbytes started to look for any information he could get at the computers.

"I think I found something. There seems to be a sort of diagram of the *Iron Warrior*. I can see a defensive system right there. For what I understand there are three barrels, one on each side and one in the center."

"But where are they supposed to be exactly?" asked Billy. They felt another jolt.

"As I told you, it says here that they are one on each wing and another one just at the center of the ship."

"And what are you waiting for? Let's use them," cried Maggie again.

"I will go to the one on the right, Billy, you take the one on the left and you, Maggie, try to take the center one."

"I think you'd better take the center. It seems a little more difficult. Mary, I take the other wing."

Once again they felt a huge shudder. It was as if a big earthquake was making the ship tremble. Turning to his friends Bruce replied with an angry voice, "Will you please make up your minds before we blow up in a thousand pieces!"

"It's on."

Billy opened the small gate to a tiny cabin in one of the wings. He entered it ducking and sat on the chair which took almost all the space in it. Looking around him he saw that he was surrounded by all kind of computers. He looked up and caught sight of something like a telescopic device attached to the barrels. Through the big front window they could see the huge outer space opening in front of them.

"Wow! This is incredible!"

"Tell us your opinions later, Maggie. Now just use that barrel," shouted Bruce without taking his eyes from the driving control.

"And how can I make this thing work? And it's so dirty," cried Maggie.

Mary came near her and observed the panel. "Forget about that. Just imagine you are playing those video games you like so much. Pretend that you are playing Space Invaders. After all, it's exactly what all this is about, isn't it?"

Billy shouted from his place, "Only that this is quite real now."

Another shudder moved the ship.

"Enough jokes and blah blah. We'll die if we don't hurry," shouted Bruce.

"Everyone in his place please," asked Billy.

The group was attuned. Maggie was on one wing, Billy on the other and Mary in the center. Bruce drove the spaceship and Nailbytes managed the main computer. They knew it was the only way to get out alive and return home.

"Do you all have full power to initiate the defense?" asked Nailbytes.

"How do we know we have it?"

"You can read it on the screen in front of you, Maggie," explained Nailbytes.

"Maintain your distance, Bruce. Get ready, everyone."

"Okay," replied Billy, "my barrel is fully operative."

"Okay, Billy. How is yours, Maggie?" asked Nailbytes.

"I told you, it's covered with dust."

"Will you please stop with that nonsense. Clean it with your sleeve and see if your barrel is ready to shoot?" shouted Bruce without taking his eyes from the space ahead of him.

The ship continued to shudder.

"Start to shoot to the ships on your sides," cried Nailbytes.

"Mary, you have one right in position for you."

"I've seen it, Billy. Come, come…"

They felt another tremor, a little stronger than the previous ones. "That came from your side, Maggie. It went right next to me but it was too fast."

"Okay, Billy, it's right within my sight. Let's see, come a little closer… There you are."

One more explosion lit the sky.

"Well done, Maggie."

"There is another one coming towards us," cried Billy.

"Wait until it comes nearer to you."

"You think you are an expert already, don't you, Maggie? Here it comes."

Two explosions sounded on the outside.

"I got it!"

"Well done, Billy and Mary."

A loud blow shook the *Iron Warrior*.

"They have a good aim too."

"Are you sure, Nailbytes? I hadn't notice it."

"It's just a comment, Bruce, you don't have to be so sarcastic about it."

"Did our ship suffer much, Nailbytes?"

"Other than my poor nerves?" shouted Maggie.

"This affects all of us," answered Billy from his position.

"This is a mess. There are ships coming from everywhere."

"Just drive and keep quiet, Bruce."

"You shut up, Maggie!"

"Stop fighting and focus on the situation we are in," asked Mary. "Nailbytes, can you see if we can get in touch with someone from the Liberator's Forces?"

"Hey, I have one on sight but it's the old plane model. Do I shoot it?"

"No! Wait, Maggie!" cried Nailbytes.

Another blow shook the ship.

"It seems that they are not so willing to wait," commented Maggie.

"Just a moment, I'm trying to get into their frequency."

"I have them. Hello, we are Esther Balag's friends, did she tell you about us?"

"Esther Balag? Yes, she just did. So you belong to the Liberator's Forces. Help us to fight this battle."

"Of course we will. What's your name, please?" asked Nailbytes.

"I'm Rentail. I'm a good friend of Esther."

Once more a blow shook them.

"You'd better stop your social life and ask them how we are going to organize ourselves."

Nailbytes made a gesture to Bruce signing him to keep quiet and continued his talk with the other spaceship. "Do you have an attack plan?"

"We have to form attack groups. You are on the powerful *Iron Warrior*, I will give you four escorts so that you will attack the

Socavon, the mother ship from which all those Diabolical Diamonds, the DDs, come from."

Bruce turned and, putting his hand on the microphone, he said, "What's he talking about?"

"He's talking about that. Look at your screen. That big spaceship over there is the *Socavon*, that's where all those DDs pop out from. We have to destroy it," explained Mary.

"Well, you sure make it sound easy. But how are we going do that?"

Mary, who had dropped her barrel and was standing behind him now, just shrugged her shoulders.

Bruce doubted for a second but spoke firmly, "Okay, Rentail, but be sure to give us good escorts."

"No problem, here they go. Air F 2, 3, 4 and 5, escort the *Iron Warrior* to attack the *Socavon* station." Bruce nodded his head in agreement and Mary returned to her attacking position at the barrel. "Ready, there they go."

"Thanks, Rentail. I'm Bruce."

"Okay, Bruce, good luck."

"*Iron Warrior*, do you copy me? This is Air F4 and I'm Commander Sinloy, in charge of this fleet. That ship next to you is Air F 5. His pilot is Olman."

"I copy you. Stick to us and we'll make a first attempt," replied Bruce. Then, without turning to them, he shouted to his friends, "Be prepared for whatever might come, guys."

"Hold on, Bruce," shouted Nailbytes, "you have Esther on your frequency."

"Hello, Esther, what is it?"

"I have two squadrons after me. I need reinforcements."

"Okay, Esther, we'll be with you. Air F 4 and 5, we have an emergency to attend first. Esther Balag needs our help."

"No problem, Bruce, we'll follow you."

"Thanks, Sinloy," answered Nailbytes.

The *Iron Warrior* and the two escorts went to help Esther who was trying hard to avoid the attacks with dedicated maneuvers and shooting in the best way she could.

"Be careful, Esther, there's one just next to you," shouted Denise.

"Yes, I've seen it. Come over here, come, come…"

A loud explosion shook the *Sinister Phantom*.

"Here we are, Esther."

"Thanks, Bruce. You take care of the ones behind me and I'll attack the ones in front."

"Understood," replied Bruce, driving the ship towards the spaceships flying behind Esther.

"Air F 4, this is Air F 5, let's split up a little to attack. The others go after them. You, *Iron Warrior*, advance a little and leave your radio on this frequency."

"Okay," answered Nailbytes with enthusiasm.

"Hey, Bruce, you're commanding like an expert," commented Mary.

"It's not that. It's more like playing a video game," replied Bruce.

"But here if you fail you die," replied Billy from his barrel.

The five spaceships, including the *Iron Warrior*, split up to initiate the attack.

"Let's go!" cried Bruce.

"Air F 5 you have one just on top."

"I saw it. Here I go."

A loud explosion was heard.

"Well done, Sinloy."

"One is coming into your position, Mary."

"I've got it, Nailbytes."

However, the *Iron Warrior* was attacked first and the blow shook the ship.

"You'd better hurry."

"Yes, Bruce, I have it. One, two and... take this!"

The enemy ship exploded in front of them.

"One more. Come a little nearer... That's it."

"Well done, Billy."

"From what I see on my screen Esther has a very good aim. She finished with almost all of the enemy's spaceships around her," commented Nailbytes.

"Yes, she's good. And the ship she's on is very powerful too. It's our turn now," added Bruce, maneuvering the ship. "There are more coming, guys."

"One for each of you," said Billy.

A blow shook the *Iron Warrior*.

"That was supposed to be yours, Maggie," shouted Bruce.

"Sorry, I can't always be perfect."

Bruce just made a grin.

"Nailbytes, tell Air F 4 that a DD is going straight to him."

"Air F 4, you have…" It was too late. They saw a big explosion in front of them.

"It can't be," sobbed Mary with half her body hanging from her barrel's seat.

"I can't believe it," cried Nailbytes.

"I'm afraid we have to. They destroyed Sinloy's ship," added Bruce.

"Why didn't he react faster?" asked Billy.

"I don't know," replied Mary.

"*Iron Warrior*, do you copy me?"

"Yes, Esther, we do, but we are quite affected with what just happened."

"So are we, Nailbytes, but Sinloy died for a good cause and we must go on."

Mary was surprised at the cold tone of Esther's voice

"It seems that the Air Fs doesn't have the powerful shield of the *Iron Warrior*," said Billy.

"That's a good observation. Olman, we lost Sinloy, we only have three ships now to attack the *Socavon*," said Bruce.

"Unfortunately, it is so. You go in front, I'll cover your back and the other two will fly by your side."

"Okay, Olman, here we go," answered Bruce and, turning to his friends, he shouted, "Are you all ready?"

They looked to each other sadly but answered firmly, "Yes, we're ready to go."

"Here comes one. It's going towards you, Mary," shouted Billy.

"I saw it. You have another coming for you."

"Just take the position I want you to take."

Two explosions were heard outside.

"Congrats, Mary and Billy," cried Nailbytes. Bruce just smiled at his friends.

For a while, Mary, Billy and Maggie went on defending their ship from the attacks and shooting at the enemy's spaceships on their way, although the *Iron Warrior* had its share of impacts itself.

"Bruce, try to get a little closer," said Nailbytes.

"I'm trying, but it's not easy. Olman, do you copy me? I'm going to try a cleaner approach."

"Be careful, Bruce, if you get too near you'll be within range of their weapons. That will be fatal."

"That's true, Bruce, look at your screen. The *Socavon* has four defensive barrels, two on each side, and all of them seem to have good mobility," added Nailbytes. "What was that blow?"

"I don't know but I hope it wasn't Olman," cried Bruce. "Olman, do you copy me?"

"Yes. They got Toplon of the Air F 2. You have just me and Air F 3 as escorts, now."

"Can we ask for some more?"

"I don't think so, Bruce. The DDs are very powerful and we don't have many ships left."

They all looked to each other, not knowing what to do.

"Can you help us, Esther?"

"I don't think that would be convenient, Bruce. If I go with you I'll bring along the enemy ships that are after me. I'd better stay behind and try to destroy them. In that way you'll have fewer obstacles to fight against."

Putting his hand on the microphone Bruce turned to his friends. "What do we do now?"

"The only option we have is to try it ourselves," said Mary from her barrel.

"Well then, let's go!"

The *Iron Warrior* was attacked.

Bruce yelled, "In positions, everyone."

"We're ready."

The *Iron Warrior* approached the *Socavon* but it was received by the ships which were on guard.

"Try to avoid them, Bruce," shouted Billy.

"That's what I'm trying to do."

"Mary, you have one just on top of you," shouted Nailbytes.

"I have it."

An explosion followed Mary's words.

"Excellent, Mary."

"What's the matter, Bruce, can't we get any closer?'" asked Billy.

"I'm sorry, I have to avoid their shots."

"Air F 3, you have one below you," shouted Nailbytes.

"Okay."

"Mary, it's your turn now. Shoot!"

Her shot wasn't too effective and they started to feel discouraged.

"I think we have to get closer," said Nailbytes.

"It sounds very easy but I can assure you it isn't."

"I didn't say it is, Bruce, it's just that we are too far from the *Socavon* to cause it any harm. It seems to have the same shield as our ship."

Once more, the *Iron Warrior* was attacked and they all had a good shake.

"It feels stronger each time," commented Mary.

"Billy, there's one coming into your position."

"I see it. Come a little more over here… There you go."

"Well done, Billy. Now it's your turn, Maggie.

At that precise moment a strong attack shook the ship fiercely.

"My barrel isn't working!" shouted Maggie.

"Just tell us what you see on your screen," said Mary.

"Defensive system damaged."

"The main computer says exactly the same. That last blow damaged Maggie's barrel," confirmed Nailbytes.

Mary took her head off her barrel's viewer. "Well, then we'll fight with two barrels."

"I'm afraid that's not the only problem we'll have to deal with. It says here that the oxygen system is also damaged," explained Nailbytes.

"What do you mean?" asked Billy from his position.

Nailbytes looked at his screen and answered, "It means that we don't have much air, so please try to keep your breath as much as possible."

Bruce shook his head with a worried expression. "One barrel less and only a little air left."

"This is getting quite complicated and dangerous," added Nailbytes with a deep sigh.

Chapter 24

A VERY RISKY ATTACK

"Bruce, do you copy me?"

"Tell me, Esther. What's on your mind?"

"I have an idea. I think you won´t accomplish anything attacking the way you have been doing it until now. The DDs won´t allow you to get near the *Socavon*, you'll have to avoid their ships and, of course, their barrels." Esther continued her talk with Bruce, displaying her plan, which would allow him to get closer to their target. The others listened in silence.

"I've got it," replied Bruce.

"It's a very risky plan. If it doesn't work we'll all die," exclaimed Billy.

"There's no time to look for other options. There's too little oxygen left. I think it's the only alternative we have right now," commented Mary. They looked at each other with a worried expression on their faces.

"Well, I think I won't be able to see my dad at the golf tournament after all."

Her friends interrupted her with a loud cry. "Shut up, Maggie, we must be positive."

"Are we ready to carry out Esther's plan?" asked Bruce.

"I think we are," replied Mary.

"I'm not quite convinced about it but I agree we don't have time," added Billy in a firm voice.

"That's it. Keep your distance from the DDs shoots," advised Nailbytes.

"I'm on it. Hold tight, guys."

"I have a DD in my position. Do I shoot it?" asked Maggie.

"Wait."

The *Iron Warrior* suffered a strong blow.

"Turn off the initiation systems. I'll release a trail of carbon dioxide so it will look as if we are out of combat," said Nailbytes.

"And let's cross our fingers and hope it works," replied Mary from her barrel.

Bruce did as told and shouted, "Hold tight, everyone."

The ship swooped down towards the *Socavon*.

"We are falling," shouted Maggie.

"Just hold on tight," shouted Nailbytes.

The *Iron Warrior* continued on its way down while the enemy ships, assuming it had been destroyed, didn't bother to attack.

"Are you ready?" asked Nailbytes.

"Yes, I think this is as near as we are going to get. Here I go," replied Bruce.

"One, two..." said Nailbytes. He shouted, "Ready? Three!" shouted Nailbytes.

Bruce turned on the systems.

"Can you handle it okay again?" asked Mary.

"Yes, I think I can," cried a sweating Bruce, concentrating himself on the driving devices in front of him.

"Shoot now!"

"Here I go."

Once more, a loud and bright explosion followed her words.

"Evasive action accomplished," shouted Nailbytes.

The *Iron Warrior* started to fly away, leaving behind the *Socavon* turned into pieces. Shouts of joy sounded all over the spaceship. "We did it!" cried Billy.

"Yes, Esther was right," added Mary with a broad smile.

"I assume we can go back home now, can't we?" said Maggie.

"That will be our next move," replied Billy.

"Esther, do you copy me? Your plan was a complete success."

"I copy you. I can see that, Bruce, it may have been my plan but you were the ones that made it possible. Congrats. We have given a strong blow to Eliom's forces and to his lieutenant, Lonar Mayer. The destruction of the *Socavon* will certainly weaken their space army."

"Well said, Esther. We're going for Denise now."

"That's it, Nailbytes," shouted Mary from her barrel.

"Esther, we are waiting for Denise, what do we have to do now?"

"Prepare for a space docking. Put your ship just under mine, Bruce."

"Wait a second, Esther, I'm putting it in your same speed first."

Nailbytes and Bruce managed to place the ship under Esther's. "Here we go. Activate the Eldano tube. You'll see the switch at your left."

"What's that supposed to be?" asked Mary.

"It's alright, Mary, it's the transportation tube. Don't worry."

"I'm sorry, Esther, of course I trust you."

"It's okay. Ready? Initiating transportation maneuver," said Nailbytes.

A large tube came out of the upper spaceship and went down directly to the roof of the *Iron Warrior*. A small opening appeared and the tube came into the ship.

Inside the *Sinister Phantom* Esther and Denise were saying goodbye. "Take care. I wish we will be seeing each other again some time," said Esther.

"So do I. Thank you so much for everything you have done for us. I hope we will meet again. Give our love to Centi and all your family." They embraced for a moment.

"Ready?" Esther walked to the controls and looked at Denise who had gone into the tube. Denise was wiping the tears from her face and Esther, as she waved her hand to her, realized that, incredibly enough, she was doing the same thing herself. She then turned to the control panel. "Transporting, here she goes." Denise went down smoothly from one ship to the other.

As soon as she was inside the *Iron Warrior*, Denise and Mary hugged for a few moments. Their friends stood around them smiling at the tender scene. "My little naughty sister. I came to think we would never see each other again."

"How can you say that? You really thought you could get rid of me so easily?" Mary just smiled at her sister, nodding her head.

At that moment something caught Mary's attention. The light on the Sathaye was blinking. She thought to herself, What's the matter with this? Is one of my friends a Shigabell devil? How is that possible? What does this mean? But she remained silent.

"Okay, Esther, it's time to say goodbye," said Billy.

"This is getting to an end," added Bruce, attentive to the driving wheel.

"I'm afraid you're wrong at that. This is not over. I'd say it's just beginning. The plan to invade the Earth is still on their minds. It's true that we have beaten the enemy very hard but, unfortunately, the truth is we have just delayed them for a while," replied Esther.

"What are you talking about?" asked Billy with a scared voice.

When Maggie heard Esther's words she cried, "Forget it, Billy. Let's just go home. We've had enough."

"If you say so, Maggie. Have a nice trip, all of you," replied Esther.

The communication went off and they all looked at each other in silence.

"Esther, what do we do with the *Iron Warrior* once we get home?" asked Nailbytes.

"No problem. I'm going to give you the coordinates for a returning remote control program. It will send the ship to Intimay, a colony quite far from Esmadis. There is a strong contingent of the Liberation Army over there."

"Well, I'm waiting for your coordinates, Esther."

Shortly after, Nailbytes had everything he needed on the computer and was ready to program the ship as Esther had indicated. "Okay, let's see. Nailbytes, look out if you have now the coordinates on your screen so that I can activate…"

"We have to activate the Xfay speed, Bruce."

"And what is that supposed to be?"

"It seems to be some degree of speed, but I don't really know how fast it will be."

"Don't ask, just activate it."

"Okay, it's ready. We are initiating our journey back home. Hold on tight, all of you. Let me find the ship memory so I can put it in the starting point position," said Nailbytes.

"Do you mean that it will take us back to the lake where this incredible adventure began?" asked Denise.

"I hope that´s exactly what this ship will do."

They all went to their seats and fastened their seat belts. In a few seconds the *Iron Warrior* was in Xfay speed, on its way home. "Everything is white out there," cried Maggie.

"That's obvious. We're traveling at light speed I think," replied Nailbytes.

"Don't talk too much. Remember we're short of oxygen," said Billy. They all obeyed at once.

After a while, they could see on the panel that they were approaching the Earth. "It says here that the Xfay speed is over and that we are back on manual controls," said Nailbytes, "Let me put on the coordinates."

A short time later the *Iron Warrior* entered the Earth's atmosphere without any problem. Then it landed exactly on the lake it had landed before. It was dark around them.

"Home sweet home at last," cried Maggie.

"Yes, it's incredible," said Billy.

In a few moments the *Iron Warrior* was floating on the lake. Billy's parents were near the shore. There was a heavy rain but they were both under an umbrella. As soon as they saw it they ran towards the ship. Billy and Maggie, who had already left the spaceship, ran to embrace them. "Where were you?" shouted Jaime. "What happened with you?"

"Okay, guys, you have to tell me everything now," demanded Henry Nearne.

They all started to talk at the same time. Henry and Jaime looked at each other, unable to understand a word. After a few minutes Henry interrupted shouting, "Wait! We don´t understand a thing you are saying. Let Mary and Billy tell us what happened."

Mary and Billy told them everything that happened from the moment the spaceship had taken off. "And do you expect us to believe that story?"

"But, Dad, where do you think this ship came from?"

"And now what do we do with it?" asked Jaime.

"No problem, Mum, it will go away in a minute."

Nailbytes said, "Now let´s get out of here."

They all walked away from the ship. In a few seconds the ship was gone and out of sight.

"Wow! If I hadn't seen it I wouldn't believe it."

"Please, Henry, do you realize what has happened? According to our son and his friends they have been to a far away galaxy, they saved the planet from an invasion and..."

"Some creatures helped us, Mum. Esther, for instance, she and I made a plan to escape and she helped Denise to get out from the Atilkawa Fortress."

"That's not so important now," replied Maggie. "Tell us what happened here. My mum must have gone mad with worry knowing that her perfect daughter was out somewhere for so many days trying to save the Earth."

"Well, it hasn't been too long since you went away you know."

"But, Mum, we were there for over a couple weeks, maybe more. There were a lot of darkness and brightness."

"But, dear, you have only been away for six or seven hours at the most," answered Jaime, looking at her watch.

"Then it means that the perception of time is not the same here as in that galaxy. And now I understand. According to the *Iron Warrior*'s computer, Xfay is a speed much faster than light," commented Nailbytes.

"Are you telling us that that ship could do that? How is that possible?" asked Henry.

"With the most modern technologies, definitely. I think the Xfay speed is faster even than time or light speed," exclaimed Nailbytes.

"But that's impossible," replied Henry.

"Impossible for us, sir, but it's exactly like that. You see, according to the calculations I was able to make, light's speed is..."

Bruce interrupted, "That's fine. But please, we've had enough of all this science talk. The good thing is that I will be able to go with Dad and Alex to the rugby game this Sunday. It will be..."

"That's the only thing you can think about now? We were almost killed in that horrible planet, and..."

Jaime interrupted, "I think that's enough. We all need to go back to our normal lives."

Henry asked, "What's that mark on your face, Bruce?"

"That idiot Elisa gave it to me."

Jaime commented, "Well, in spite of all you were very lucky, it could have been worse."

Everybody talked at once.

"Okay, guys, that's enough. You must realize that maybe someday you won't be so lucky, and then you won't be able to tell anyone about your adventures."

"I know, Mum, but it was awesome. Nobody would believe what we've been through. People would think that we are all crazy."

Henry agreed. "You are right, son. Who's going to believe that six school friends traveled by themselves to a far away planet, tried to save the Earth from an invasion and came back home in one piece?"

"Well, I can't believe it myself," said Nailbytes.

"It was fantastic. Far away planets, galactic battles, a terrible fortress and all those incredible creatures. And imagine traveling faster than time," commented Mary.

"And don't forget the sabotages," said Billy.

Denise added, "I just hope Esther is safe together with Edison, Centi, Yami…"

"I'll always remember Master Cantelot," added Mary.

"Who was that?" asked Billy.

"An old camel with a bow tie, eyeglasses and a beret," explained Bruce.

"That's a good description. You forgot his Victorian fashioned clothes," replied Nailbytes.

"We saw a similar creature in the infirmary," commented Billy.

"That must be Master Cantelot's daughter, Camila," replied Mary. "I hope she will recover and she and her son will succeed in running away along with Master Cantelot."

Billy put up his eyebrows in concern. "I really don´t know. She was all tubed."

Mary put a worried face. She felt sad thinking of her friends in that far away planet.

"Well, I'll never forget Esther," exclaimed Denise with a deep sigh.

"Talking about Esther, do you remember what she said before we parted?" asked Nailbytes.

"She said the Earth was not safe because Lonar Mayer had not been defeated, and that, sometime in the future, they would plan another invasion to our planet."

"If that happens, Mary, it's not your problem anymore. You have other things to worry about in your lives."

"You're right, Mum," replied Billy. "However, we are the only people on Earth who know whay that planet, Esmadis, is like."

"I can say that you certainly showed an effective way to confront the tyranny of that Lonar Mayer or whatever her name was. You found the way to defeat or at least to sabotage her evil plans, not only against the Earth, but also against other planets. It's…" remarked Henry Nearne.

"Okay, that's enough, guys. This shouldn't be our concern anymore," replied Jaime Nearne.

"Yes, Mum, we just wish that Esther and her family are okay. It's for sure that those Roman soldiers will know that she helped us out."

"They were not the only ones. Many creatures out there helped us in one way or another," said Mary.

"That's true. I hope we will able to see them again someday," added Denise.

Henry stopped for a moment and spoke very seriously to the kids gathered around him. "Please, guys, I just want you to be aware of the fact that you have gone through an exceptional adventure, full of incredible and unknown perils. You were able to achieve all that without any special powers using only your personal skills smartly and efficiently. Fortunately, you have come back home sound and safe but, my friends, you might not be that lucky next time. You must be conscious of this and go on with your lives."

The lives of these friends recovered little by little and their daily routine took over, but for how long?

THE END